THE ... R

THE HOYT WAR

PETE BIEHL

First hardcover edition December 2022

Cover Art by Joseph Gruber
Map by Joseph Gruber

The Hoyt War

ISBN 978-1-7365286-6-2 (hardcover)
ISBN 978-1-7365286-7-9 (paperback)
ISBN 978-1-7365286-8-6 (ebook)

www.petebiehl.com

For Joe Gruber,
Thanks for turning my mind mush into works of art.

Books by Pete Biehl

The Rawl Wielder Trilogy
The Path of the Rawl Wielder
The Throne of Thornata
The Hoyt War

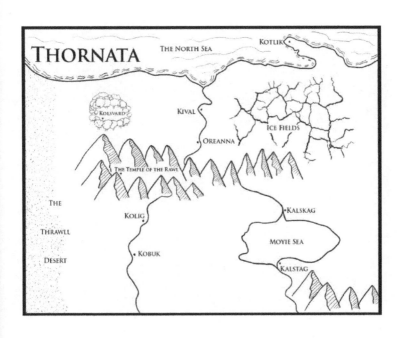

Chapter One

Captain Thad Dunstan stalked through the dimly lit stone corridors of Fort Oliver, hurrying to the main gates as swiftly as his rapidly aging legs could carry him. An Imperial Army veteran of over twenty years and a dozen great battles, he was the fortress's ranking officer. He walked with a slight limp, an injury from many years ago coming back to haunt him in his advancing age. It was one of the many scars that pained him more with each passing year. As the years went by, he continued to try, with less success each year, to conceal the effects of his old wounds from the men under his command. He had always believed a commander should exude strength and confidence, not frailty and pain. The intensity of the pangs told him that rain was likely on the way in the next day or two. He took some small comfort from the fact that at least the aches had their occasional uses. He had appreciated the beauty of rain in his youth, but now the extra discomfort it brought with it made it more of a hindrance with every passing year.

Fort Oliver sat on the southeastern border of Thornata, at the foot of a mountain pass separating it from the neighboring province of Verizia to the south. The fortress existed for the sole purpose of keeping the peace between the neighboring regions, though there had been no conflict between Thornata and Verizia in several centuries. These days, such fortresses played more of a symbolic role than a practical one. It was a role the younger men stationed at them found dull and battle-weary veterans like Thad Dunstan found relaxing. These young ones would have their taste of bloodshed and death soon enough. Younger men craved the thrill of battle, and there was always conflict for the Imperial Army to give them. Their captain had already had his fill of fighting long ago. Dunstan could happily live the rest of his days without going back to the table for another helping.

He had been the commanding officer of this fortress for nearly two years. He had been part of a surge in Imperial troops along the Thornatan border due to the growing threat of the Hoyt outlaws. In times past, it was not uncommon for Fort Oliver to be manned by a token force of as few as twenty men; now it was home to just over a hundred. Their orders were clear: do not become involved in Thornata's infighting, but do not allow the Hoyt problem to spill over into the neighboring provinces. The Empire rarely became entangled in internal politics within any of its regions unless they failed to pay the proper taxes. Still, it held a strict position about such conflicts impacting others. If the Hoyt were to show any intention of expanding their reach into Verizia, Captain Dunstan and his men would have no choice but to act. Thus far, it appeared the Hoyt harbored no such intentions, which served Dunstan perfectly well.

In the two years he had spent at Fort Oliver, Dunstan had never needed to engage the Hoyt in combat. The outlaw gang's attention had been focused on Thornata's large cities, far to the north and west. The Imperial fortresses were so remote that they seldom saw visitors until it was time for resupply from Imperial High Command. Thornata was a remote region of the Empire, and most travelers entered the province by river or sea. In two years, only a few dozen traders had entered by way of the mountain road from Verizia. However, if the rumors his men had brought him that morning were true, their days of living in boredom might soon come to an end.

The five Imperial fortresses that sat within Thornata's border exchanged messages via rider once every week. The scheduled rider from Fort Baker was two days past due, and such a delay was uncommon. His men were beginning to talk, spreading rumors of a Hoyt assault on Fort Baker, an attack which may have been coming for them next. As far as Dunstan could tell, there was no weight to the rumors as of yet; soldiers in dull assignments such as this were prone to senseless gossip. Still, the tardiness of the rider made him uneasy. In these remote regions of the Empire, the Imperial Army took communication seriously. If there was no news by nightfall, he would have to send out a search party in case the rider had taken a fall from his horse.

He reached the main gates of the fortress and called out to a nearby corporal, who hurried over and snapped a salute. Dunstan, never one for such formalities, waved him off. He had always felt the Imperial Army could run much more efficiently if they spent more time on proper preparation and less time on pomp and ceremony. *Try telling that to those bloated old fools at Imperial High Command. I doubt any of them even remember what it feels like to hold a weapon in their hand.*

"I received word that I was needed at the gates. What is happening, Corporal?" he asked.

"Sir, Cason just returned from his morning check around the fortress. He came across twenty men from Fort Baker. Almost all of them are wounded, and they claim they are the only survivors of an attack. He rode ahead to tell us; they should be arriving any minute now," the corporal replied.

"Attacked by the Hoyt?" Dunstan asked.

"From what Cason says they told him, it was the Hoyt, along with Thornatan soldiers."

This was not a reply Dunstan would have thought to hear. The Thornatans and the Hoyt had been locked in a bitter conflict for several years now. What could possibly have prompted them to join forces, and against Imperial interests no less? Imperial High Command would never stand for such an outrage. Even with their combined forces, the Thornatan Army and the Hoyt must've realized the Imperial Army could annihilate them in short order if given a reason to do so. The reasoning was irrelevant, he supposed. Anybody who came to this fortress looking for a fight would soon realize they had bitten off more than they could chew.

"Sir, they are approaching!" someone cried from the walls.

"Open the gates and send for the healer. I'm sure some of them will need his attention right away. Then go to the officers and instruct them to meet me in the planning room. I have a feeling we will have much to discuss shortly," Captain Dunstan ordered before turning his attention to the gates.

The gates swung open, and twenty men in Imperial uniforms stumbled into the courtyard, most of them looking rather the worse for wear, several of them unable to walk without support from their comrades. Captain Dunstan could see several visible wounds, and the men looked physically exhausted. Their uniforms were caked in a dried mixture of mud and blood. None of the men looked as though they had rested in days. Whatever they had been through, it had clearly taken a heavy toll on them. As soon as they were safely inside, Dunstan gave the signal to seal the gates once more. It did not appear that there was an immediate pursuit, but he couldn't be too careful.

"Please sit and rest, soldiers. Our healer is coming to tend to your wounds. I am Captain Dunstan, the commanding officer here. Can somebody please tell me what happened at Fort Baker?" he asked.

"A force of Hoyt and Thornatan soldiers arrived three days ago, around 120 of them. They requested an audience with Captain Sheelan and told him they were evicting us from the province. He explained to them that they had no authority over us and we weren't going anywhere. They argued for a bit, but they left without too much of a fuss. It was surprising to us that they left so meekly after making such a long trek. They just sat around outside our fortress for the rest of the day, though they made no move. They must have gotten a man inside the walls somehow because that night, we came under attack. The gates just opened up for them. A man on the inside is the only explanation. They must have helped him scale a wall somehow. How they managed to do it under our noses, I don't understand. We had tightened our security. There wasn't exactly time for an inquiry. As far as we know, we're the only survivors of the attack," one of the men explained.

"Do you have any idea why the Hoyt and the Thornatan Army are working together? Our last intelligence said they were locked in a bitter war."

"The ones who came into Fort Baker to treat with our captain said Idanox is the duke of Thornata now. Our eviction came on his orders. That's all the information we have on their reasoning."

"You think this force is coming here now?"

"No, sir, they are still manning Fort Baker. We were lucky enough to repel down one of the outer walls and escape when it became clear the battle was lost. But they told us all Imperial forces are being expelled from Thornata, so we wanted to warn you that another force is likely coming right for you as we speak. This fort is more remote, but I can't imagine it will take them much longer to get here. You have to get word to the other fortresses as well. Hopefully we aren't too late to warn them."

The soldier could hardly speak anymore; it was clear these men had suffered a difficult journey to get here. Fort Baker was over twenty miles away, and it was challenging terrain to cover on foot, even for men in the best of health. Dunstan decided there was little else of value they would be able to tell him, and it was better to get them the healing they required. Perhaps with the proper care, some of them would be well enough to fight in the event of an attack.

"You men have served the Empire with honor and distinction, and you have my thanks, all of you. My men will see to it that you are fed and your wounds are treated. Send for me if there is anything I can do for you. Please excuse me; I need to make preparations for a possible assault." As Dunstan walked away, he shouted out orders, calling for the watch on the walls to be doubled at once. Whatever was coming for them, he did not want to be caught unprepared. Captain Sheelan, the commanding officer at Fort Baker, was a good man but known for being lax with security. Dunstan had a bad feeling that carelessness had cost him his life.

Leaving the wounded to be tended to by the healer, Captain Dunstan made his way to the planning room. If Fort Baker had fallen two days ago, it would only be a matter of time until Fort Oliver found itself under attack as well. They were more remote, but it was possible an attacking force could arrive as early as today. He would not be yielding his fortress to any attacker, but there were preparations he needed to put into place. They would likely be outnumbered, and though their walls gave them a strategic edge, he couldn't discount the fact that Fort Baker had fallen under similar circumstances.

He arrived in the planning room, a large stone chamber situated in the center of Fort Oliver. At its center was a massive oak table ringed with a dozen chairs. Most of these chairs would sit empty; he had only four lieutenants stationed here with him. It would fall on the five of them to devise a plan to repel the coming assault. The lieutenants filed in shortly after his arrival, punctual as always.

Dunstan was a well-liked captain, but he was known for running a tight ship. His men knew better than to leave him waiting, especially with the possibility of such a threat looming over them.

"Gentlemen, as you have likely already heard, we have a situation coming our way. We are likely to be attacked soon by the Hoyt, along with help from the Thornatan Army. We will most likely be outnumbered, though if some of the arrivals from Fort Baker are fit to fight, the odds against us may not be so great. If it were just a mob of Hoyt scum, I wouldn't be so concerned, but with trained soldiers backing them, we may be in danger. Our walls give us an edge, but Fort Baker had the same advantage and has already fallen. We would be fools to think it could not happen to us," he said, not wasting time on the lengthy preambles favored by most Imperial officers.

"Any soldier who aligns himself with Hoyt rebels against his people is unworthy of the uniform he wears," Lieutenant Rigel spat in disgust.

"You will hear no argument from me, but their motivations are of no concern to us. We need to concern ourselves with how to stop them. If it comes to a siege, how much food do we have stockpiled?" Dunstan asked.

"We have enough stores to last us through the next winter, but if the men from Fort Baker are staying, we would likely run out before the snows thaw," Lieutenant Pavery replied. "Assuming we are all still alive, of course.

The next resupply from Imperial High Command is not due until spring."

"I want the gates closed and barred from this moment on, and they are not to be opened without my direct order. The men from Fort Baker say the Hoyt and Thornatans attempted to treat with them first. We will not give them the satisfaction here. A member of their delegation may well have slipped away unnoticed and stayed hidden until they could open the gates for their comrades. No such mistakes are to be made. I also want every inch of our walls guarded day and night. They may try to slip a man over so he can open our gates. We will not have that happen here. It will mean long shifts for the men, so make sure we have rest time scheduled for each of them. We need to be sharp," Dunstan said.

"Sir, if I may make a suggestion, perhaps we would be better to take a different course of action," Rigel said, much to Dunstan's surprise. Rigel was typically not a planner; his skills fell under the purview of committing violence more so than planning it.

"What is your suggestion, Lieutenant Rigel?" Dunstan asked. He was skeptical, but he was always willing to hear his lieutenants out. It was a trait which set him apart from most Imperial captains, and his men respected him more for it.

"Perhaps we should allow their delegation inside to treat with us. If we do not care for their terms, which I assume we will not, we kill them. Assuming they send high-ranking members of their force, we will cut off their leadership, as well as lessening their strength in numbers."

"This is a tactic Imperial High Command would frown upon." He did not care for the suggestion one bit, but he was forced to acknowledge to himself that it did have its merits. "But it may be our best hope for defending this fortress. If we take out some of their leadership, their force may not be organized enough to defeat us. And any dent we can make in their numbers would be a boon for us. I will consider your suggestion, Lieutenant Rigel. Thank you for proposing it."

Truthfully, the proposal did not sit well at all with Thad Dunstan, who considered himself to be an honorable man. But if forced to choose between a black mark on his honor or the lives of his men, there was no decision to be made. He would win the battle to come at any cost, because the alternative would be the deaths of the men who had served him so well over these past two years. Most of these men were young with bright futures ahead of them, and he would not sit idly by and watch them be butchered for the sake of something as trivial as his honor. The massacre at Fort Baker would not be repeated at his fortress. He would do whatever was necessary to make sure of it.

"I want our best archers stationed on the wall in shifts. If an attack comes, they are all to gather there. Have every arrow we have brought up; I don't want them lacking ammunition. Pavery, I want you in command on top of the wall. If a force arrives, do not open fire unless I order you to do so. If they fire on you first, you have full authorization to shoot with intent to kill. Anybody not fit to fight needs to be moved to the infirmary at once. If the gates are breached and we are forced to fall back, that will be our last stronghold. Rigel, I want you and a dozen of our best men guarding it, protecting our path of retreat. Jaxson, Quincy, you two will be in the courtyard with me and the rest of our men. If they breach the gates, we will make them earn every last inch of ground. Is everybody clear on your assignment?"

"Yes, sir!" came the uniform reply.

"Perfect, gentlemen. The fortress is officially under lockdown. Nobody is to be roaming about without being fully armed and armored from this moment onward. Anything out of the ordinary is to be brought to me at once. Let's keep our wits about us, and we will be just fine. You are all dismissed. Long live the Empire," he concluded.

"Long live the Empire!" they all repeated as one before dispersing to see to their assigned tasks.

Thad Dunstan made a beeline for his quarters, seeking a brief moment of rest. He was not an old man by any traditional measure of the word, but the conflicts he had seen had aged him well beyond his years. He had considered retirement only a year prior, but he enjoyed the men he served with here at Fort Oliver and had signed on for an additional four years of service. He had never thought to see serious combat here on a simple border-policing assignment. He realized now that assumption might well end up costing him his life.

When he reached his chamber, he made himself a cup of strong tea and sat back in his favorite chair to enjoy it. He was anxious, eager for the impending attack to arrive and be over. He did not fear battle—not for himself, at least. He had seen enough of them over the years that he had grown numb to the prospect. He did fear losing men he cared for, but such was the risk every one of them had agreed to take when they had enlisted. As long as he did all he could do to protect them, he knew he would be able to walk away with his head held high. *Assuming the Thornatans don't kill you*, he thought darkly to himself.

Finishing his tea, Dunstan made his way to his armor stand and began donning his battle gear: black plate armor emblazoned with the Imperial star sigil, a shield with the same design, and, of course, his sword and spear. If the Hoyt arrived suddenly, he would not have time to armor himself, so he felt it best to do so now. As he was preparing to return to the central courtyard to check on preparations, the sound of a horn split the silence. The trumpet was only blown when suspected enemies were approaching. Their attackers had arrived even sooner than anticipated.

He strode past the infirmary on his way to the courtyard, pleased to find Lieutenant Rigel already in position with his dozen handpicked fighters. Rigel assured him as he passed that the infirmary would be well protected, but Dunstan simply nodded and walked by. There was no time to respond now. He emerged into the courtyard to find the archers lining up on the walls above him, Pavery directing them into position.

Inside the courtyard, the rest of the men—around forty-five of them—were taking defensive positions. If the gates were breached, it would be up to this group of men to defend the interior of the fortress. The surviving archers would come down from the wall to help, of course, but by the time they reached the courtyard, it may already be too late. Lieutenant Jaxson rushed over to Dunstan as soon as he spotted him.

"Sir, the preparations are made. The men on the wall report roughly 120 fighters outside, both Hoyt and Thornatan Army. They've spotted a battering ram; they've come prepared to smash open the gates if we decline to open them," he said.

"They are welcome to try." As always, Dunstan would not allow his inner doubts to show to the men who were counting on him to lead them through this. "Thank you, Lieutenant Jaxson. You have done fine work. Send word to Pavery that he is to open fire if the enemy tries moving the ram toward the gates."

"Captain Dunstan, sir!" The voice was calling to him from atop the wall. It was Pavery, waving his arms so his commander could find him in the crowd of archers. "They have sent a party forward with a white flag; it seems they want to negotiate. There are ten men total in their party," he called out.

The Hoyt War

Thad Dunstan hesitated for the first time in a long time. He was a man of swift, decisive decision-making, but this gave him pause. He knew what he must do, but even so, he was reluctant to do it. Still, he reminded himself once more that the lives of the men under his command were more precious to him than his honor ever could be. There was only one thing to be done, and there was no point in delaying it. He would give his men their best hope of survival, no matter the consequences it brought upon him. Steeling himself, he gave the word.

"Open the gates. Allow the negotiators to enter, and then close the gates behind them," he commanded with a meaningful glance at Jaxson and Quincy. They knew as soon as the words left his mouth what he intended to do. He would not have allowed the gates to open for any other reason. They moved off to discretely give the word for their men to be ready.

The men in the courtyard hurried to unbar the gates and swing them open. A party of ten men strode into the fortress, half of them bearing the gray-and-red garb of the Thornatan Army, the others the black leather of the Hoyt. Once they had entered, Dunstan nodded for his men to secure the gate. The envoys came toward him, their arms spread wide in a gesture of peace. Dunstan noted that they had not seen fit to remove their weapons before entering the fortress, despite their allegedly peaceful intentions. They stopped within a few feet of Dunstan, the Hoyt in the lead smiling wide.

"Good day, my good man. I assume you are the commander of this fine fortress?" he asked.

"Captain Thaddeus Dunstan. To whom am I speaking?"

"We come bearing a message from Idanox, the duke of Thornata. The men I have gathered here with me are both Hoyt warriors and Thornatan soldiers, come to represent the newfound unity between previously bitter rivals," the man replied, the sneering grin never leaving his face.

"I see. What message is it that the duke would send such a large contingent of fine men such as yourselves all this way to deliver?" Dunstan asked, already growing weary of the charade.

"No need to be concerned, Captain Dunstan. These regions can be dangerous, and Duke Idanox did not want to put his men at risk of unnecessary harm. You and your men have served with distinction here on the border, and no man can deny it. The duke has asked me to relay to you that your service is appreciated but no longer required. You may gather your men and equipment and march home." The Hoyt's words were harmless enough, but his tone had changed to reflect just the slightest threatening hint. Thaddeus Dunstan never trusted a man who showed so many of his teeth while smiling, and this Hoyt was no exception.

"I understand. Please thank the duke for his kind words, but our orders come from Imperial High

Command, not from the ruler of any individual province. This ensures we remain impartial in the affairs of the provinces, as I am sure you understand. I am afraid that until our orders from Imperial High Command are changed, we cannot accept the duke's most generous offer," Dunstan replied. He was trying his utmost to remain calm and seem at ease, as though their actual intent were a mystery to him.

"My apologies, Captain Dunstan. Perhaps I did not make myself clear enough. I'm rather new to politics, so please be patient with me. You and your men are being expelled from the province of Thornata, effective immediately. You are to vacate this fortress by dusk and make your way immediately across the border. If you do not, we will forcibly remove you. That would be most unfortunate, in my opinion. I do not see any need for hostilities between us," the Hoyt spokesman said.

Dunstan paused, wanting to choose his next words carefully, knowing they could well be his last before giving an order he did not relish. The Hoyt was an arrogant fool, no question about that, but he still had no desire to spill this man's or any other man's blood on this day, nor would any man who had seen as much death and bloodshed as he had in his life. Still, he saw no other means out of this predicament. The fate of Fort Baker made it abundantly clear.

"I am afraid we must continue to politely decline your request, my friend. This fortress is the property of the Empire, and we cannot yield it without direction from the proper authorities. Please command your forces to withdraw from our walls immediately. I also see no need for hostilities between us. If your duke wishes to meet with a member of Imperial High Command to discuss this matter in person, I would be happy to help arrange it."

The Hoyt fighter did not look surprised or even angry. *No doubt he wanted this outcome*, Dunstan thought. The Hoyt had a reputation for bloodlust; surely the thought of killing them all was one this man savored. Still, he was somewhat shocked to find Thornatan soldiers had been swayed to join such a cause. No sooner had the thought passed through his mind than the foremost soldier lifted his spear into an attacking position. Dunstan clenched up, his shield coming up in defense, the order to attack already moving to his lips. To his shock, the soldier did not attack him. Instead, he plunged his spear directly into the back of the Hoyt emissary's skull.

The Hoyt dropped without a word, dead before he struck the ground. His Hoyt companions stared down at him, bewildered before reaching for their weapons, but it was too late. The remaining soldiers were striking now, their spears thrusting into their Hoyt allies before they could react. All five Hoyt were dead within seconds, their blood pooling beneath them on the ground. The Thornatan soldiers immediately flung their weapons to the ground, raising their hands in surrender as the Imperials drew their own.

"Please, Captain Dunstan, we mean you and your men no harm!" one soldier cried out.

"I suspect these men thought you meant them no harm as well, so you will forgive me for being a bit skeptical," Dunstan replied, still mildly in shock. His spear and shield were raised defensively in front of him, and he had to intention of lowering them until he was sure of the Thornatans' intentions.

"We have no love for the Hoyt, any of us. We do not serve them willingly. Please, sir, please hear us out. If we delay much longer, the Hoyt outside will begin to suspect something is awry. These negotiations were not expected to be lengthy."

"If you have something to say to me, say it quickly."

"None of us wish to serve the Hoyt. We march with them because Idanox threatened the lives of our families if we did not. He seized control of Oreanna with murder and the aid of black magic. None of us have any love in our hearts for him. Please believe us, Captain Dunstan. We need your help. Please allow me up onto your wall. If I give a signal, my men outside will slay the remainder of the Hoyt forces who are with us, and we can speak without fear of attack. Please give me just five seconds atop your wall." The man was quite desperate; that was easy enough to see. Dunstan nodded his consent, signaling two of his men to accompany the soldier.

The soldier hurried up the stairs to the wall. Pavery looked down at him, looking quite befuddled, but Dunstan merely signaled for him to allow the man to pass. The

Thornatan soldier looked down from the edge of the wall and raised one arm to the air with three fingers extended upward. Dunstan could not see anything happening on the other side of the wall, though he could hear the faint clash of weapons in the distance. The expressions of his men stationed above told him everything he needed to know. The Thornatan soldier had been true to his word.

The Thornatan soldier returned moments later, a broad smile splitting his face. He hurried toward Captain Dunstan, extending a hand, which Dunstan cautiously accepted, still on his guard for a possible betrayal. Early in his career, he had learned to never take any man at face value. There were so many out there who were so skilled at concealing their true intentions. These soldiers had burst into his fortress, threatening to attack. Now they were acting as though they were the best of friends.

"I cannot thank you enough, Captain Dunstan. You have helped to liberate us from our captors. But now I must ask one more thing of you. My comrades and I wish to return to Oreanna and retake our province from that lunatic Idanox, but we are only one hundred strong. There is another force making its way toward Fort Woodson. If we can help them eliminate their captors as well, we will double our strength," the man said.

"I suggest you get moving then, soldier. Fort Woodson is a hard march from here. We can spare a small amount of provisions for each of your men if needed," Dunstan replied.

"Captain, respectfully, I would ask that you consider mustering your own forces to join us on this march," the man said, to Dunstan's amazement.

"I am sorry, soldier, but the Imperial Army has no place in the infighting of Thornata. We are here to keep the peace between the Empire's provinces, nothing more," he replied.

"With all due respect, Captain Dunstan, I believe this is your fight as much as ours. Fort Baker has already fallen. I apologize for it, but not all of our fellow soldiers were as bold as us to make such a move against the Hoyt. Your fellow Imperial soldiers are in jeopardy at Fort Woodson. Are you going to sit idly by and trust us to save them? Beyond that, if the Hoyt are allowed to rule Thornata unchecked, how long until they look to expand their reach? How long until they advance into Verizia and beyond? You don't have enough men to stop them if they do, but you could make a difference now, before things go too far."

He made a reasonable enough point, but Dunstan was still hesitant. Becoming involved in a province's inner war without approval from Imperial High Command was a risky move. It could end with him locked in a stockade for the rest of his life, or even swinging from the end of a noose. Still, the man was right: other Imperial lives were in harm's way. Could he really turn his back on them? He did not look to his lieutenants for advice. He knew this was a decision he must make on his own, and he would not have them bear any of the blame for a mistake that was his to make.

Captain Thaddeus Dunstan had lived his life and served his Empire, trying to do the right thing. It was the only life he had ever known. He wanted to do the right thing here. But for the first time in a long time, he was not confident he knew what the right thing was.

Chapter Two

The sun was swiftly dropping behind the western horizon, and Alsea's spirits were sinking along with it. She could not bear to face the horrible truth that was overwhelming her even faster than the blackness of night was enveloping the sky. She had been waiting since dawn, perched near the top of an old willow tree overlooking the Kival River just south of the city of Kolig. She could see the agreed-upon rendezvous point, and her eyes had not left it all day, yet still there was no sign of her friends. She had gone without food, water, or rest, and with each passing second, she feared more and more that it had all been for naught. She knew in her heart that Adel and Ola would have come by now if they were able.

An entire day had passed since she had successfully slipped out of Kolig with General McLeod and two of his soldiers. Each moment that had passed with no sign of Adel or Ola had been nothing short of torture. Their escape through the Kolig sewers had been unpleasant, but nothing compared to the pain of not knowing where her friends were or if they were even still alive. With a full day having passed since their flight from the treacherous General Bern, each moment that passed with no sign of them seemed to reinforce the message that the pair had not been able to escape the city.

The thought of the two of them still trapped inside Kolig with the army pursuing them was unbearable for Alsea. The notion they had possibly been captured or killed was far worse. It was the unknown that hurt her the most. Were they still alive? Had they been caught? Were they still trying to find a way out of Kolig? The same questions had run through her head thousands of times while she had sat in the tree, waiting for their arrival. Now, with nightfall imminent, she felt certain they were not coming. She did not know where they were or what had happened to them. She only knew one thing for sure: her friends needed her help.

Alsea blamed herself for whatever predicament in which Adel and Ola were caught. If she had not gotten separated from them, she could have led them safely out of the city, or at the least she could have been captured along with them, assuming they were still alive at all.

Stop it! Of course they were still alive, and she could not allow herself to believe otherwise. Adel and Ola were not easy people to kill, no matter how great the odds against them. But something had obviously gone wrong in their escape, and they needed her help. There was no point in keeping them waiting any longer.

After descending from the tree, she made her way back to the small river cave where Supreme General Randall McLeod and the men loyal to him had hunkered down to await her return. She did not fail to note the looks of disappointment on their faces when she entered the cave alone.

"No sign of them at all?" General McLeod asked, even though he already knew the answer. The question annoyed her. Obviously, she would not have returned alone if there had been. She had saved his skin the night before; he could at least have something more helpful to say. Alsea knew this line of thought was not fair. General McLeod had done everything he could. But she did not care much about fairness at the moment. Anything not related to helping her friends was something she did not have time to entertain.

"There's been no sign of them all day. Fortunately, there's been no sign of any enemies either, so I don't think they know where we planned to meet. I'm afraid our worst fears may be realized: I don't think they escaped Kolig. Either they have been captured, or they are unable to find a way to get out of the city," she replied, the words leaving a bitter taste in her mouth. How could she have allowed this to happen?

The general did not reply for a moment, his brow furrowed in thought. About twenty men had gathered here with him last night, fewer than half the men he had instructed to meet here. If the men who hadn't reported to him were serving General Bern, this area was not safe. Every moment that went by was a moment they risked discovery; Alsea knew this. Even if the men had tried to come and been captured, Bern would no doubt already be interrogating them. Every hour that passed placed them further at risk. It was entirely possible that Bern knew where they were and was waiting for the cover of darkness to move against them. They would need to move soon, but first, they would need to find out where Adel and Ola were. This meant the unpleasant prospect of venturing back into Kolig.

"I think we should march to Kalstag, gather what forces we can muster to our cause, and then begin our march on the capital," General McLeod said after a long silence, shocking Alsea. "We can try to rally men from Kalskag as well on our way north. I've thought about going to Kobuk first, but the garrison there is relatively small, and it will take a lot of time that we don't have. Besides, that may be the next place Bern expects us to head. Better if we don't do what he is expecting. We don't have much in the way of supplies, but I think we can make it to Kalstag if we ration responsibly."

"You can't possibly mean to leave Adel and Ola behind after all they have done to support you?" Alsea demanded, not bothering to show the respect she would normally display for a man of McLeod's stature. He was a good man, but she could not accept that he planned to leave her friends behind. He could make all the plans he wanted; she would have no part of them.

"Please try to understand, Alsea," McLeod began, looking everywhere but directly at her. "Even if they are alive, which you must admit is very much in doubt, we do not have enough men here to go after them. We have no hope of getting back into Kolig unnoticed. Bern will have the garrison on high alert for any sign of us. They are quite resourceful, and if they are unable to get to us on their own, there is likely little we can do to help them. Adel has his powers, and Ola is an exceptional warrior. What can we possibly do for them that they would be unable to do for themselves? We would only be putting ourselves in jeopardy. The people of Thornata are depending on us to rid them of Idanox. I do not like the idea of leaving them behind, but this is what circumstance requires of us. We have to act in the best interest of the people of Thornata, no matter the cost."

Alsea could scarcely believe what she was hearing. All three of them had nearly died multiple times fighting for this man, and now he was refusing to help them when they needed him most? They had viewed General McLeod as a man of honor, a belief she doubted more by the second. She did not bother to attempt to conceal her fury when she spoke again. It took every bit of restraint she still possessed to keep from screaming in his face. If it were not for the risk of discovery, she would have.

"With all due respect, General McLeod, I have fought and bled for you, just like Adel and Ola have. I almost died in that warehouse in Kalstag after we walked into the trap your intelligence led us into. I almost died again fighting to defend your wounded men from that mindless monster when it attacked our camp. I will bear those scars for the rest of my life. Do you wish to see them? If those actions mean nothing to you, that is your business, but I will not be leaving my friends behind. If you do not wish to help me, I will find them myself." She could not tell if the look he gave her in return reflected admiration or exasperation, nor did she much care. She was already thinking about her next steps while retrieving her pack from the back of the cave.

"You think that the sacrifices the three of you have made mean nothing to me?" General McLeod asked, stepping in front of her. Alsea tensed at his approach. If he thought to stop her from leaving, she would be forced to hurt him, which was something she did not want to do, no matter how disgusted she was with his attitude. "You are sorely mistaken on that count, Alsea, but the lives of every man, woman, and child in this province could be at stake here. If Idanox is allowed to rule Thornata unchallenged, why have we been making these sacrifices? If I knew that I could help Adel and Ola, I would do so in a heartbeat. But I have no information that leads me to believe this is the case. For all we know, they have been found and killed. I know it is not what you want to hear, and believe me when I say I do not want to believe it. But it is the truth. I will march to Kalstag and try to muster more men to march on Oreanna, because that is the only option I have which makes any sense."

He was right, but it changed nothing for her. He was not telling her anything she didn't already know, but her brain would not win out over her heart. McLeod was not a heartless man, but he was a cold and calculating one. A man in his position could be nothing else if they wanted to live for very long. He saw her friends as assets that had been lost in the service of a greater good. While they may have been gone, for McLeod, the fight for that greater good had to continue. But she would not allow herself to see them this way. If there was even the faintest hope that she could help her friends, she would try to do so. It did not matter how great the odds were stacked against her.

"I understand and respect your decision, General McLeod. I hope you will understand and respect mine not to join you this time. I will not be able to live with myself if I turn my back on my friends, so I will try to find them and help them in any way I can. I hope the three of us see you again when the time comes to put an end to Idanox and the Hoyt. If we don't make it, I hope for nothing more than for you to succeed against them. As you said, the people of Thornata are depending on you to save them from this nightmare," Alsea said, already starting to make her way toward the cave entrance.

Darkness would fall soon, and she wanted to reach Kolig before it consumed the sky entirely. General McLeod did not move to block her this time, but he did call out to her one last time as she walked away.

"Alsea, wait just one moment, please. What you want to do here is admirable, and I respect it. You possess the type of courage I look for in my own men. I just hope you have thought this through completely. Getting yourself killed will not do Adel and Ola any good. I respect your decision, but I also urge you to reconsider it."

But Alsea's mind was not to be changed in this matter. Neither Adel nor Ola would leave her behind, and she would not leave them behind either. She sincerely hoped that General McLeod succeeded in his mission, because the future of Thornata depended on it. But his mission could not be hers—not this time. She would go her own way, no matter how dangerous the decision would prove.

"I appreciate your advice, General McLeod, but my mind is made up," she said. "If I do succeed, the three of us will find you. We will keep our word and help you put an end to Idanox and the Hoyt. I believe in my heart that all three of us will be at your side when you reach Oreanna. But by myself, I would be of limited use to you anyway.

The best purpose I can serve is to try to reunite you with Adel and Ola. It is they who have the skills you truly require at your disposal. Especially Adel. You will need his powers to help you overcome the Hoyt, especially now that Idanox has turned the bulk of the army against you. I am doing what is right for me, but I hope it also proves to be the right choice for Thornata."

"I strongly disagree with you on one count. Your use would never be limited in my eyes, Alsea. After spending all this time with you, I realize how asinine it is that we do not allow women to serve in the Thornatan Army. I doubt there is a man anywhere in this force who is tougher and more determined than you. I hope I live long enough to push for an end to such outdated rules. However, I understand that there is nothing I will be able to say that will change your mind. Is there anything I can provide that will aid you?"

"A few days' worth of provisions and a few more arrows would be much appreciated if you can spare them."

So, the general and his men gathered the requested supplies and prepared to make their own departure. They could not risk staying in this cave any longer. If they were discovered, it would perhaps be the end of any hope of overthrowing Idanox. They were ready to depart in short order; most of these men had been fortunate to escape Kolig with their lives, let alone many possessions. *At least they won't have a lot of extra weight to carry along with them*, Alsea thought. They would march at night across the plains toward Kalstag and hope no Hoyt or men loyal to General Bern would spot them. Before parting, General McLeod pulled Alsea aside for one final word, out of earshot of his men.

"Alsea, if you do succeed in finding Adel and Ola, I plan to gather as many loyal men as I can find on the southwestern edge of the Ice Fields. It's the best place I can think of for an encampment. Such terrain will make a direct assault against us nigh impossible. We will stay there until the time comes to march on Oreanna. I hope you will join us there," he said.

"Returning to the scene of your greatest triumph?" Alsea asked, referring to the general's famous victory on the Ice Fields decades earlier.

"Perhaps the Ice Fields will bring us as much luck as they brought me all those years ago. We're going to need it. All these years later, I still have a hard time admitting how lucky I was." The general smirked. "Don't ever tell anyone I told you this, but I thought I was going to die that day. As the bandits advanced on us, I was sure I had led those men to their doom. A strategy that went down as brilliant could just as easily have been considered the worst blunder in the history of the Thornatan Army."

"History is kind to the victors. We may need you to be so lucky once again," Alsea said, clasping the general's hand before turning away.

Alsea did not waste any time putting ground behind her, heading back toward Kolig as rapidly as her long legs could carry her. She estimated that she would reach the city just as the darkness of night fell entirely, which served her purposes well enough. She was not concerned with being noticed moving around the city. It seemed the Hoyt had little knowledge of her. Unlike Adel and Ola, no bounty had been placed on her. The possibility existed that some soldiers may recognize her from her time serving with General McLeod, but that was a gamble she was willing to make. She would keep her head down and talk to nobody. It was her ears, not her mouth, that were needed to find her friends.

Her plan was relatively straightforward. She would head into taverns frequented by Thornatan soldiers and listen to their conversations. If she did not hear anything of consequence at one, she would move to another. From her experience, soldiers loved to boast about their accomplishments, and drink made their tongues even looser. Sooner or later, she would hear a bit of news about what may have happened to her friends, and she would act accordingly.

What would that entail? Alsea had not spared a great deal of thought on what exactly she would do if her friends had been captured. She would need to free them, of course, most likely from the prison in the city of Kolig. It was a formidable structure, but one she was confident she could breach if necessary. Getting them back out would be another challenge, but she would be able to find a solution. Alsea had spent the better part of her life relying on herself, and she had never failed to accomplish what was needed. Ola had told her once when she was young that where there was a will, there was a way. She had found it to be a true statement over the course of her life. She was good at slipping in and out of places undetected, and the Kolig prison would be no different. If that was where they were, she would find a way in, and woe to anyone who tried to stop her.

The possibility existed that Adel and Ola had been killed, of course, but this was not a possibility she allowed herself to entertain for long. She had spent the better part of the last day shoving it to the back of her mind. In truth, it was more than simple denial. It was a logical line of thinking that made her believe they were not dead, contrary to what General McLeod might have assumed. Alsea suspected the ambitious General Bern would crave the additional credit that would come his way for delivering the fugitives to Idanox alive. Such an achievement would ingratiate the traitorous Bern in the eyes of Idanox.

If either of her friends had been killed, she vowed to herself that General Bern would pay for their lives with his own, even if it was the last thing she did. But there was no time to dwell on such things now. She forced the albeit pleasant image of twisting her knife into Bern's eye socket from her mind. She needed to focus, but she was finding that rather difficult. Her mind was scattered in a million different directions, and there would be no clarity until she knew what had happened to her friends. Once she did, she would have no trouble focusing, but for the time being, the endless possibilities were maddening.

Her thoughts turned to Adel. The young man had grown so much in the short time she had known him, not only in the mastery of his power, but in his development as a man. When they had first set out from the Temple of the Rawl, he had still been a boy, naive about the world in many ways. He had been shielded for most of his life, protected from the challenges of a grim reality she had known from a much younger age. But he had been thrust into impossible situations, and he had come out the other side of them stronger than ever. She admired that. Though he was older than she had been, his journey mirrored her own in many ways.

He was in love with her; any fool could have seen it. Concealing his emotions was a skill he had not yet managed to develop in the time she had known him. Alsea had not spoken to him about his feelings. She felt it best to allow him to resolve them in his own time. Besides, she had not cared to admit just yet that they were feelings she shared. Ever since the Battle of Kolig, she had found herself more and more enamored with the young Rawl wielder. Her feelings had only grown more intense when Ola had told her of Adel recklessly trying to save her in that burning warehouse in Kalstag. His selflessness and courage were attributes that would make the world a better place if more people shared them.

Perhaps she should have told him how she felt, taken the onus off him to do so. But she had resolved to allow him to come to her when he felt comfortable doing so. Now he may never get that chance, and if he didn't, then neither would she. It was just another tragedy in the long string of them that had been her life. Perhaps she was doomed to spend the rest of her days wondering what might have been.

She scolded herself again for allowing such negative thoughts to creep into her head. Adel was not dead, and she was going to find him, no matter where he was. Anyone who tried to get in her way would meet an unpleasant end. She was drawing near to Kolig now, and the wooden bridge that had been hastily constructed after the Hoyt had demolished the old stone pathway was within sight. She briefly considered entering the city via the sewers instead of the main gates but brushed the idea aside. Time was of the essence. She was not a well-known fugitive like Adel or General McLeod; she should be able to get into the city unnoticed through the main gates.

There were perhaps a dozen soldiers near the gates, examining the face of every man who was exiting the city. Alsea surmised they must've been searching for General McLeod, unaware he had escaped from the city the night before. *At least his men haven't given him up yet.* They were paying no attention to anybody entering the city, and Alsea was able to stroll through the gates without issue. *They must not expect anyone fortunate enough to get out would be stupid enough to come back*, she thought sarcastically to herself. She set off at once for the first tavern she had decided upon. It was time to go to work.

Chapter Three

Darkness and disorientation were the only things
Adel could recognize as he was shoved along.
The hands propelling him were none too gentle,
and several times he stumbled to the ground. His captors
seemed content to let him fall hard to the stone before
pulling him roughly back to his feet and shoving him forward once more. The black sack they had forced over his
head blocked out everything about the world around him.
He desperately searched for anything he could use to summon his power—a sound, a smell—but there was nothing.
Every time he slowed his pace even slightly, the hands
shoved him forward once more, and his handling grew

even rougher. His captors clearly had no interest in allowing him to slow down and find his bearings. Any time to find a way to bring his powers to bear against them was not going to be allowed. His confusion was their most powerful ally at that moment, and he was forced to admit dismally to himself that it was serving them well.

The soldiers had shoved the sack over his head as soon as he had let his sword clatter to the ground on the docks. He had known nothing but darkness from that moment, as they had not removed it since. Nobody had spoken a word to him, the only communication the rough shoves propelling him along. He had no idea if Ola was still with him or even if the ogre was still alive for that matter. He assumed the sack was meant to prevent him from using the power of the Rawl and was forced to acknowledge that it was an effective means of doing so.

Without being able to see, hear, smell, or feel any of the world around him, Adel had no method of using his power to manipulate it against his enemies. Since he had learned to use his power, he had always assumed it would be there to save him, even in the direst of circumstances. It was a depressing thought, a force as mighty as the Rawl neutralized by something as simple as a burlap sack. Still, he took heart from the fact that they had not killed him yet, and as long as he lived, he had hope.

They had stopped walking once for several hours, and Adel had been tempted to try to lift the sack from his face. But he had not forgotten their threat from the previous night. If he was being watched and he made such a move, they may kill Ola in retaliation, assuming the ogre was still alive at all. The fact they had not bothered to tie his hands was not lost on him. The army must've felt as though they had a more effective means of keeping him under their control. This, at least, gave him hope that Ola was alive.

If anything had happened to his friend, Adel vowed to himself that every last one of these treacherous scum would pay for it the moment they removed this sack from his head. He suspected they would make good on their promise not to harm Ola for precisely this reason. The ogre was their only means of controlling Adel, after all. The threat of harm to his friend was the only thing stopping Adel from ripping off the sack and launching a devastating, instinctual Rawl attack against his captors.

Unwilling to risk harm to Ola, Adel stood in silence, straining his senses, searching for anything that could be of use. The sack over his head was thick, and he could not even smell anything through the stench of the musty canvas. He strained his ears, hoping for the sound of a nearby river or a cackling torch, but there was nothing. His training had taught him ways of manipulating the world around him to devastating effect. But it had taught him nothing to help him in this situation. How could he manipulate the world around him if he had no idea what was there? He fought hard to keep the despair from overwhelming him. He told himself repeatedly there was a way out of this; he just had to find it.

After a rest of several hours, hands clasped around his arms and propelled him forward once more. Keeping the pace that his captors were setting without the use of his sight was a challenge. Adel stumbled twice, almost losing his footing completely. On each occasion, the hands steadied him and then shoved him forward once more. *At least they didn't just let me fall this time*, he thought. Wherever they were going, the soldiers must've been in a hurry to get him there. No doubt he was not a prisoner they relished having in their custody. *I wouldn't want to try to hold me either. One mistake, one slipup, and I will make them pay for this, even if it's the last thing I ever do, the traitorous scum.*

Just when Adel thought they would never stop walking, his shins collided with a hard surface, sending shock waves of pain radiating through his legs. He fell forward, crashing down onto another hard surface, which felt like it was made of wood. Hands grasped his legs, lifting him slightly and shoving him farther onto the surface. Then came a loud crash, the sound of metal colliding with metal—a cage perhaps. That would make sense; they would want him contained in a manner he could not easily escape.

Within moments he was moving again, the ground beneath him lurching awkwardly. He must've been in a cage in the back of a wagon. Where was the army taking him? He was mildly surprised they hadn't killed him yet. They would surely have been able to collect the bounty with his dead body just as easily. Why go to all this trouble? They were keeping him alive for a reason, and he was sure whatever that reason was, it was no good thing for him. He did not know General Bern well, but he had seen nothing to indicate that the foul man would allow him to live for no reason. His thoughts were interrupted as the wagon hit a bump, and the force sent him careening into the bars of the cage.

They had not secured him in the wagon in any way, so he was thrown continuously about the cage with every lurch, repeatedly slamming into the metal bars. The sack over his head prevented him from seeing properly to ward off the impacts. Within an hour, no part of his body was not aching horribly, and there was no indication the journey would end anytime soon. He tried to grasp for the bars to steady himself, but the wagon never held still long enough for him to establish a firm grip. He was silently grateful for the fact that the soldiers had not stripped him of his armor. The hard leather protection that had been gifted to him by the Children of the Rawl was likely the only thing saving him from broken bones. Occasionally his head would absorb the impact, leaving him dazed and confused for long minutes afterward.

He had no concept of time, but he surmised it must have been at least several hours before the wagon came to a halt at last. Had a full day passed since their capture? Adel had no way to be sure. He tried to stretch his limbs to relieve some of his aches, but his body was so battered that

- 42 -

he found he could hardly move a finger without pain washing through his extremities. He had not had anything to eat or drink since they had fled the abandoned shop after Bern's betrayal, and his weakness did little to help the pain. Even if he could see, he doubted he would be able to summon his power in this weakened state. It was probably precisely what the army wanted, he realized. A Rawl wielder without the Rawl was no more of a threat than any normal man.

They had been stopped for several minutes when the sounds of clattering metal told him the doors of his cage were opening. He felt the wagon rock once, twice, three times and assumed that three men had just climbed into the cage with him. He held his breath, not sure what was going to happen. Were they going to kill or torture him? At last, he received an exhilarating rush of fresh air as one of the men loosened and then lifted the bottom portion of sack off his face so he could hear.

"We are going to remove the sack so you can eat and drink, boy. Don't get any funny ideas. If we suspect you are even thinking about using your power, the pet ogre dies, and you don't eat for the rest of the journey. If you think we're bluffing, just try us. Do you understand?"

"Yes," Adel gasped, his throat so parched he could barely understand his own response.

The light of the midday sun burned his eyes as the sack was removed. He blinked furiously against the blinding sunlight, trying to adjust his sight. It took nearly a full minute for him to begin to make out anything around him through the tears welling up in his vision. When he was finally able to see, he felt a rush of relief wash through him.

There was an identical wagon parked directly next to his, and a similar iron cage was mounted to the back. Within the cage was Ola, looking right back at him. The ogre was alive, if not entirely well. His head was bruised and cut where the spear had struck him the night before, two nasty wounds. He had been wounded in the ambush, struck unconscious before he could make a move to defend himself. It appeared the soldiers had only bothered with the most rudimentary dressings possible for the injuries. Both looked as though they were in danger of infection if not treated properly. Unlike Adel's, Ola's wrists were chained to the bars of the cage. Two Thornatan soldiers stood just outside of his cage with their spears pointed straight at the ogre. The message was unmistakable: Adel had better behave himself if he wanted his friend to keep breathing. Adel chanced shooting his friend a brief smile, but the ogre's expression did not change, his face as unreadable as it had been on the day Adel had met him. Did Ola blame him for their capture? Or was he merely trying to remain an enigma to their captors?

"If you're done exchanging loving glances with your pet, you can hurry up and eat now," the soldier who had removed his sack snapped at him, delivering a gentle kick to Adel's side. "Get a move on, or the sack is going back on."

Adel's eyes snapped to the floor, where the men had set a cup of water and a few chunks of bread and cheese. It was not much, but Adel was happy for anything he could get. He suspected the small portion was an intentional effort to keep him as weak as possible. Malnutrition would be the most effective way of keeping him from summoning the power of the Rawl. The less sustenance they gave him, the less of a threat he would be to them. He drank the water first, his parched throat screaming in protest as it went down. As he drank, he allowed his eyes to wander, examining the prison they had placed him in. The cage seemed to be of solid construction, but he was sure he could find a way to open it with the power of the Rawl. He would first need to rebuild his strength, which would be problematic if this was all they planned on feeding him.

He willed himself to eat as slowly as possible, resisting the urge to devour the meal as ravenously as his body was urging. As he ate, he continued to survey his surroundings, trying all the while to be as discreet as possible. If his captors suspected what he was doing, they would no doubt confiscate the rest of his food. As he chewed, he allowed his eyes to take in everything they could find of the camp around him. The sight that met them was far from a welcome one.

He dared not take the time to count the number of soldiers, but there had to be dozens, perhaps even more. At least two dozen of them were mounted on horses, filling him with despair. Even if he and Ola did somehow escape these cages, they would not be able to outrun mounted men. There were too many of them to fight, and their hopes of flight were slim to none. If they continued to mal-nourish him, he would not be able to count on the Rawl's power to help even the odds.

"Hurry it up, boy. This isn't a feast in your honor. One more minute and the sack goes back on," the soldier snapped.

He rushed down the rest of his food, knowing he needed all the nourishment he could get. Before he knew what was happening, the sack had been forced back over his head and cinched tightly around his neck. The iron doors clanged shut, and off they went again. The aches and pains soon set in once more as he was tossed around with every jolt of the wagon. He wondered if Alsea and General McLeod had escaped Kolig. There had been no sign of them when he had been able to see his surroundings, and this gave him a twinge of hope. He felt if they'd been there, the army would have made sure that he could see them. The more of his friends they held prisoner, the more power they had over him. If they were not here, he could only surmise that they were still alive and free of the army's clutches. Perhaps they would still be able to overthrow Idanox without him.

Thinking of Alsea brought him both comfort and pain. He was relieved she was not here with them, that there was still hope for her. But the thought of never seeing her again pained him so much more than the aches of being thrown around inside this steel cage. The regret of never sharing his feelings with her was overpowering. He had been such a fool. Or had it been cowardice that had kept him quiet? He had no way of knowing for sure where these soldiers were taking them, but he could assume there would not be a happy ending waiting for him at the end of this journey. They weren't keeping him alive out of the kindness of their hearts. They hoped to profit off of him in some way.

He took some comfort from the fact that if Alsea and General McLeod had indeed escaped Kolig, they would continue the fight against Idanox and the Hoyt. It would not be easy for them, but there was hope as long as the fight continued. If he was going to be killed at the end of this journey, at least he would have died for a just cause.

And at least I managed to make life difficult for the Hoyt for a while, he thought, allowing himself a brief moment of humor. If Idanox had put such a massive bounty on him, he must have gotten under the Hoyt leader's skin. He had to allow himself to be proud of what little he had managed to accomplish in this struggle.

He took a moment to consider how ridiculous this truly was. Just over a year ago, if somebody had told him this was where he would end up, he would have laughed in their face. His life as a cabin boy had been a simple one, but one he had enjoyed nonetheless. There had been quite a few times over the last year that he had yearned to be back in that life, longing for the simplicity of delivering cargo to its destination. It was ironic, considering most of his time on the barge had been spent imagining the grand adventures he would go on one day. If only he had known how good he actually had it. But the Hoyt had stolen that peaceful existence from him. It was disappointing to think he was not going to be able to see through his plans to put an end to them. They deserved to face justice for their crimes, and Adel could only hope that another would be able to deliver it to them.

His thoughts distracted him from the physical pain this journey was inflicting on him, but the emotional pain taking its place was no better. He knew he shouldn't have been thinking like this; self-pity did him no good, nor did lying back and accepting the inevitable. He should've been working on a way out of his predicament, not waiting for his fate to come to him. He should've been scheming an escape attempt. If he was doomed to die, he would rather do so fighting and trying to escape. Adel had never in his life given up, and this was no time to start. If they wanted to kill him, he was going to make them work for it. Once again, he thought of Alsea, using the thought of her for strength. She would never lie back and meekly accept her fate, and neither would he.

Every time they took the sack off to feed him, he would see more of his surroundings, a little more each time. Eventually, he would spot a way to set them free. He wished he could talk to Ola. The ogre always had keen observations. No doubt Ola was also searching for a way to get free of their cages. Just like Alsea, Ola would never give up. But Adel was the one who possessed the power of the Rawl; he was the one who might be able to give them an advantage over their captors.

Wait, maybe I can talk to Ola, he realized. The ogre possessed hearing far beyond any human, and it had saved them multiple times in their travels together. He would not be able to respond, of course, but perhaps Adel could get a brief message to his friend. The opportunity to escape could come at any time, and it would be preferable for Ola to be prepared for it to happen. It was a risk, trying to communicate, but he felt it was the best choice he had. Fighting to keep his voice as quiet as possible, barely a whisper, Adel said the only thing he could think of to reassure his friend.

"Ola, we're going to get out of here. Keep your eyes open, and be ready."

Adel had no way of knowing for sure if Ola had heard. He could only hope. He had tried to sound as confident as possible. In truth, he had no idea how they were going to manage such a feat when they were surrounded by the Thornatan Army. But he had to believe they would find a way, or at least die trying.

Chapter Four

Idanox stalked back and forth, pacing the entire length of the reception room, his aggravation growing with each passing second. His men had woken him from a restful sleep in the middle of the night, telling him important news had arrived from the south. He had been pacing this same stretch of the floor for the better part of the past hour, waiting to hear what this supposedly urgent news could be. The incompetent fools under his command had been mistaken regarding the urgency of communications numerous times in the past. The longer the delay lasted, the more he feared this was doomed to be one more such case. He had been sleeping peacefully for the first time in days, and if they had no legitimate reason for waking him, somebody would pay the price for disturbing him.

He had looked at himself in the mirror before leaving his chambers, and the sight had been one he was still stewing over. His once-black hair was streaked with thin lines of gray, streaks that were growing more noticeable each time he looked. It even appeared as though it was beginning to thin near the top. He could not bear the thought of going bald; he had always been a vain man, though he would have never admitted it to anybody else. There had been a time when he had assumed such deteriorations were the burden of lesser men. His appearance needed to project strength and confidence to those under his rule. The lines crisscrossing his once-smooth face were another painful reminder of all the hard work he had invested in the Hoyt over the past few years. They also reminded him of the value of his time and how much of it his men were wasting at this very moment. Every second a man like Idanox had was valuable, a fact none of these oafs seemed to recognize. He had never liked to be kept waiting for any length of time, but these brutal reminders of his aging only intensified his anger at the waste of his precious time.

If they had woken him over yet another trivial matter, he would have them flogged or worse. He spent the next few minutes imagining the horrible punishments he could inflict upon his men in payment for their foolishness. He had refrained from dishing out such summary punishments in his time as duke, but perhaps it was time to remind his men that his mercy and patience had their limits. At last, just as his patience was about to run dry entirely, there was a knock at the door, and several Hoyt fighters entered, accompanying a Thornatan soldier. The man looked tired, as though he had been traveling for days. The Hoyt had relieved him of his weapons, and two men flanked him on each side. Perhaps they weren't as stupid as he had assumed. At least they possessed enough wits to spot a possible assassination attempt.

"We are sorry to disturb you at such a late hour, Duke Idanox. But we knew you would want to hear what this man has to say right away," one of the men said, pointing to the Thornatan soldier. Idanox glanced over his shoulder, reassuring himself that the two monstrous bodyguards that now followed him everywhere were present. His men had no doubt searched the man, but still, he could not be sure this was not a ploy by the soldier to make an attempt on his life. Most of the Thornatan Army now followed his orders, though none of them had any love in their hearts for him. The sight of the imposing monsters would give any would-be assassin second thoughts.

"Thank you for receiving me, Duke Idanox," the soldier began with a deep bow that brought the Hoyt leader no small amount of satisfaction. He had been in control of Oreanna for several weeks now and had found that seeing people simper and bow to him did not get old. He was finally growing used to hearing himself referred to as the duke, a position he had craved his entire life. While his years of toil and hardship had taken their toll on him, they had also born him the rewards he had sought. "I have been sent here by General Bern, who is stationed in the city of Kolig, with urgent news for you."

"Very well, soldier. What news do you have for me?" Idanox asked. He had never heard of this General Bern, though he was the first man of such a high rank to reach out to him since he had seized the capital. Idanox could not help but be curious about what the man could have to tell him. He doubted the soldier would have bowed to him if the message were meant to be disrespectful in nature. The Hoyt leader's mind was already going to work; a general who was willing to serve his cause could be a valuable tool. Thus far, his efforts to bring the Thornatan Army to heel had not gone well. His only allies were unwilling men he had blackmailed with the threat of harm to their loved ones.

"I rode here with as much haste as I could muster to bring you news that I think you will find most welcome. General Bern has captured the Rawl wielder you seek, along with his ogre friend. As we speak, General Bern is making his way toward Oreanna with the captives in tow to deliver them to you personally as a token of his loyalty. General Bern asked me to inform you that he sees no reason for the Thornatan Army and the Hoyt to continue the senseless bloodshed between us. He feels neither side has anything to gain by continuing to fight the other. He hopes this gift will begin to heal the rift between our rival forces and usher in a new era of peace and prosperity for the people of Thornata."

Idanox dared not believe it could be true. After all this time, had the Rawl wielder finally been captured? He had long given up any hope of having a chance to speak with the young man alive; he had assumed the boy would die fighting against him. Even the indestructible monster the mage Srenpe had created at his behest had been unable to bring him the boy, dead or alive. Now an opportunity he had long thought dead was breathing once more.

Furthermore, he was shocked that a Thornatan general had turned to his side without being coerced or intimidated. General Bern was clearly an intelligent man who recognized a lost cause when he saw one. Idanox had not thought to find such a man within McLeod's ranks. Exciting plans were already forming in Idanox's mind, ways to use this turn of events to its fullest potential. The possibilities were endless.

The boy would be invaluable to him no matter what his attitude. Idanox still held out hope that he could sway the boy to join the Hoyt, for a powerful ally could be made of him. He had not forgotten the threats of the Thrawll emissary, and the boy could be a valuable ally against such creatures if they decided to move against the Hoyt. If he refused to see reason, he could be handed over to the Thrawll as a token of goodwill. Their emissary had made it clear their patience with Idanox was waning. The boy could be a gift that would immediately turn their feelings toward him. No doubt the Thrawll could force the boy to give up the location of the Temple of the Rawl. Of course, none of this could happen if the boy was not transported safely to him. He turned his attention back to the soldier.

"Thank you for delivering this message to me, soldier. You have served your province with honor and courage. Every man, woman, and child of Thornata owes you a debt of gratitude, and I will do everything in my power to see that debt is repaid in full. My men will see to it that you have a comfortable bed and warm food tonight to rest from your long journey. I will also see to you it that a purse of gold is delivered to you as a bonus payment for your hard ride. May I ask, how were the boy and the ogre captured?"

"Thank you, Duke Idanox. General Bern suspected that Supreme General Randall McLeod was conspiring with them to rebel against your leadership. McLeod was in Kolig mustering a sizeable force for purposes he would not share with the other officers. The suspicion was that he planned to use this force to attack the capital and take control of it away from you. General Bern had him followed, leading us right to the Rawl wielder. The boy attempted to flee the city, but we were able to capture him before he could escape," the soldier explained.

"It is reassuring to know such treachery will not be tolerated in the ranks of the Thornatan Army, even from the highest of its officers. Thank goodness for loyal officers like General Bern and, of course, honorable soldiers such as yourself. Such men will lead Thornata into a new age of peace and prosperity. Was General McLeod captured or killed as well?" Idanox asked, eager to have the Supreme General removed from the picture.

The old man was a loose end that needed to be tied up as soon as possible. Randall McLeod had a history of inspiring men against impossible odds, and Idanox did not care to see him do so once more. Idanox did not think McLeod could muster the numbers he would need to overthrow the Hoyt, but he would still feel a lot better knowing McLeod was dead and buried. As long as he was out there plotting, the Hoyt's hold on Thornata was in potential jeopardy.

"Regretfully, McLeod had not been found at the time I left Kolig. He split away from the boy and the ogre during our pursuit. Our primary focus was on capturing the Rawl wielder, so we decided to devote the majority of our forces to that pursuit. Our men continue to search but thus far have found no sign of McLeod in Kolig," the soldier said, his shaking voice betraying that he was wary of disappointing the Hoyt leader. Idanox did not fail to note the hurried glance the man made toward the two beasts standing a few feet behind him. But Idanox saw no need to call them into service just yet. An opportunity he would never have dreamed of had fallen into his lap; it was best not to jeopardize it with a rash overreaction.

"The correct decision was made, soldier. I understand the reasoning, and it makes perfect sense. I would expect no less from the fine men of the Thornatan Army. The boy is the greater threat by far. McLeod is a bitter old dinosaur who cannot bear the thought of his province moving into a new age of prosperity, leaving him behind to wallow in the memories of his countless failures. After decades of failure to his people, seeing me succeed must eat away at him. Rest assured, he will not be allowed to continue his treason to the province of Thornata for much longer. We will find him and deal with him soon enough, no matter where he tries to hide. Tell me, my good man, how are the boy and the ogre being transported?"

Idanox did not allow his frustration to show. The boy was indeed the more significant threat after all. McLeod could be dealt with when the opportunity presented itself. The old fool would make a critical mistake sooner or later. The boy possessed a power far more destructive than anything the old man could bring to bear against him.

"General Bern is leading the expedition himself along with two hundred Thornatan soldiers. Both are being transported in caged wagons and are guarded day and night. We have been able to effectively neutralize the boy's powers by covering his head. It seems he cannot use them properly without being able to see, hear, or smell anything around him.

"The ogre is also being kept alive as a means of controlling the boy, who has been told that the ogre will die if he attempts to use his power to escape or attack us. General Bern's immediate thought had been to kill the ogre and merely bring you its head for verification. But after some thought, he decided it was more useful to us alive for the time being."

"Very good, my friend, quite intelligent indeed. I am grateful to have such brilliant men willing to do the hard work that is required to keep their people safe. I wonder if you would do me a favor and return to General Bern with a message from me?" Idanox asked, and the soldier nodded. "Tell General Bern his loyalty is most appreciated. He and those who have helped him will be rewarded most richly for the service they have done for their people. I will send two dozen of my own Hoyt men with you to help bolster the security of the transport. We don't want to take any chances with such dangerous prisoners. Go now and rest, my friend. My men will come to you with fresh horses in the morning for your departure. Thornata thanks you for your loyal service. Long live Thornata."

The soldier bowed once more, and it was a sight that Idanox once again suspected he would never tire of seeing. Fully awake now, and quite delighted to have had his rest disturbed, he sent for one of his highest-ranking lieutenants. He ordered the man to assemble two dozen of his best men to ensure the boy arrived in the capital without incident. He would feel better once there were Hoyt eyes on the operation to transport the Rawl wielder. This General Bern was wise to capture the boy, but there was always the risk that others in his company would have heroic ideas in their heads. Better to have Hoyt men on hand to have their eyes open for such attempts. While he may question their intelligence, he never doubted their loyalty. Once this was done, he poured himself a glass of the duke's finest wine and took a moment to savor the taste of his victory.

He had won. He had succeeded at everything he had set out to do. He was the duke of Thornata. The army had been successfully bent to his will, thanks to this General Bern. Now the last threat that had remained was coming to him locked in a cage. It was as complete a victory as Idanox could have possibly imagined. Soon the Imperials would be forced from the province, and his deal with the Thrawll would be fulfilled as well. The forces he had sent out to attack the Imperial forts should complete their work any day now.

There was, of course, the possibility that the Empire would respond to the Hoyt forcing their soldiers out of Thornata. The Thrawll had undoubtedly hoped this would be the case. If a sizeable Imperial force marched on Thornata, he would need to be prepared. They would likely turn around and march home as soon as the Thrawll did whatever it was they intended to do with the Imperial Army otherwise occupied, of course. That was what their emissary had assured him. But still, he might have to hold them off for a short time. But this was not his primary concern right now. Even if the Imperials did decide to attack, it would take weeks—if not months—for them to muster a force. The boy had to be his primary concern. Everything else could wait.

The Rawl wielder did still present a significant threat, of course. There was the chance he could attempt to use his powers once he arrived in Oreanna in a desperate attempt to escape or to kill Idanox. He would need to be prepared for this possibility. He decided he would send for Srenpe once more. Idanox despised the arrogant man, but he would feel better having the mage present while he met with the boy. He did not care to imagine what type of price the mage would demand this time, but it would be worth it. Between Srenpe and his mindless, monstrous bodyguards, the boy could be contained—he was sure of it.

There is still the matter of General McLeod, he reminded himself. The messenger had reported that McLeod had been attempting to muster a force against him, a threat he could not afford to take lightly. He would triple the bounty on the old fool; that would be sufficient to turn any soldiers who might still be clinging to their old loyalties. Idanox had found over the years that gold was worth far more than loyalty to most men. It was merely a matter of finding the right amount to sway them. Poorly paid soldiers were ideal targets for tantalizing bribes.

Then there was the matter of the future leadership of the Thornatan Army. It was a task that required more attention than he was able to give by himself. If he were to invest the necessary amount of attention, other matters that required his personal touch would suffer. He trusted none of his Hoyt to have the intelligence required of a man in such a position. If this General Bern was sharp enough to capture the Rawl wielder, perhaps he would be a suitable candidate to fill the Supreme General's now-vacant position. Clearly, he was smart enough to see Idanox's rule was a good thing for Thornata. When General Bern arrived with the Rawl wielder, Idanox would carefully assess the man and examine him for the traits he sought in his servants, namely a lack of moral qualms and an endless supply of blind loyalty.

There was one last complication with which he had to contend. He had promised the Thrawll emissary that he would give the Thrawll the location of the Temple of the Rawl. While the Hoyt had developed an educated idea of where the ancient temple could be found within the Bonner Mountains, he was not certain. The scouts he had sent to the area had repeatedly gone missing. Giving the Thrawll inaccurate information would be sure to enrage them, and their patience with him was already beginning to wear thin. He must be sure before he handed over the information.

The boy would be able to tell him the correct location, of course. Hopefully he would do so willingly, and if not, he would have to be persuaded by other means. Srenpe would no doubt have ways of making the boy talk.

If not, the boy would be handed straight over to the Thrawll. No doubt they had their own methods of loosening the boy's tongue. This boy had killed his men, thwarted his plans, and been an overall thorn in his side since the day Idanox had first heard of him. It gave him a feeling of immeasurable pleasure to know that the foolish boy would soon be paying the price for his crimes, one way or another. The Rawl wielder would either be his servant or his method of payment. Just like all the others who had dared defy the Hoyt, the boy had lost.

Chapter Five

The Wilted Lotus was far from the most unsavory establishment Alsea had ever found herself in, but it was still not an environment she would choose to expose herself to under normal circumstances. She had been in the tavern for most of the morning, seated in the darkest corner she could find with her head down and her ears keen. She had been listening intently for any piece of information that might prove useful. Thornatan soldiers had come and gone all morning, but thus far she had learned nothing of value. It was frustrating; she had thought it would only be a matter of time until she overheard some hint of what had happened to her friends. With each passing hour, she doubted more that she would discover anything here. If anybody in this tavern knew anything about Adel and Ola, they weren't talking out loud about it.

Instead, she had learned a great deal that she would have never cared to know under any circumstance. Unfortunately, information such as where the soldiers were developing rashes or which serving girl they wished to enjoy alone time with was of no use to her. The men frequenting this establishment were a far cry from those she had fought beside under General McLeod. She had suspected this would be the case, and such was her reasoning for choosing establishments like The Wilted Lotus. She did not want to go where the good and honorable men could be found. Such men would have no valuable information for her; they would currently be trying to elude capture by their traitorous brothers-in-arms. She needed to find the places with seedy reputations and the clientele that went along with them.

But almost an entire morning had passed with nothing, and Alsea was already planning her next move. There was another tavern closer to the barracks called The Rotten Apple, and its reputation was no better. Perhaps men fresher off duty would be more inclined to let sensitive information slip through their lips. Resolving that nothing of value would be learned here, she left a few coins on the table and made her way to the exit.

The brightness of the late-morning sun hurt her

eyes, causing her to realize just how long she had been sitting in one place. *I stayed inside that tavern too long*, she scolded herself. She should have realized sooner that there was nothing to be learned there. Every minute wasted was a minute that Adel and Ola may not have to spare. If they had, in fact, been captured, the army could decide to kill them at any moment. Her eyes darted in every direction, stopping at last on a trio of parchments nailed to the wall of a nearby shop: three wanted posters, one each for Adel, Ola, and General McLeod. Could this possibly mean that Adel and Ola had escaped? She thought not. There was no way they would not have met her by the river if they had. She was overthinking things; the army had just not taken down their posters yet. The army had captured her friends. Alsea was sure of it. She just needed to find out where they were being held so she could plot her rescue operation.

She had given thought to heading straight to the Kolig prison and trying to find information there. If they had been captured, that was most likely where the army would hold them. The only other possibility would be the army barracks, but that would be risky. There may still have been men loyal to General McLeod who would try to help them escape. The prison would be an environment that was easier for General Bern to control. But it was no sure thing, and her chances of being recognized loitering near the prison were much higher than they were in these seedy, dimly lit taverns. This was a situation that required a certain amount of patience, and she needed reliable information with which to work. Spending hours spying on the prison only to discover that they weren't there would not be a better investment of her time.

She made her way to The Rotten Apple, noting once more the distasteful names these establishments tended to have. Not that Alsea hadn't seen worse, of course. Her work for the Children of the Rawl had taken her to a great many places she would rather have never entered. She had once been to a place in Kalskag called The Purple Dinosaur with Ola that made these wretched establishments look clean and hospitable by comparison.

Once again, she took a seat in the corner and ordered a bowl of stew from a passing serving girl. She was no good to anybody if she wasted away from hunger, and she had been neglecting to eat these past few days. With so much else to concern herself with, it had seemed unimportant. Once settled in, she started to listen to the conversations around her once more.

"I swear, she said it was the biggest she'd ever seen. You calling me a liar?"

Alsea rolled her eyes. Nothing to be learned there.

"I'm sick and tired of bunking underneath that hog. He tosses and turns all night. How am I supposed to get any sleep? Not to mention he snorts like a pig. It takes me hours to fall asleep. If I oversleep one more time, I'll end up court-martialed. You think Gunderson would give me a transfer?"

Again, nothing there.

"Notice how Bern goes on and on about what's best for us and what's best for the people, then, first chance he gets, he waltzes off to Oreanna to lick Idanox's boots? I've been telling people that man ain't nothing, least of all a leader," a man was saying at a table to Alsea's left, drawing her attention.

The serving girl arrived with her stew. Alsea thanked and paid her before resuming her eavesdropping. Any information about General Bern was information that might serve a purpose for her. If nothing else, she would love to know where to find him so that she could acquaint him with the blade of one of her knives. The man was a traitorous weasel, and she fully intended to repay him for separating her from her friends at the first opportunity.

"You're being too hard on him. Bern's just wanting to make sure the job gets done right is all," the man's tablemate was saying.

"Since when has Bern cared one wit about a job getting done right? He nearly got a whole bunch of men killed after the Hoyt took control of this city, or did you forget about that? I was in one of those boats, and Bern was leading us right into the trap Idanox had laid for us. If it weren't for that Rawl boy, all of us on the water would be fish food at the bottom of the river right now. So how does Bern repay him for that? Turns around and stabs him in the back! I'm not a fan of the boy's magical powers; I think it's unnatural for anyone to do what he can. If I had my way, those types would be sniffed out and put down at birth, the unnatural beasts. But the kid has done nothing wrong by us, as far as I am concerned. That's not to mention betraying McLeod, who has led this army for decades! How the hell can you think a man like that is gonna do right by us?" The first man was clearly not a fan of General Bern. Alsea liked this, setting aside his offensive comments about Adel and his powers.

"Hey there, beautiful. What's a pretty thing like you doing in a run-down old place like this?"

It was the first man she had eavesdropped on after her arrival. Despite her efforts to blend in, he had taken notice of her and made his way over to her table with a leering grin stretched across his face. She did not have time for this; she had finally found her best chance of useful information yet. She had to get rid of this distraction quickly.

"Not interested," she snapped, motioning the man away with a dismissive wave of her hand.

"I didn't ask if you were interested in anything there, girlie. That's kind of a rude thing to say. Don't you have any manners? Just don't see many pretty ladies in here is all. Wanted to chat a little. Is that so wrong? You should be grateful; there are men that ain't as noble as me that would try to take advantage of a sweet little thing like yourself in a place like this."

His voice was growing louder, drawing a few eyes toward her table. Alsea could not afford to have this kind of attention focused on her. The more eyes were looking at her, the more people would realize she was not this tavern's typical clientele. Her presence would elicit the type of questions she did not want to answer. Even worse, somebody might recognize her as having been with Adel or General McLeod.

Alsea looked closely at the man's face for the first time. He was obviously quite drunk and even uglier than she had initially suspected. She pondered for a moment if the handle of her knife protruding from his eye socket would improve his appearance but dismissed this idea. Killing him in public would bring all sorts of unwanted attention, no matter how greatly it would enhance his personality. Once again, she would have to act with patience. She would have to handle this differently. What kind of incompetent fool was this drunk at this hour of the morning? No matter, she would have to turn on the charm.

"I'm so sorry, handsome. It's been a rough couple of days. A sweet fellow like you doesn't deserve to be snapped at like that. It's so kind of you to check on me. Not many men would do that. I'd love to talk to you, but do you think you could do a girl a small favor first?" she asked, forcing herself to smile at him.

"What can I do for you, darling? Anything to see you smile," the oaf said, what she could only assume was intended to be a charming grin splitting his face.

Oh, yes, I'm sure my smile is what you are interested in, Alsea thought.

"I've been looking in all the markets for some

pretty yellow flowers to give to my mother. I've looked everywhere, but I can't find any. Do you think you could find me some? I'll pay for them, and I would be oh so grateful if you did. She is ill, you see, and I just know that would brighten her day. Yellow is her favorite color, and I haven't seen them anywhere. The markets in this part of the city can be a bit scary for a girl like me, but I've looked everywhere else," she said, trying her utmost to sound as naive and innocent as possible, hoping he was too drunk to take note of the belt of knives at her waist and the bow and quiver resting by her feet.

"Don't you say another word, beautiful. You just sit right there, and I'll be back before you know it," the man said, a grotesque grin splitting his face. He was gone a moment later, staggering out into the street on the mission she had assigned to him. Alsea was able to turn her attention back to the table on her left. Hopefully she could get what she needed and be gone before he returned.

"All I'm saying is you gotta cut Bern just a little bit of slack. McLeod was gonna get us all killed with the way he was carryin' on. Notice how most of those elite soldiers he took with him when he left last fall didn't come back? The ones that did have all kinds of stories to tell, the kind I would write off as gibberish if I hadn't seen some of their injuries. They say they ran into some sort of unkillable monster out there. Do you want to fight something like that? Besides, they were out there all winter, and they still weren't able to find Idanox, were they? If they had, he wouldn't be sitting in the duke's palace! Makes me question McLeod's ability to lead this army. Maybe he's gotten too old. If Bern hadn't stepped in, McLeod would have had us in open war with the Hoyt. How long you think we'd last if they have monsters fighting for them? The way it had to happen is sad and all, but Bern did what had to be done," the skeptical soldier's companion was saying.

"But McLeod is still out there, isn't he? If Bern hadn't insisted on going into that shop and gloating about his brilliant plan, we would have gotten all of them quick and easy. Bern blew the whole thing with that overblown head he's always had. It's not enough for him to beat someone. He's got to make sure they know about it. He just can't help himself. You know as well as me that he wouldn't be in his position if his daddy weren't good pals with the duke. Or should I say the former duke," the first soldier replied.

"Look, I ain't gonna sit here and act like the man's not an arrogant twat. Everyone who's ever spent two minutes around him knows what he is. But we got the Rawl boy and the ogre, didn't we? It may not have all gone according to plan, but we got 'em," his companion said, and Alsea's ears perked up at the mention of her friends. "From what I hear, they're both on their way to Idanox now, and I don't envy the reception he'll have for them. We don't have to worry about them causing any more conflict with the Hoyt. At least not anywhere near us, which I, for one, am grateful to hear. Look, I don't like it better than you do, but the Hoyt run things now, and we might as well get used to it. It's better than dying in an unwinnable war, least as far as I'm concerned. And they'll find McLeod sooner than later, you mark my words. Best thing we can do is keep our heads down."

Alsea had heard all that she needed. General Bern was taking Adel and Ola to Idanox in Oreanna. It was up to her to make sure they did not reach the capital. No doubt Bern would have a sizeable contingent of soldiers with him; he would not want anything to go wrong. Freeing them would be difficult, but Alsea had never been one to shy away from a challenge. She would get them out, and if Bern or anybody else got in her way, they would not live long enough to regret their mistake.

How would he transport them? He would have two options: by boat or by wagon. Traveling by river would be faster, but it would be more challenging to bring a large security force with them by boat. Traveling on the water also gave Adel more ways to use the Rawl against them. Bern had seen the devastating effect of Adel's power with his own eyes, and he would not want to give the young man a chance to use it against him. Bern would most likely have chosen to travel by wagon, and this suited Alsea just fine. It would be easier to catch up to and attack a caravan of wagons. Their defenses would be thorough, but not impenetrable—not to someone like Alsea. She would find a way through them no matter what it took.

She could spend the day gathering supplies and

then leave Kolig at night. She would need enough food for at least a week, including extra for her friends once she freed them. The army was not likely to keep them well-fed. She could also use more arrows. McLeod had given what he could spare, but she was still running low. Darker clothing would also play to her advantage. If she could find some all-black garb, it could be beneficial. This was most likely going to be a rescue she would have to undertake late at night.

The army wagons would need to stop at night to rest their horses, and she could gain ground on them while they slept. At most, they had a one-day lead on her, and she was confident she could make that up in no time. There was an inn nearby where she was friendly with the innkeeper. She could find a few hours of rest there before setting out. It would probably be her last chance at sleep until after she had freed Adel and Ola. With no time to waste, she got to her feet and began to make her way discreetly to the exit. She had what she needed; she didn't want anybody to notice her now.

Alsea was almost to the doors of the tavern when they swung wide, and there was the blundering oaf she had asked to bring her flowers. She had apparently underestimated his intelligence. She had thought she would be long gone by the time he returned. But there he was, the same stupid grin plastered across his ugly face and a large bouquet of yellow flowers in hand. Alsea had neither the time nor the patience for this nonsense.

"Thank you so much," she said, setting a gold coin in his hand and taking the flowers. "I have to be going. Why don't we meet here tomorrow at this time for a little chat?"

"Hold it right there, girlie. Not so fast. I think I would like to have a little chat right now," the soldier protested, leering at her again with his awful grin. For the first time, she noticed that he was missing several teeth. If he did not tread lightly with her, he would soon be missing several more.

Enough is enough, Alsea told herself. She had more important things to deal with, and this fool was not going to stop. She would prefer to avoid a scene, but it seemed unavoidable if she was going to get rid of this oaf and get to work. *No point in delaying the inevitable. Just don't hurt him so bad that the rest of these soldiers come running after you,* she told herself.

"Of course, you're right. I'm so sorry, sweetie. I've never met such a big, strong man who is also so kind. Just look at these flowers you found for me; they are so pretty!"

She shoved the flowers forward as if to show him, waving them directly in his face. The moment of obscured vision was all she needed to take two quick steps closer to the man. The same second that she pulled the flowers away, she landed a vicious elbow strike directly above his left eye. She'd turned her arm as the blow landed, just as Ola had taught her many years before, making sure to strike with the sharpest point of the bone. His forehead was cut open instantly, blood flowing down into his eye. He fell to his knees, yowling in pain, his vision obscured. As he collapsed, she landed a hard knee to his ribs for good measure, not wanting to take any chances that he would get up and try to chase after her.

She had not expected him to cry out quite so loud; she feared his fellow soldiers would rise to his defense. She tensed up, her hand flashing close to the knives on her belt. On the contrary, most of them burst out with laughter, quite amused to see their fellow dropped so effortlessly by a woman. Confident that she could leave unchallenged, Alsea began to walk out the door. At the last moment, she turned to take a look at the cut she had given the man. It was quite deep, sure to leave a noticeable scar. *Such a shame.* She chuckled to herself.

"Something to remember me by," she whispered to him, patting the side of his face as he let out a befuddled whimper. Without further delay, she stepped out of the tavern and into the next phase of her rescue mission.

Chapter Six

The sound of the iron doors clattering open was unmistakable by now, though the timing of it caught Adel by surprise. It had not been as long as usual since his last feeding, and the Thornatan soldiers had not made a habit of giving him food and water often. He was sure this unexpected visit could not mean they were increasing the frequency of his feedings. There was no way this could mean anything good for him. The wagon rocked once, twice, three times, which was also a bit odd. After the first feeding, only two men had been climbing into the cage with him at feeding time. Rough hands loosened the sack and then lifted it slightly from the bottom of his head. This time, a new voice hissed in his ear, one he had not heard before.

"Don't even think about doing anything stupid, and by anything stupid, I mean anything at all. One wrong move, one wrong glance, and your pet ogre dies, and then you do. Keep your eyes forward, and we won't have any problems. If you think we are bluffing, try your luck, magic boy."

Before he could respond, the sack was pulled from his face. For once, his eyes did not need to adjust to the sunlight. The night sky was a welcome sight; the tears which normally accompanied the blinding glare of the sun were not missed. He tried to discreetly glance at his sur-roundings, as always, but this time his efforts were met with a hard slap to the face. His vision blurred momentarily from the force of the blow, his skin stinging from the im-pact. His eyes watered slightly. *So much for a tear-free breath of fresh air*, he thought sarcastically to himself.

"I said keep your eyes forward, boy. That's your only warning. Do I need to break a few fingers to get my point across?"

Adel focused his gaze straight in front of him, sur-prised to find the face of General Bern looking back at him. One of the general's massive bodyguards was standing slightly in front of him; he must have been the one who had delivered the slap. He dared not turn around, but he could feel another large presence behind him and assumed the other bodyguard must've been there. He noted that the bodyguard he could see looked unfamiliar to him; he had not seen this man before. He remembered with a small sense of satisfaction that Bern's last protection detail had met an unfortunate end as their general betrayed General McLeod in the abandoned shop. Hopefully this new syco-phantic follower would meet an end similar to that of his predecessors.

"Good evening, General Bern. My apologies, I would normally rise and bow for a man of your stature, but I fear your friend here might overreact to such a threaten-ing gesture," he said, earning another hard slap across the face. He had braced himself this time, suspecting his lip would cost him, but it still hurt, his ear ringing from the force of the blow. Adel forced himself to look up and smile, not wanting to show even the faintest hint of weak-ness to the despicable traitor masquerading as a Thornatan general.

"Hey!" a rough voice cried out from behind the general.

Bern and his guard turned as one toward the source of the voice, leaving a small gap between them for Adel to peer through. It was Ola, sitting perhaps a dozen feet away in a cage of his own. His wrists were still chained to the bars. Adel had seen him every time the guards had re-moved the sack, but this was the first time the ogre had spoken or shown any hint of emotion. The enraged look on his face was terrifying to behold, even for Adel. It was primal and beast-like, his eyes filled with murderous intent.

He locked his gaze on each of the men in turn before finally coming to glare at the one who had struck Adel.

"Look at me, big man. Take a long look at my eyes. I'm going to kill you, you sniveling coward. These eyes will be the last ones you ever see. That's a promise," Ola said, his voice almost a growl. In all their time together, Adel had never heard Ola so angry. He did not envy the bodyguard if Ola managed to get free of his cage.

"Or maybe I will come over there and kill you right now, ogre," the bodyguard spat, reaching for his sword in what he clearly thought was an intimidating gesture. "Your pelt would make a fine pair of boots." This last insult reminded Adel of one a Hoyt fighter had once hurled at Ola. That encounter had not ended well for the Hoyt, and Adel could only hope this soldier would meet a similar fate.

"Why don't you come and take your best shot? I'm right here, and I can't even lift my hands. Come show me what a big strong man you are," Ola taunted in response, his massive hands clenching into fists, his teeth bared. For the first time, Adel took a long hard look at the chains around his friend's wrists. They looked rather thin for restraining a man as strong as he knew Ola to be, and Adel suspected that if the bodyguard was foolish enough to enter Ola's cage, he would be in for a nasty surprise. He could feel his heart racing in anticipation. As satisfying as it would be to see Ola dispatch the arrogant bodyguard, it could throw their chances of escape to the winds. Adel tried to make eye contact with his friend, trying to silently warn him to calm down, but Ola's gaze did not leave the body-guard for even a second.

The man started to move toward the door of the cage, but General Bern placed a hand on his shoulder, stopping him in his tracks. Adel breathed a sigh of relief. The bodyguard would get what he had coming to him soon enough. Now was not the right time. Once they were free of the cages, there would be plenty of time to repay a great many people in full.

"Enough of this. Stand down. The ogre has more value to us alive than dead. Stand there and shut up. I did not bring you with me so you could provide your input. You are not required to say anything more," Bern barked at the bodyguard, who moved into the corner of the cage, seething at the criticism.

"My apologies for that nonsense, Adel. Sometimes my men forget their place. I will tell you it is the bane of a general's existence, something I am continually struggling against every day. I'm sorry you are being transported in such a manner, but I'm sure you understand the need we have to take such precautions. You are quite a dangerous young man after all. We can't afford to take any chances with you," General Bern said.

His voice was far more cheerful than Adel had ever heard it during their previous encounters. Bern was talking as though they were old friends making small talk. Adel suspected this had nothing to do with a changing attitude on the part of the general, which left him with only one assumption.

"What do you want?" Adel asked bluntly, in no mood to deal with the insufferable man. Bern was a traitor to his army and his people. Adel could not imagine that such a man had anything of value to offer him. If he still had his sword, he would be sorely tempted to plunge it into Bern's gut, even here, surrounded by hostile soldiers who would kill him for the act.

"I can understand why you might be suspicious of me, but rest assured, such suspicions are misplaced. After all, I already have everything that I could ever want, Adel. If you think about it, I suppose that is the difference between you and me. Do you remember the first time we met, in my encampment after the Battle of Kolig? You were quite disrespectful to me on that day too. I had put a tent over your head and provided you with food and water. I even allowed our healers to treat your pet over there, though my first instinct was to let it bleed out from its injuries. But still you felt the need to be rude to me. You were dripping with arrogance from the moment we met. I am sad to see that your personality has made no improvements. No doubt your powers have given you an inflated sense of importance. McLeod lavishing praise upon you has likely inflated your ego as well. I suppose you never imagined that you would be in the position you find yourself in now, did you? If you had, perhaps you would have shown a general the respect a man of his rank deserves." Bern was obviously enjoying himself immensely, grinning wider with each insult he hurled.

"You're right about that, Bern. I was mistaken, and I will admit it," Adel began, causing one of Bern's eyebrows to arch quizzically. "I thought you were an arrogant, stupid piece of human garbage who was unworthy of the uniform you were wearing. But I never suspected you to be a traitor to your people. You surprised me, all right. Well done." Adel was already bracing for his punishment the moment he finished talking.

The bodyguard moved forward as if to slap him again, but Bern waved him away. The arrogant smirk faded for the briefest of moments after Adel had insulted him, but Bern was quick to don it again. *Not used to being on the other side of your smart-mouthed comments, are you, Bern?* Adel knew he might be dead before too long, but at that moment, he promised himself he would do everything possible to take this traitor with him. Perhaps then he would at least be able to rest in peace, knowing he had rid the world of such a despicable man. It wasn't Idanox, but it would be the next best thing.

"Adel, I feel you misunderstand me, though I cannot place you entirely at fault for it. After all the time you spent with Randall McLeod, I can see how I may appear to be a traitor in your eyes. This belief is misguided, and if you will only hear me out with an open mind, you will see this for yourself. You must understand, I am doing only what I feel is best for my people," General Bern said, trying to reason with him. Adel laughed derisively.

"By bowing down to Idanox and the Hoyt? How does that benefit your people exactly?" Adel spat.

"Is endless war a good thing for the people of Thornata, in your opinion, Adel? How much death and destruction can our province bear in the name of this conflict? How many innocent farmers, merchants, and stable boys need to die before you can see this conflict for what it is? Sometimes the best thing we can do is set aside our pride and choose the less desirable path in the name of the greater good. War is not always ended with swords, spears, bloodshed, and death. Sometimes it is ended by recognizing the need to set such things aside. The needs of my people outweigh my personal needs and ambitions," Bern replied.

Adel would have laughed out loud if his body were not in excruciating pain from spending the day being thrown about the cage like a sack of hay. Had Bern managed to wipe the arrogant smirk from his face for even a second, his monologue may have been a slightly believable story. Adel seriously doubted whether anything had ever outweighed Bern's personal needs and ambitions in the greedy man's mind. No, his actions had not been born out of selflessness.

"Do they really, Bern? You claim you are setting aside your pride and making sacrifices in the name of your people. The greater good, that's what you said, right? It seems to me like you have done quite well for yourself in the Hoyt era. You claim to set aside your ambitions, but here you are, personally escorting two wanted prisoners all the way to Oreanna. Why would a man of your position make such a trip yourself? I don't think it is to enjoy the scenery of the Thornatan countryside. I think it is because you want Idanox to shower you with praise, to see you as the hero, just as you have always seen yourself. Spare me your speeches about the good of the many, General Bern. You cannot fool me. You care only for yourself; any fool could see it."

Adel was already growing weary of dealing with the insufferable man. He would've rather been sitting in silence with the sack back over his head than listening to the insufferable traitor ramble on about the sacrifices he was making in the name of his people. Bern had still not revealed his purpose in having this chat, and Adel was growing less interested by the second. Seeming to sense this, Bern plowed forward.

"You could learn something from me, Adel. When we reach the capital, you could choose the same path I have. You may not like me, and I will openly admit that I do not like you. But the wisdom of the decisions I have made cannot be denied. When we arrive in Oreanna, you will have the option of joining the Hoyt. They would gladly accept someone of your prowess, regardless of your prior conflicts with them. There is no need for you to die in the name of a lost war. Why die when you could live and still do some good for the people of Thornata? What good will your death bring for the people that you sit here and so righteously claim to be a champion of? Why not serve to unite our people?"

Unable to contain himself any longer, Adel finally laughed out loud at the sheer absurdity of Bern's suggestion. Bern could not possibly harbor any real hope that Adel would do as he was suggesting. Perhaps Bern believed that if he could sway Adel to join the Hoyt, he could ingratiate himself even further in the eyes of Idanox. The traitor's career ambitions meant nothing to Adel. As far as Adel was concerned, he should have let Bern burn to death in the fire after the Battle of Kolig.

"You are wasting your breath, General Bern. Allow me to make myself as clear as I can possibly be so that you will not waste it any further. I will not join the Hoyt, and I will not cooperate with Idanox. I have nothing to learn from a coward and a traitor such as yourself. If I ever have the opportunity to kill you, I will take it without hesitation, and I will draw great pleasure from watching the life leave your eyes. Now put the sack back over my head and leave me in peace," Adel said. He shoved himself back against the bars of the cage, pushing his way past the bodyguard stationed behind him. *Enough of this pointless debate.* He needed to rest if he was going to find the strength to escape.

"I am disappointed that you are unable to see things beyond your own limited perspective," Bern said, turning toward the door. "I tried to help you, Adel. Please remember that when you meet your fate in Oreanna."

With that, the sack was placed back over his head and cinched tightly around his neck. The door clanged open and then shut, and at last, he was alone again. Though he had grown to despise the smell and feel of the sack on his face, it was preferable to listening to and looking at General Bern. He did his best to find a comfortable position on the hard floor of the wagon but struggled to do so, just as he had since leaving Kolig. Sleep had proven elusive to him since their capture. He knew he needed to rest, needed to build his strength if he was going to muster any sort of legitimate escape attempt. It would do him little good to break free of this cage if exhaustion caused his power and body to fail him as soon as he was out.

Thus far he had found few weak points in his captor's defenses, though his opportunities to look had been limited. The nearer they drew to Oreanna, the more daring he was going to need to be if he hoped to escape. If the soldiers got them inside the walls of the capital, it was over. He could occasionally smell campfires at night, though he could not see them. If he could identify their location, he could potentially use them to create a diversion. A sudden fire raging out of control could be just the distraction he and Ola needed. He did not know precisely how large this camp was, but he believed that a disturbance of as little as five minutes could give him and Ola the opening they needed to slip away. Hopefully they would be able to get their hands on weapons on their way out. As exhausted as he was, he could not count exclusively on the power of the

Rawl to get them away from the soldiers. If the power failed him, he would need a sword, and the soldiers had confiscated the one Captain Boyd had gifted to him before leaving the barge.

Adel constantly tried to reassure himself that he still had time to think of a plan. His brief glances around the encampment had told him that they had not yet reached the Bonner Mountains. He knew the journey through the mountains might be the best time to make his move. There was a lot of rocky terrain where they would be able to elude pursuit. The army's horses would not be able to run them down, especially in the dark. They could even flee toward the safety of the Temple of the Rawl if necessary. Once the caravan was north of the mountains, it would not take long to reach Oreanna. The flatlands north of the Bonners also did not present a surplus of escape options. They would quickly be run down by the horses on flat terrain.

He wondered where Alsea was and if she and General McLeod were working on a plan to overthrow Idanox. He wished he had her help to get out of this situation; she was by far the most resourceful person he had ever met. While plotting their escape, he had often tried to imagine what Alsea would do if she were in his shoes, what plan she would form to extract herself. The girl did not possess the power of the Rawl, but she would have an abundance of ideas—she always did. Though it was just as likely that Alsea would never have found herself in this predicament to begin with, he reminded himself.

The thought of the young woman pained him. The regret he felt had not faded in the least. He had spent most of this journey reminding himself what a fool he was for not sharing his feelings with her when he'd had the chance. He could only hope that he would have the opportunity again, but there was no point in dwelling on it now. His energy would be better spent on formulating his plan of escape. Rather than dwelling on his regrets about his feelings for Alsea, he should've been fighting to make his way back to her. If he wanted to see her again, he was going to have to get out of this cage and away from his captors the hard way.

"Ola, I think our best opportunity will come once we reach the Bonner Mountains," he said in the same hushed tone he had used to communicate with his friend previously. "We need to be ready to go at any moment, though I think our chances will be best at night. I may be able to use the Rawl to buy us a few minutes, but we have to expect resistance. I would rather die fighting these traitors than at the hands of Idanox, and I'm guessing you feel the same way."

He hoped Ola could hear him, though he knew the ogre could not risk a response. He needed Ola to be ready. Their first opportunity to escape would come soon, and they were not likely to get a second.

Chapter Seven

Idanox was not a man who had accumulated his vast wealth by ever allowing himself to feel comfortable. Complacency was the predecessor of failure. The longer he spent as duke of Thornata, the more he found the challenges of ruling a province similar to those that came with building and maintaining a fortune. Though the trials were familiar, he could not allow himself to become content, even in the midst of his victory. Idanox was pleased to hear the Rawl wielder had been captured and was being brought before him. But he was also no fool; he recognized the coming meeting presented a new set of risks. Wise leaders could never assume anything to be as simple and straightforward as it may appear on the surface. So it was that he paced his quarters restlessly, once again waiting on the ever-late mage Srenpe.

Every encounter he had with this mage led him to dislike the man more than the previous one, but Srenpe had proven himself invaluable time and time again. Idanox had not seen Srenpe in several weeks, an absence which had not made the heart grow fonder. His men reported the mage continued to spend much time in the former government's vaults beneath the palace. Idanox had given him free pick of the magical artifacts found within them, and apparently, he had made good use of the time. His men had reported it was not uncommon for the mage to stay locked within the vaults from dawn to dusk, emerging with a satisfied grin across his face each time. Idanox scowled. Anything that made Srenpe so happy could not possibly be a good thing for the Hoyt.

Idanox had requested that he arrive hours earlier, though he had held little hope for an on-time arrival from the mage. The arrogant man had made a point of emphasizing to Idanox at every meeting that he did not work for the Hoyt and cared nothing for their cause. Now that Idanox was the rightful duke of Thornata, the behavior showed no signs of changing. His constant refusal to afford Idanox the respect a man of his stature was entitled to was just another of Srenpe's qualities that made the Hoyt leader despise him. Idanox was not sure what the mage's definition of work was, but he had provided the Hoyt services in exchange for a significant amount of gold. Each time, Idanox hoped it would be the last. He yearned for the day when he could finally have the mage killed and never be forced to suffer his insolence again. Now, with the Rawl wielder within his grasp, that day may have been fast approaching.

Srenpe arrived, at last, no fewer than four hours late, strolling through the door as though he had not a care in the world. His crimson robes were the same as ever, but Idanox took note of the new staff the mage was carrying. Like his old one, it was black, but it was longer, and the top was twisted into a gnarled design he could not identify. Idanox also noted several new pieces of golden jewelry. The mage had clearly spent some of his vast earnings. A new ring stood out as well: a white band adorned with a stone the color of the blackest night.

"Hail, Idanox, the duke of Thornata and savior of the common people!" Srenpe cried out, dropping into an exaggerated bow and then rising again with a fanciful flourish of his arms.

"How kind of you to join me, Srenpe. I trust your time scouring my vaults has proven fruitful," Idanox said, not bothering to admonish the man for his tardiness. If anything, Srenpe seemed to enjoy his reprimands. There was no point in giving the mage the satisfaction of delivering a sarcastic reply to the rebuke.

"Oh, quite fruitful indeed, Duke Idanox. It's rather sad to see the things your predecessor saw fit to keep from his subjects. Did you notice my new staff? The former government of this province must have seen fit to confiscate this from some poor mage. I know you can't tell the difference from my old one, but it is quite an upgrade for me. The ring as well, a find I am pleased to have come across. I won't bother telling you what it does; you wouldn't believe me if I did. More examples of why this province needs your wise leadership. Can you imagine seeing fit to lock such things away, where they can do no good for anybody? Your men have shown me much hospitality, and it is greatly appreciated."

Idanox was tempted for a moment to ask the purpose of the ring but decided upon reflection that he would rather not know.

"I am glad to hear it, Srenpe. You have served our cause well and have earned your reward many times over. I have called you here to ask if you would be interested in earning more for yourself," Idanox said.

"Of course. I would not have bothered to come if I had no interest whatsoever. The level of my interest will depend. To be blunt, it will hinge on what you are asking of me and what you are willing to pay in exchange for my services. I am a man of means now, Duke Idanox, so keep in mind that it may take a high price to entice me to end my relaxing retirement. I do hope it is not overly forward of me to say this. I hope we have come to a point in our relationship where we can be open with each other."

It was much the response Idanox had anticipated. Srenpe was a proud man who would never admit to needing anything from anybody. He was a powerful mage, possessing powers Idanox could never hope to understand. However, he was also quite greedy, a trait which Idanox understood perfectly well. It was one he valued in those who served him. A greedy man was a predictable man and one who could be easily controlled. It had been more difficult with Srenpe than it had with others, but that had not stopped Idanox from getting what he needed from their partnership.

"It would seem the Thornatan Army has captured the Rawl wielder who has been such a thorn in my side. Do you remember the one, Srenpe? The same young man your beast, the one I paid a hefty price for, apparently failed to slay. But it is all water under the bridge, is it not? One of their generals is making his way to Oreanna as we speak, transporting the boy to my custody," Idanox explained.

"Why bother bringing him to you alive at all? He is a threat to your rule, perhaps the only legitimate threat left outside of the Imperial Army. Why not simply kill him and move on with your life? Forgive my bluntness, but this type of shortsighted thinking may be the reason you never managed to ascend to the level of duke without my assistance."

Idanox scowled. The mage's questioning of his decision-making at every turn had worn on him. Srenpe was a clever man—there was no denying it—but he was nowhere near as clever as he believed.

"I have shared your line of thinking for a long time, and I admit it was my first instinct when I heard the news. But when I first heard of this boy last year, I had hoped to persuade him to consider joining our cause. There is no denying that if the Imperials do see fit to interfere with my rule, the boy could be a powerful ally. I still believe there is hope for this, Srenpe. I wish to give him this opportunity before killing him," Idanox explained, fighting back his irritation at the disbelieving sneer that crossed the other man's face.

Who did Srenpe think he was to question Idanox's judgment? Idanox had won the right to rule this province using nothing more than his own ingenuity. The sneering mage was wealthy because Idanox had made him wealthy. On his own, he had achieved nothing more than being expelled from the Order of Mages. His skill at his craft was impressive, but it had not been enough to raise him from a life of poverty before Idanox had hired him.

"Your men have pursued this boy across this province and killed men who have fought beside him, yet still you think he will consider joining you?" Srenpe did not bother to hide his skepticism. "Everything I have heard about this boy suggests he is far more intelligent than the rest of your followers. While I am sure their blind loyalty serves its purpose well, they are not exactly the type of people who would make good scholars, and you must realize that. If not, I hate to be the one to break the news to you.

The boy will see through whatever silver-tongued offers you may levy at him."

"I can be quite persuasive, Srenpe. Do you think I would be where I am now were I not?" Idanox snapped. "In any case, he has no option. He will join my cause, or he will die. Do you think a mere boy will honestly choose the latter? Young men have so much life ahead of them; they are not so quick to throw it away."

"This boy is a trained Rawl wielder who has fought you for over a year, winning more often than not. He is not one of the simpleminded peasants you manipulated into joining your militia with promises of glory and riches," Srenpe retorted. "He has shown a repeated willingness to risk his life fighting your forces, yet you are willing to set all of these facts aside in your quest for more power. If there is a brain in that oversize head of yours, take this advice. Have the soldiers who are transporting him put a spear through his neck right now, and be done with it. It would be the wisest decision you have ever made."

Perhaps calling on Srenpe again had been a mistake. Maybe it would have been best to leave his partnership with the mage behind for good. He had never tolerated such disrespect from any other man, and had he not needed the mage's help, he would have put an end to Srenpe long ago for his insolence. He had his monstrous bodyguards; did he still need Srenpe? Still, the boy had slain one such beast before, and having a backup plan was never a bad thing. Swallowing his pride, he continued, pretending as though he had not heard Srenpe's insult.

"Your point is a valid one, Srenpe, but I still wish to proceed with my attempt," Idanox said, biting back the angry reply that he knew would only escalate the animosity between them. "All I am asking is whether or not you would be a match for the boy if he were to attack me or my men somehow."

Srenpe did not reply right away. He studied Idanox quietly, his expression unreadable. Idanox could only assume the mage was mulling exactly how much he was going to charge for this service. *Yes, Srenpe. By all means, charge as much as you would like. It is not as though you do not already owe me for everything you have.* Idanox's patience was about to run out when he finally began to respond.

"The boy has powers I do not possess, but that is a knife that cuts both ways. I do not doubt his abilities, nor the extent of his powers. But I am far more experienced at utilizing mine than he is his. He has never faced a foe with my particular skills. I promise you he would not find it as simple as decimating your simpleton Hoyt brutes, or even facing one of my beautiful creations. I understand the extent of his abilities far more than he will understand mine. Given enough time to plan and prepare, I believe I could neutralize the boy as a threat. As a matter of fact, some of the spellbooks I found in your vaults may well prove useful for such an undertaking. You see? It has all come full circle.

I knew you would not regret giving me access to such treasures. How long until he arrives?"

"They are bringing him from Kolig, so you should have at least a week to prepare for his arrival. Is there anything you need for your preparations?" Idanox asked, relieved that the mage seemed to be coming around.

"Not so fast, Idanox. Before we get into too many specifics, I feel we should discuss my payment," Srenpe replied, shooting him the familiar smirk.

There it was. Idanox had known it was coming. Srenpe did not do anything for free. His first beast had cost Idanox no small amount of gold. The group he had created for the attack on Oreanna had required that the mage be given full access to the artifacts within the Oreanna vaults. What could he possibly need now? Idanox dreaded discovering the answer.

"What would you like this time?" Idanox asked, not bothering to argue the point. The sooner he could end this conversation and get the infuriating mage out of his sight, the better. He needed Srenpe's help, but that did not mean he had to like the man. He would pay whatever price was necessary to ensure his continued safety.

"As you may have heard, the Order of Mages was quite unkind to me several years ago. It is the reason I am no longer in their service. I know a great many rumors are floating about the reasons for my expulsion. Most of these are bald-faced lies. The simple truth is that they felt some of my experiments did not fall within the overly oppressive guidelines they had set for me, so they expelled me from their order and cast me out into the world alone. As I'm sure you can imagine, my feelings were quite hurt. I don't appreciate that, and I want my friend, the new duke of Thornata, to do something about it," Srenpe said, trying and utterly failing to convey just how deeply his feelings had been wounded.

"Oh, so now you consider us to be friends? The Order of Mages does not fall under the rule of Thornata or of any other province. They answer only to the authority of the Empire. Their stronghold in Kotlik is just one of several, as I am sure you are well aware. I cannot force mages in other provinces to recognize you as a member of their order," Idanox snapped, irritated by the lunacy of the request.

"Fear not, Duke Idanox, for I could not possibly care less about the recognition of mages in far-off provinces. I simply ask to be readmitted to the stronghold in Kotlik, perhaps in a new role?" Srenpe again refused to state his request outright.

"What role might that be?" Idanox asked, already suspecting the answer but wishing Srenpe would just spit it out already.

"Every Order of Mages stronghold has a high mage to lead their mission and guide their followers along an appropriate path. The man currently in that role is far too old, and the sanctum in Kotlik has made no progress in their studies in many years because of it. They require somebody who is willing to boldly blaze them a new path. I have learned much in these years since my expulsion, and I believe I would be well suited to this task. Just think, it could be the beginning of a new, fruitful working relationship between the Order of Mages and the duke of Thornata. Such a partnership could prove to be mutually beneficial."

"Why not just conjure up some more of your beasts and take it for yourself?"

"Do you take me for a butcher? I would not be much of a high mage if I were to murder all of my prospective followers, would I? I would much rather handle this matter in a diplomatic manner. The duke of Thornata will make a request to the order that I be inserted as the high mage of Thornata. I feel as though the request will be more convincing if several hundred of your men travel to Kotlik to make it on your behalf. The Order of Mages will not be happy at first, but they will accept your request. I am certain of it. They are stuck in their ways, but they still have a strong desire for self-preservation. They will yield to the request to save their own skins. The doddering old fool won't want to step down, but the younger mages will force him to do so," Srenpe explained.

Idanox had expected to pay a hefty price for the mage's services yet again, but he had not anticipated this request. Attempting to place Srenpe at the head of the Order of Mages could create a new enemy, one he was not prepared to face. But having the Rawl wielder here in the capital without the mage's support was by far the more imminent danger. If he must find a way to deal with the Order of Mages later, it was a price he was willing to pay—assuming, of course, he did not see fit to simply have Srenpe killed once he had served his purpose.

"This is the only thing I can offer you in payment, Srenpe? I will tell you bluntly that our hold in Kotlik is tenuous at best at this point. The city is so remote that it will take time and likely a visit from a large force to bring them fully to heel. It may be quite some time before I can honor your request." Idanox was desperate to find another suitable form of compensation. A new enemy—particularly one as powerful as the Order of Mages—was an issue he would rather avoid if at all possible.

"Do you understand what you are asking me to do, Idanox? You are asking me to stand with you in the presence of a Rawl wielder and use my power to fight against him if necessary. This young man has proven himself more than formidable. The price I have asked is one that is appropriate for the amount of risk I am putting myself at," Srenpe shot back. "If you need to send a force to bring Kotlik in line, they can handle my affairs at the same time. It's rather convenient, isn't it?"

It was true; Srenpe was a man who preferred to stay out of the middle of the action. The prospect of possibly being needed to fight the Rawl wielder was a dangerous one. Even a mage as powerful as Srenpe would not be able to defeat such a foe easily. The risk of angering the mages was one he was willing to take if it meant increased security for himself. Perhaps he would get lucky and the pair would destroy each other if it came to a fight. Then the Rawl wielder would be no threat, and Srenpe would no longer be an annoyance.

"Very well, Srenpe. I agree to your terms. Once this matter with the Rawl wielder has been dealt with in one way or another, I will demand you be admitted to the Order of Mages in Kotlik as their new leader. Once you are in that role, I trust you will do everything in your power to keep them out from under my feet?"

"Under my leadership, the order will not have time for such trivial matters as interfering with your absurdly capable rule," Srenpe replied, yet another far-from-innocent smile crossing his cunning face. Idanox did not know what the mage had planned for the Order of Mages, but he had a feeling he would need to deal with it sooner or later.

"Very well. You have my word, Srenpe. Stand with me when the Rawl wielder arrives, and you shall have your prize," Idanox said, knowing he had little choice in the matter.

"Excellent, my fine duke. It is my understanding that the former duke of this province built a bunker for himself to hide in should the city come under assault. Is this true?" Srenpe asked.

"Yes, it is true," Idanox replied, bewildered.

"It's fortunate my creations helped you sack the city before he could get there. The naivety of those in power can be quite useful, can't it? I recommend you have the boy brought to you there. The fewer natural elements he has at his disposal, the better off we will be. Only a few torches for light, and no water. The door should be sealed to prevent him from conjuring up too much wind power. Keep your bodyguards close by as well; they will be of great help should he become aggressive. The fewer options he has available to him, the easier he will be for me to control," Srenpe rattled off. "I will begin making preparations for his arrival immediately. Rest assured, Duke Idanox, by the time the Rawl wielder gets here, I will have already defeated him."

Idanox agreed to the mage's suggestions and bade him goodnight. He hated to rely on the arrogant man once again, but he reassured himself that this would be the final time. The Rawl wielder would be his ally, or he would be dead. Once that was done, his uses for Srenpe were gone. He considered again for a moment the idea of killing the mage instead of paying him at that point but scolded himself for thinking that far ahead. It was essential to live in the present, now more than ever. Srenpe would be dealt with when the time was right, one way or another.

Idanox poured himself a stiff drink and reflected for a moment on all he had achieved. *More impressive accomplishments are soon to follow*, he told himself. The Rawl wielder would soon be no threat, and the Imperials would soon be removed from the province, fulfilling his deal with the Thrawll. Things could not be going much better, and it filled him with a sense of pride more significant than any that the forever self-important man had ever felt. He had always thought he was born to rule, and now he knew that he had always been right.

Chapter Eight

Alsea slipped through the early-evening shadows as silently as a ghost. She was completely unknown to the men standing close enough to hear her breathing if they bothered to stop and listen. Her experience over the years had taught her that most people rarely took the time to truly see the things right in front of their eyes, let alone things that were concealed even slightly. She had made a living in the service of the Children of the Rawl, listening in on those too preoccupied to know they were not alone. The Thornatan soldiers who were assigned as sentries over this caravan were no different, and she had suspected this would be the case. They assumed their strength in numbers was all they needed to guard their valuable prisoners. After all, no sane person would ever try to act alone against such a large force. *It's a good thing I'm capable of setting my sanity aside when necessary*, Alsea thought to herself. *Otherwise it might get in the way of what I'm about to do.*

It had taken Alsea most of the last three days to catch up with the army caravan. She had set out before the sun crested the horizon each morning and marched on long after it had set each night. She did not stop for even a moment of rest during the day, knowing her friends were counting on her to reach them before it was too late. For a time, having seen no signs of the caravan, she'd worried she had guessed wrong, that her friends were being transported by the river after all. But on the morning of the second day, she came across tracks that could have only been made by a massive contingent of men and horses. Recognizing this was the type of group General Bern would use to escort his prized prisoners, she immediately picked up the trail and quickened her pace.

She had spotted them for the first time earlier that day and had followed at a careful distance, knowing that getting too close in broad daylight was certain to doom her mission. So, she had been content to shadow them from afar for the remainder of the day. Thankfully, the army had remained unaware of her presence thus far. With two such valuable prisoners, Alsea was surprised the caravan had not sent scouts out wider. Silently thanking General Bern for his incompetence, she followed all day without issue. Alsea only dared to draw near enough to see the caravan as the sun began to fall from the sky. The wagons had stopped for the evening, and it was time for her to do some reconnaissance.

Her early findings were less than promising. Despite their lax security during their march, the Thornatan soldiers were taking few chances with their prisoners at night. She had spotted Adel and Ola easily enough from a distance, the purpose of the caged wagons unmistakable. The Thornatans had Ola chained to the bars of his cage, and Adel had a sack placed over his head, no doubt to dull his senses and prevent him from using his power. The pair were kept in the center of the encampment, presenting no small number of challenges. At least four men were stationed close to them at all times, and often there were more. To her dismay, the army had brought dozens of mounted men along with them on this journey. This would complicate their escape once her friends were free of the cages. She needed a way to ensure they would not be pursued immediately, or the horses would swiftly run them down. She had no intention of springing her friends free from their cages only to end up in one with them shortly after.

Alsea had already made a rough count and found the caravan was made up of roughly two hundred Thornatan soldiers. She had spotted the despicable General Bern as well and hoped she would have an opportunity to see him face-to-face before too long. But his two hundred men had to be her primary concern. This was no time to look to settle a personal score with the hated man. There was no way she could hope to kill them all by herself, and if she moved against General Bern, that was what she would have to do if she wanted to survive. She had to go about this in a calculated, intelligent way. If she was going to set Ola and Adel free, she had to find a way around the soldiers rather than through them.

Or did she? Her companions were far from help-less children after all. Perhaps if she merely gave them a small window of opportunity, they could free themselves from their captors. The pair were guarded constantly. But if she could cause even a moment's distraction, it could be enough for them to free themselves from the cages. She doubted there were four men anywhere who could stand against the pair of them once they were free of the cages. All she would need to do was ensure they had a relatively clear path to freedom once they were out.

If only I had a way to communicate with them, she thought to herself in frustration. If her friends did not re-alize what was happening, they might miss their oppor-tunity to break free of their captors. *Wait, maybe there is a way I could talk to them after all*, she realized, kicking herself for not recognizing it sooner. Ogres possessed hearing far beyond the abilities of other races. Was it possible Ola would be able to hear her if she spoke to him? She would have to find a spot close enough to the camp to give him a chance at hearing her while still being far enough away to avoid detection. It was a risk, but one that she felt was worth taking.

There was no time to waste. Alsea immediately began making her way to the nearest vantage point she could find, a patch of oak trees situated on a hill overlooking the encampment. Shaking her head once more at the sheer ineptitude of General Bern for not having placed a guard on top of such a vantage point, she began to climb. Within minutes she was on top of the hill and up to the top of the tallest tree. Looking down at the army camp, she found she had a clear view of her imprisoned friends. They were far away, but she could still make out their shapes and a few of their features. *I might as well give this a shot*, she thought. She glanced around one last time, making sure there were no army patrols within earshot. When she spoke, she spoke in a normal tone, as though she were talking to somebody right next to her. The noise would not carry to the nearest Thornatan sentries, but it just might be picked up by Ola's keen ogre ears.

"Ola, can you hear me? It's Alsea. If you can hear me, turn your head to the left," she said, staring intently at the ogre.

There was no response, no indication he had heard her. The noise in the middle of the camp must've been too loud for him to hear her over. She would have to try again, but louder, clearly enough that he could recognize her voice over the hustle and bustle of the encampment. She glanced furtively in every direction once again, ensuring that no soldiers were within earshot. Raising her tone slightly, she tried again.

"Ola, can you hear me? It's Alsea. If you can hear me, turn your head to the left," she repeated, continuing to stare intently. After a moment's pause, to her great relief, the ogre slowly turned his head to look to his left. He could hear her, which would make organizing this escape much more manageable. The remainder of her plan was already falling into place in her mind.

"I can see they have you shackled to the bars, but those chains and bars don't look all that strong. I am assuming you could extract yourself from that cage in a hurry if you had to. Tuck your right knee into your body if I am right about that," Alsea said, her eyes still sweeping the nearby terrain every few seconds for any sign of approaching soldiers.

Once again, to Alsea's great relief, Ola complied with her instructions. If he was indeed able to get himself out of his cage without help, it would make matters much more straightforward. The plan was already beginning to finalize in her head, but there were still a few small details to be worked out. She could not risk much more talk; just one stray soldier passing nearby could ruin everything. She glanced around one last time, paranoid she would be discovered at any moment.

"I can't talk much longer; they could find me at any time. I'm nearby, and I'm going to get the two of you out of there tomorrow night. We should be close to the Bonners by then, and I have a few places in mind where we could hide. Once we are in rockier terrain, their horses won't be able to give chase, especially in the dark. I'm going to cause a distraction; you will know it when it happens. I probably won't be able to talk to again; you will have to trust your gut. When it does, get yourself out of that cage and get Adel's cage open too. Get yourself a weapon if you can. Hopefully Adel has enough strength to use his power as well. The two of you need to get to the western edge of the encampment as fast as possible. I'm going to do everything I can to make sure you have as little resistance as possible. I'll find you there. Turn your head to the right if you understand everything I have said."

There was a brief pause, but then Ola's head turned to his right. No doubt he was skeptical, but she could not risk explaining further. Every word she uttered increased her risk of discovery. In truth, she was still working out the logistics of her plan for herself. Breathing a sigh of relief, she climbed out of the tree, her plan still coming together as she did. She had not been able to lay out a plan as thoroughly as she would have liked, but with such a fluid situation, there was nothing to be done about it. It also worried her that Ola would not be able to communicate any of this to Adel in advance. But the young Rawl wielder was fast to adapt to challenges; he had proven it time and time again, and he would do so once more. She was sure of it. Ola and Adel were resourceful, and they would be able to handle themselves. They just needed her to give them a chance to make their move. She needed to turn her attention on creating the distraction that she needed.

A fire would serve her purposes well. A blaze on the eastern end of the encampment would draw many of the soldiers in that direction to fight it. This would move most of their forces away from the area where her friends would be making their escape. With any luck, Adel would catch on to what she had done and use the Rawl to help spread the flames even more rapidly. General Bern had shown an inability to effectively lead a response to such a disaster after the Battle of Kolig. He had needed Adel to step in and save him. Hopefully he would prove to be just as inept this time around. By the time the soldiers realized the cages were empty, all three of them would be long gone. Of course, the army may suspect that Adel had started the fire. Sack over his head or not, suspicion for any sudden fire may immediately fall on him. She would need to choose her target with care so as not to arouse suspicion.

The few sentries posted around the camp posed a problem. She would spend this night counting how many sentries there were and their rough positions around the caravan. The next night, she would eliminate them before they could raise the alarm or interfere with their escape. Alsea already knew they were stationed in pairs. She should be able to manage this as long as she chose her moments and strategies carefully. For a moment, she considered eliminating only those stationed on the western edge of the camp, where her friends would be making their escape. She immediately dismissed this idea. She also needed to be able to move freely around the outskirts of the encampment. They would all have to go in order to ensure she could do this without being discovered. She would take no pleasure from killing them, but nor would she feel much in the way of guilt. They had chosen their fate when they had chosen to betray their people.

How would she go about starting the fire? Scanning the encampment below, she noticed several supply wagons situated near the eastern perimeter. She would need to bring in some extra kindling, but she should be able to make those go up in flames with relative ease. She noted that several groups of soldiers were starting camp-fires perilously close to the wagons. With luck, she could make it appear as though one of their fires had simply gotten out of control. The soldiers would take the blame, and nobody would have time to suspect Adel until it was too late. Having more eyes on the young man was the last thing she needed. General Bern would no doubt hurry over to berate the careless men, not realizing that his valuable prisoners were slipping away as he did. Her most challenging task would be slipping away after she had set the wagons ablaze and making her way around the camp to meet up with her friends. Again, the chaos ensuing from the fire would have to be her ally.

They would have several options once they were free of the soldiers. The Temple of the Rawl was a hard two-day journey, but one they could make if their other options were taken from them. If the army was foolish enough to pursue them there, Klaweck and the giants would see to it that they received a much-deserved welcome to the valley beneath the temple. But Alsea understood her friends were not likely to be in the best of health after their ordeal. The army was likely not feeding them much or treating them with much care in their transport. They would need rest and time to recover from their imprisonment. The Temple of the Rawl was too far to afford them these necessities. They needed to hide out someplace closer.

There was a small village Alsea knew of. It was tucked away in the foothills of the Bonners, a town she doubted the army was even aware existed. The journey to get there would take them through some steep and rocky terrain. It would be hard on her friends after their captivity, but it would be nigh on impossible for men on horseback to pursue them. She had passed through the village many times on her journeys to and from the Temple of the Rawl. There was a small inn there, and Alsea was friendly with the innkeeper. They could stay there for a few days to give Adel and Ola time to recover. This would also give the army time to take their search elsewhere. Once they were rested and the coast was clear, they could make their way north to rejoin General McLeod and put an end to the Hoyt—and General Bern, unless they were truly fortunate and he died in the fire the following night.

She was getting too far ahead of herself, she knew that, but failure was not a possibility Alsea was willing to consider. She would not fail; she could not fail. Her friends needed her to succeed. They had always been there for her, and she would not fail them now. She would not be alive if not for the pair of them. Ola had found her wandering the wilderness alone as a small child after bandits had murdered her father and left her for dead. It was Adel who had lit that warehouse ablaze after she had been shot in the Hoyt ambush. It was Ola who had carried her safely out of that inferno. She owed them her life several times over.

***

That night, Alsea made her way cautiously around the entirety of the Thornatan encampment, taking a count of every sentry on duty. In the end, she had counted six pairs spread out widely around the large camp. The Thornatans obviously did not feel there was much to worry about in the way of an attack. Their complacency would work to her advantage, and their overconfidence would be their undoing. She was confident she could eliminate all twelve sentries without alerting the soldiers within the camp. Once that was done, the rest of her plan should unfold smoothly enough.

Alsea slept in a tree that night, a small length of cord secured around her waist to ensure she would not fall to an untimely demise. Her heart raced in anticipation of what was to come, and her overactive mind strained against her desire to sleep. But she knew she would need her strength for the following night. It may be several days before she would have another chance at rest, and she knew she must take advantage of this last opportunity.

She awoke the next day to find the caravan had already departed, though it was of little concern to Alsea. By noon, she once again had the slow-moving wagons within her sight, and then it was merely a matter of maintaining a proper distance. Just as she had the day before, she needed to be close enough to monitor any developments but far enough away to avoid detection. It was an easy enough task for somebody such as Alsea, who had experience at watching and listening while remaining undetected. She had spent most of the last three years in Thornata's major cities, listening for any rumors of Rawl wielders so she could alert the Children. Her years of practice served her well here.

Alsea moved leisurely, staying close to a mile away from the caravan at all times, taking no chance of discovery. The slower pace also allowed her to conserve her energy, which she knew she would need later. She gathered kindling as she went, making preparations for a plan that played out in her head hundreds of times as she walked. Her mind raced the entire time, going over every minute detail over and over again. The day passed without incident, but it was far from peaceful inside Alsea's head.

Just as she had suspected, the caravan came to a halt that evening deep within the shadows of the towering Bonner Mountains. The following day, they would begin winding their way through the mountains by way of a narrow river canyon, stripping her of her ability to keep watch on them while remaining undetected easily. Once they were north of the Bonners, matters would be even worse. The flatlands beyond would give them few options for making a clean escape. This night was the best opportunity they were going to get. They had to get this escape right on the first try because Alsea understood there was unlikely to be a second.

If everything went according to plan, their flight should be straightforward enough. The three of them could vanish into the rocky foothills, out of the reach of the horses. With good fortune, they would reach the village that Alsea meant to head for by morning. She made one fast circle of the encampment, identifying the six sentry postings just as she had the night before. She would not act until darkness had fallen completely but wanted to ensure she knew their exact locations. The blackness of the night sky would create disorientation for the Thornatan soldiers, but her familiarity with this country would turn it to her advantage. Her scouting finished, all there was left to do was wait.

It occurred to Alsea as she settled down in some boulders thick with underbrush that perhaps she should speak to Ola again. It was already too dark to see the ogre, but she could at least try and hope that he heard her. He was already on the lookout for her distraction, but if she could give him more specifics, it could improve their chances of success. In her mind, it was worth the risk to try. Adjusting her voice to a similar tone to the one she had used the day prior, she spoke, hoping he could hear her.

"Ola, it's Alsea again. I have everything in place; the plan is going to happen tonight. When you smell smoke or see fire, that means it's time to get yourself and Adel out of those cages. Make your way over to the western edge of the camp as fast as you can. I can't see you, so I don't know if you can hear me, but if you can, good luck. I'll see you soon." She paused and considered saying more before deciding too many words could risk exposure. Ola was more than capable of figuring out the rest. Everything she knew about surviving such situations she had learned from him as a young girl.

There was only a quarter moon that night, a small sliver of light high above the rather thick clouds. This played well into Alsea's hand. The first pair of sentries never had a chance; she crept up behind them, a long knife tucked behind her back until the last moment. The first man was dead before he knew what had happened. The second turned at the sound of his falling body, only to find the same knife slicing the life from him before he could even think to cry out for help. It was a ruthless, calculated attack, precisely as it needed to be. Alsea moved on without hesitation, not allowing herself to dwell on the acts this night required of her. She saw any soldier following General Bern as a traitor to his people, but she still took no pleasure in ending their lives.

The second and third pairs met nearly identical fates to the first, but the fourth pair would prove to be more of a challenge. These men apparently did not take their sentry duties seriously and stood talking to each other rather than facing outward as any good sentry should. With the men facing each other, she would never be able to slip up behind them unseen, no matter how dark the night sky. Instead, she crept to the nearest vantage point she could find, an exposed hillside roughly thirty feet away from them.

There was little in the way of cover, but she had no time to waste. She needed to get Adel and Ola out of the camp as quickly as possible to maximize their time under the cover of darkness to make their escape. Drawing her bow and two arrows, she lined up both of her shots, making them a hundred times in her mind before ever pulling the string. She would need to be as fast as she had ever been, and both shots would need to be flawless, with hardly any light to guide her aim. If one shot was not instantly fatal, if one of these men cried out for even a second, everything could be lost. Taking one last deep breath, she drew the bowstring and let the first arrow fly. Without waiting to see if it would find its mark, she pulled back the string once more and sent the second winging forward as well, praying that neither man would happen to move at the wrong moment.

There was a pained grunt followed by another a split second later. Both men slumped to the ground, and Alsea waited for several agonizing moments to see if either of them would be able to cry out. As the seconds passed by, she was able to breathe easier. She had placed both shots perfectly. She moved on to the final two pairs of sentries, both of which she was able to dispatch without issue.

The final pair had been the easternmost. She had moved in this direction intentionally to place herself near to her hidden stash of kindling. She knew she needed to hurry now. If even one pair of dead sentries was found, it would complicate her plan horribly. It was unlikely the army would relieve the sentries so early in the night, but it wasn't a chance she was willing to take. She listened intently, trying to find a hint of anything going wrong around her, but the night remained as quiet as a crypt. Knowing every second was precious, Alsea gathered her supplies and began the final phase of her plan.

Chapter Nine

Blackness and agony had become the entirety of Adel's new reality. The senses he was deprived of by the sack over his head were swiftly becoming distant memories. How many days had it been since his talk with General Bern? Four or five? Or had it only been one? The soldiers had been removing his sack less often, feeding him only once a day since he had rejected the general's attempts to sway him to join forces with Idanox. Maybe they had been feeding him so well prior in an effort to butter him up so he would accept Bern's suggestion of joining the Hoyt. Each time, he was allowed only a few brief minutes to eat and drink before the sack was back over his head and he was back to the blackness and uncertainty. The last time they had removed the sack, he had tried to steal a glance at their surroundings. His food and water had been taken away, and the sack had been shoved back over his head instantly in punishment. *You should have strung him along more. He would be feeding you better at least.*

If there was a part of his body that did not ache from the continued wagon ride, he could not identify it. Each day felt like an eternity; his battered body was tossed about the iron cage like a sack of potatoes with no end in sight. He scolded himself repeatedly each time he caught himself longing for the end of the journey. He reminded himself that nothing happy was waiting for him once he left the wagon. An increasing scratching sensation against the inside of the burlap sack told him he had been a prisoner long enough that a beard was starting to grow in earnest. He would look quite unkempt when brought before the new duke. *They should at least allow me to shave before I meet Idanox*, he thought sarcastically.

The inevitability of his situation had begun to weigh down on him like a heavy boot pressing an ant deeper and deeper into the soil. Early in his captivity, he had felt no doubt that he and Ola would find a way to escape this predicament, but each passing day had stolen more of his hope. With the soldiers feeding him so rarely, he had virtually no time to observe his surroundings. With no time to look, there was no way to find a way of using the Rawl against his captors. Even if he could use his power, the sporadic feedings had begun to take their toll on his body during the ride. The injuries he had suffered while being tossed around the cage had sapped him of most of the little strength he still possessed. He doubted he would be able to use the Rawl for more than a few moments, even if they gave him the opportunity.

He knew stewing in this depressed state was not doing him any good, but with each passing day, it became harder to fight. His mind kept going to dark places, wondering how many days were left until he arrived in Oreanna, how many more days until they killed him. They must've been drawing close to the Bonner Mountains by now. This meant they were close to their best chance of escape. If only there was something he could do to make it happen. But with no clear idea of their surroundings, he had no idea how to use what little power remained in him to its fullest potential. Perhaps he should just call down a thunderbolt on top of them with the last of his strength. He would die too, of course, but at least he would be able to take most of these traitorous scum with him. At least Idanox would not get the opportunity to gloat over him as he died. He would go out on his own terms.

He would not join the Hoyt, no matter what threats were levied against him; he knew that much. He regretted that Ola would die along with him. He wished he could speak to his friend one last time. Adel knew the ogre's death would fall solely on his shoulders, knew that Ola was only in this war because of him. He wished he could have done more when they were captured. Perhaps if his instincts had been better, he could have fought off their attackers with the power of the Rawl.

The ogre had not said a word since their chat with General Bern, so the sound of his voice caught Adel entirely off guard. It took a few seconds to fully register that Ola was speaking to him.

"Adel, get that sack off of your head now!" Ola was crying out.

The urgent tone of the ogre's voice prompted Adel to follow his instructions without question. He may have thought it was a dream or a hallucination, but at that moment, he was willing to take any sliver of hope he could get. Reaching up, he ripped the sack from his head, the evening air refreshing him as though it were his first drink of water in days. He took in the sight around him. Men were running past the wagon in a frenzy, clearly panicked by something.

"Put that sack back on your head right now, boy!" someone was yelling at him.

Adel did not bother to acknowledge the command. Instead, he looked straight across at Ola, still chained in the caged wagon directly in front of him. The ogre was shifting around, trying to get his body into a particular position. He tugged one of his arms against the shackle that held it to the bars of the iron cage. The chain was no match for the ogre's inhuman strength, and it snapped under the strain.

A split second later, Ola's other arm was free, and the guards around the wagons had taken notice.

"The ogre is trying to escape; kill it! Bern says it's better dead than loose!"

The guards were moving to surround the door of Ola's cage as he rose to his feet, his massive form forced to hunch within the confinement of the cage. Adel acted at once, summoning the Rawl, an act born more of instinct than rational thought. He felt the power flow through him for the first time in days, the familiar feel of its power filling him with a reassuring sense of strength he had not felt since their capture. He sent it barreling into the gathering soldiers in the form of an immense wind gust, blasting the men from their feet. He broke off the attack quickly. The Rawl had been fast to respond to him, but expending himself too rapidly could be a costly mistake.

Adel's attack had given Ola the time he needed. He threw himself into the door of the iron cage with all the force he could muster. It only took one blow for the lock to snap, sending the door flying open. Ola was out of the cage a split second later, hopping down to the ground and wheeling to face the men regaining their feet. He was unarmed and outnumbered, though if this was in any way daunting to the massive ogre, he did not show it in the slightest.

A vicious kick to the ribs sent his first attacker tumbling back to the ground, Ola's hand reaching out and snatching the spear from the man's grasp as he fell. The next man took the spear straight through his gut, Ola using the long-handled weapon to pull the soldier close enough to tear the sword from the scabbard around his waist. Ola fended off the rest of the guards with ease, the spear and sword flashing through their defenses before they could think of a way to counter. Ola must have been a blur to the men trying to kill him, but Adel's trained eye could see that his friend was moving much slower than usual. It was no doubt a result of his injuries and lengthy captivity. In the end, it mattered not; Ola's exceptional skill was too much for his attackers to withstand. Within seconds, the fight was over.

With four guards dead or dying on the ground, Ola rushed over to the door of Adel's cage. Motioning for Adel to stand back, Ola struck the cage's lock with the blade of the spear once, twice, three times. On the third strike, the lock gave way, and Adel was free of his prison at last. He lunged through the door without hesitation, immeasurably grateful for Ola's courage to launch such an attempt. Ola must have also realized that their chances of escape were dissipating. His bold move surprised Adel, but he was not going to argue, not while he was standing free for the first time in days. He would take any chance he could get of survival.

His legs nearly failed him when they touched the ground for the first time, the impact of his days of inactivity hitting him in full. He shifted his weight from one foot to the other, trying to restore the feeling to his legs and feet. His senses were fully returning to him now, though they were quite sensitive from days of neglect. There was a smell in the air. Was that smoke? It was emanating from the east; there must've been a fire, a rapidly growing one judging by the intensity of the smoke stench. Something had gone wrong for the army, and Ola had obviously pounced at the opportunity.

Willing his legs to not give out on him, Adel took one step, and then another, and then another. He grew steadier with each step, more confident in his ability to make this escape a reality.

Turning toward Ola, he found his friend right beside him, holding out the sword of one of the fallen soldiers. Adel took the blade, unsure of how well he would be able to wield it if it came to a fight, realizing his arms were not in much better shape than his legs. Still, if he was going to die, at least he could put up a fight now. Ola retrieved another sword from one of the fallen soldiers, now wielding one in each hand, his eyes darting in every direction, searching for threats. The camp was in turmoil, and Adel realized that nobody else had tried to stop them. It sounded as though almost every soldier was to the east of them, working to put out the fire. The commotion of Ola's fight with the guards had somehow gone entirely unnoticed by the camp at large.

"Adel, we need to get to the western end of the encampment before they notice we have escaped the wagons. Can you walk?" Ola asked.

"I'll be fine. Let's get moving," Adel replied, hoping he was right even as the words left his mouth. "I'm not going back into that cage. If they find us, they'll have to kill me."

"We're in agreement on that, but have faith. We are getting out of here alive. Follow me, and stay close!"

Ola led the way, Adel following as close as possible. It was clear to Adel that Ola was experiencing the same aches and pains as he was. There was a noticeable limp in the ogre's stride with each step he took. A few soldiers raced by, apparently so distracted by the fire that they did not even notice their fleeing prisoners. The pair wound their way through wagons and nervous horses, trying to stay as low as possible. They had been walking for perhaps two minutes when a man stepped out in front of them, unaware of their presence until they were right on top of him. The soldier raised his spear in shock, but he never stood a chance. One of Ola's swords swatted the weapon aside, and the other plunged deep into the man's chest before he could say a word.

Ola hurriedly shoved the man's body under a nearby wagon, trying to conceal their tracks as best he could. The grass where he had fallen was slightly bloodstained, but there was nothing to be done about that. They could only hope nobody would notice until the chaos in the encampment had subsided. They continued onward, trying to reach the western end of the encampment without further delays. Adel did not know what they would find when they got there, but anything was better than being locked in that cage. He vowed to himself once again that he would not be going back there. If they found him, they would have to kill him. He would take as many of them with him as he could if that happened.

Had the army noticed their escape yet? Adel did not know, and he was not about to go back and find out. There were no cries of pursuit; for the time being, that would have to be enough. They continued onward, trying to hurry while not drawing attention to themselves. The camp was in utter chaos, but Ola's massive frame would stand out if they were not careful.

It proved to be a painstaking process. The Thornatan soldiers had spread their camp out over a large area, often with wide-open spaces between parked wagons and tents. Every time the pair was forced to dart over a long stretch of open terrain, Adel feared somebody would spot them. At one point, a cry rang out behind them, causing Adel to spin in his tracks with his sword raised defensively, but it was merely a soldier racing in the opposite direction.

The Thornatans must've been struggling to contain the blaze to the east; the smoke filling the air was not relenting. If anything, the ashy stench only grew stronger as they fled. Realizing he could make their situation worse, Adel focused his power for a brief moment, willing the fire to worsen. He dared not hold his focus on the matter for too long. Adel knew he needed to conserve his energy. He had no way of knowing if he had succeeded from such a great distance, but he hoped he had made their lives more difficult with his brief use of the Rawl.

The horses they passed were continually rearing and crying out anxiously. Adel suspected many of the animals closer to the flames had likely bolted already. The thought caused him to smirk in satisfaction. The fewer horses the army had available to pursue them with, the better. It felt as though they must be nearing the far end of the encampment. The wagons and supply tents were beginning to thin out. Adel allowed himself a brief moment of relief; they were going to escape! What had seemed impossible only minutes earlier was going to happen. His moment of joy was to be short-lived, however, as a shout broke the night ahead of them.

"Stop right there! Lay down your weapons immediately!"

Adel's heart sunk as shapes materialized out of the smoky night air ahead of them. There must've been at least a dozen Thornatan soldiers advancing on them. Such numbers would be a difficult fight even if he and Ola had been at full strength, let alone in their current diminished states. Adel raised his sword into the defensive posture Ola had taught him, taking a deep breath of acceptance. Weakened or not, he would not make this easy for them. They would not take him back to that cage alive. He immediately began to sweep the area, searching for a way to use his power, knowing he would likely only have enough strength for one final attack.

"You almost got away. Congratulations. If I hadn't noticed your empty wagons as I ran to help with the fire, you might have escaped, boy. We have you outnumbered; look around. You cannot possibly hope to outfight all of us. Surrender, and I will tell General Bern that you were cooperative. Who knows? He may not even kill the ogre if you give up now," one of the soldiers said, his spear raised threateningly toward them.

Adel tightened his grip on his sword; he would not surrender, not again. He locked eyes with Ola and was glad to see that the ogre seemed to share his thoughts. They would fight until these attackers were dead or they were. To his surprise, Adel found he was not afraid, not like he had been when he had found himself surrounded on the docks in Kolig. He understood now that there were worse things than death in an honest battle. He reached out to the power of the Rawl, hoping he had enough strength left for one last powerful attack. He would strike the ground beneath their feet, he decided, much as he had during their flight through the streets of Kolig. If he could complicate their footing just enough, he and Ola might have a chance to overcome the seemingly impossible odds.

"We won't be your prisoners again, so kill us if you can, you rat-faced traitors!" Adel shouted, his anger getting the better of him.

The soldiers began to advance, and he lashed out with his power, turning the dirt beneath their feet instantly to mud. They began to sink—some of them all the way up to their knees—weighed down by their heavy gear. He struck again, this time turning the mud solid once more, sealing their legs underground.

The soldiers immediately began to struggle to free themselves, fighting to work their way out of the deep earth he had sunk them into. Ola was already moving, the two swords he had appropriated from their fallen owners slashing out at the men as they fought to find their footing. Three of them were dead before they could even think of raising their weapons in defense.

Adel joined the attack, fighting through the aches and pains that reverberated through every inch of his body. He rushed toward a soldier stuck in knee-deep dirt, lashing out with his sword. The man caught his first strike with his shield. Adel swung once more, swatting the shield aside and exposing the soldier's body. He struck one last time, his lunge plunging the blade deep into the man's gut. He wrenched the sword free, his eyes searching for more attackers as his first foe collapsed to the dirt.

To his right, another soldier had worked his way free of the dirt and was rushing toward him, spear fully extended. Adel backpedaled, hoping the man would over-commit to a thrust and be left off-balance. The soldier made no such mistake, pressing in on him faster than he could retreat. Adel sidestepped to the left and swung downward, catching the man's spear on the shaft, trying to split it in half. The blow caught the shaft with substantial force, but to his dismay, the spear did not break. The soldier shoved Adel with his shield, and now Adel was the one off-balance, stumbling backward as the man brought his spear to bear once more.

Adel was sure he was dead. His battered body had failed him at last, and his aching arms were unable to bring his sword around in defense. His legs gave out on him, and he tumbled backward, falling to the ground. But the man's spear never reached him, a sharp thwack ringing out, an arrow plunging deep into his neck. Adel did not have time to register what had happened; another soldier was closing in from his right. His body feeling renewed by the reprieve he had just received, he forced himself to his feet, turning to meet the new attacker.

This man attacked with a sword; Adel parried his first strike, then his second, and then finally sidestepped the third. He counterattacked, his first swing forcing the man into a stumbling backward retreat. His second attack came down as his opponent was fighting to regain his footing, cutting down through the man's shoulder and deep into his chest.

Adel spun in every direction, searching for more attackers. Ola was finishing off two more soldiers, several others dead or dying near his feet. There were several more strewn along the ground, arrows protruding from their bodies. Where had the arrows come from? Were there men in this camp who were helping them escape, men loyal to General McLeod? It was then that Adel spotted a figure approaching from the north with what appeared to a bow in their hand. He raised his sword cautiously, but as the figure drew closer, he felt the flood of recognition and joy begin to sweep through him.

Alsea slung her bow to her back and drew her knife, moving with caution around the bodies in case any of them were not truly dead. Adel began to walk toward her, fighting the incredible pain that was still rushing through his legs. Noticing him trying to reach her, Alsea moved over to him first, reaching out and placing one hand on his chest to stop him in his tracks. Her grip was firm but gentle, her touch sending waves of relief throughout Adel's aching body. Just being in her presence again filled him with happiness and relief he had never experienced before. It was as though a heavy boulder had been lifted from on top of him. He fought to hold back tears of joy as he looked into her eyes. She had come to save them, as he should have known she would.

"Take it easy, Adel. You've had a rough ordeal, and we still have a long way to go tonight. You need to save your strength," she said, shooting him the most dazzling smile he could have imagined. "Oh, and by the way, I've been wanting to do this for a long time, and I know you have too, so just shush it for a second and let me do it. Fair enough?"

Without waiting for agreement, she drew him close and kissed him. It shocked Adel so much that it was several seconds before he thought to kiss her back. For the first time, he was not concerned with his emotions or what the ramifications of them could be; he was just in the moment, and it was the most fantastic thing he had ever felt. She broke away at last, and they looked somewhat abashedly into each other's eyes. Adel managed to look away first and immediately saw Ola standing a few feet away. The ogre had a bemused smile on his face, his two bloody swords hanging at his sides.

"Oh, no, don't let me interrupt," he said with a chuckle. "Though we should probably get moving before they get that fire put out and realize we are missing."

Adel looked over at Alsea, who was still beaming from ear to ear. He could feel his own smile on his face. He couldn't help it. No matter how dire the situation, he was happier than he had ever been. But Ola was right; they would have time to talk later, but only if they managed to escape this camp with their lives. He looked at her for a second longer, trying to communicate a million thoughts in his smile, realizing she was doing the same. For the first time in days, his body felt the slightest bit rejuvenated.

"You're right, Ola. Let's get out of here," Adel said, and the three friends slipped away into the night, together once more at last.

Chapter Ten

Adel woke to find every inch of his body aching. The pain radiated from the top of his head to the tips of his toes. Their desperate flight away from the Thornatan Army camp had taken all night, a night he was still not quite sure how he had survived. He likely would not have if not for Alsea being there to keep him moving every step of the way, never allowing him to falter for even a second. Thinking of Alsea, he inched his way back ever so slightly in the bed and could not help but smile gleefully as he felt his back press against hers. He was not sure if he would ever get used to the feeling of joy that raced through his body from having her so close. The doubts that he had once harbored about sharing his feelings had evaporated at the mere sight of her. He was in the worst physical pain of his life but could not have been more delighted to be in the position he found himself now.

She had saved them and led them to this inn in a tiny village deep in the foothills of the Bonner Mountains. Once again, the young woman had astonished him with her tenacity and skills. If it were not for Alsea, he and Ola would still be locked in those cages, still trundling their way toward Oreanna and their inevitable demise. The journey had been short but far from easy. The terrain they'd been forced to scramble through in the dark had been rocky and steep. They had each taken multiple falls in the darkness but fought to push on. Adel had taken heart from the fact that the army would not be able to send its horses into such terrain, especially in the darkness of night. Alsea had planned their escape route just as well as their initial rescue.

Adel knew Idanox and the Hoyt were still out there and still needed to be dealt with, but they would have to wait. He was exhausted, and while his entire body ached from his captivity, Ola's injuries were far worse. The ogre still had wounds he had taken during their capture that the soldiers had not bothered to treat appropriately. He also bore a few fresh cuts from their fight the night before. Alsea had been able to properly treat and bind his wounds, but they still needed time to heal. It would be quite some time before they would be ready to depart—perhaps a week, if not more. Alsea had assured them that the chances of the army searching this village were slim. Considering the area where they had made their escape, the army most likely assumed they were making for the Temple of the Rawl. They could only hope this would be the case. If the army tried to make an attack there, Klaweck and his giants would be all too happy to remove them from the region.

Adel tried to rise from the bed, finding that his back and joints groaned in protest as he did. Every part of his body was telling him to stay in bed, telling him he should have more appreciation for a comfort he had suspected he would never experience again. But his mind was racing, and he felt the overwhelming urge to move. The early-morning light was beginning to creep through the shades covering the only window. He had spent the better part of the previous day and night in the bed, rising only briefly to eat and relieve himself before collapsing into a deep slumber once more. He and Alsea had entered the inn and rented two rooms, then helped Ola climb in through one of the windows. The ogre just stood out too much, and they could not risk anyone in this tiny village talking about his presence. The people of this village bore no love for the Hoyt, but the promise of gold could make men do foolish things, as they had learned. Ola had slept in the next room over while Adel and Alsea had shared this one.

The last two days had been such a whirlwind that Adel was still trying to process everything that had happened. He had been so exhausted upon their arrival at this inn that Alsea had forced him to go straight to bed. She had accepted none of his protests about his desire to talk about anything that had happened, assuring him there would be ample time for discussion later. When he had woken briefly the prior afternoon, she had fetched food for him from the inn's dining room but told him to get back to sleep after he had eaten. He could feel his strength returning with each passing hour, but the process was proving to be a slow one. He estimated it would still be several days before he was at full strength. Still, he could not help but be relieved. His aches and pains were not all that bad, considering the fate that had awaited him in Ore-anna.

He limped his way over to the table, where a half-full carafe of water was waiting. After pouring himself a cup and downing it all once, he turned back toward the bed. Alsea was sleeping peacefully, the sight of her once again filling him with happiness unlike any he had ever experienced before. He did not know what the future held in store for the two of them, but he felt blessed to have shared at least one incredibly special moment with her. Indeed, at that moment, he did not care much about the future. All that mattered was that moment and the fact that he never wanted it to end.

They had not spoken of it—their frantic escape and ensuing exhaustion had not allowed for it—but Adel had thought of little else since their arrival at this inn. Every time he had sought to make conversation with her, Alsea had quieted him, urging him to sleep. Every time, he had slipped into dreams of Alsea before those dreams gave way to the horrors he had experienced over the past year. He knew those horrors were a part of him now, that he would carry the burden of them throughout the rest of his life. At least not all of the memories were bad. His kiss with Alsea crept its way into his mind at every turn, helped by the fact that he made no effort to prevent it. There would be time to discuss such things later, she promised, but now he needed his rest.

He made his way to the door of the chamber and staggered over to the next room, giving the door a gentle tap. He did not want to wake Ola, but he was concerned about his friend's well-being. The ogre's wounds were severe, and Adel was worried that Ola might take a turn for the worse if not monitored closely. He doubted any other man he had ever met would still be alive after suffering so many grievous wounds. Immediately after his tap, he heard the sound of a shifting chair and heavy footsteps making their way toward the door. The door opened slowly at first, Ola's sharp eyes glancing through the crack, before opening completely, the ogre beckoning Adel to come in. Ola closed and latched the door behind him swiftly, clearly not eager to be discovered by the innkeeper or their fellow patrons.

"How are you feeling, Ola?" Adel asked.

"Better than I was in that cage, that's for sure," Ola replied, motioning for Adel to take a seat and pulling out a second chair for himself. "How about yourself, Adel?"

Adel limped his way toward the table, gesturing toward his legs. "There's still quite a bit of pain, especially in my limbs. I was getting tossed all around that cage like a sack of hay, though nothing seems broken at least. Please remind me to thank Elim for giving me the armor. The soldiers could have had the courtesy to restrain me in place. But at least I wasn't dealing with a head wound the whole time. Is it healing up well?"

"It will leave a nice scar, but it will heal. Alsea came in and helped me clean it out and rewrap it last night. Luckily for me, ogres are hard to kill." Ola turned his head slightly so Adel could see the fresh bandage in the spot where a spear had struck him on the night of their capture.

It was a night he had replayed in his head repeatedly during the endless hours in the cage. He could still feel his sword slipping from his fingers. The mental wound of having lost the sword that had once belonged to Captain Boyd was one he was still having a difficult time recovering from. The captain had been a father figure to him. Losing his sword felt like a betrayal of the man's trust. He knew this was silly, that all the grizzled captain would care about was his former cabin boy's safety, but he still could not shake the feeling of guilt. He felt as though the loss of the sword proved the captain had viewed him as more of a man than he had proven himself to be that night.

"We haven't had an opportunity to talk much since we escaped. I suppose we have Alsea to thank for that—both for getting us out and for making us rest and recover like good little boys. But I wanted to talk to you about something. Alsea is still asleep, and what she doesn't know won't hurt her. I'm sorry, Ola. Us getting captured was all my fault, and I'm so sorry. I've been replaying everything that happened the night they captured us in my head, and I wish I had done things differently. I should have been able to use my power to get us out of that. I could have used to Rawl to tear those soldiers to shreds, but I hesitated. No, I didn't hesitate. I froze, and I panicked. If not for Alsea, we would still be on our way to our death in Oreanna, and I would have been entirely to blame," Adel said, and Ola cut him off before he could continue.

"Have no regrets, my young friend. We are both still breathing. If anyone should have regrets, it will be the Hoyt and those treacherous soldiers who didn't kill us when they had the chance! You did what you thought was right, and nobody can fault you for it. Besides, I am not blameless in our capture. I still can't believe I did not hear them sneaking up on us. You are not the only one who has been kicking himself. I underestimated their ability to find us and never would have thought them smart enough to sneak up on us on that dock. I am old and experienced enough to know better than to ever underestimate any foe. Don't worry, my friend. There will be no more mistakes from here on out. We will pay them back tenfold for everything they did to us."

Adel grinned; he was indeed looking forward to paying their enemies back for everything they had suffered since Kolig. The three had not spoken of any future plans, but he felt confident they were all on the same page. They would leave for Oreanna as soon as they were fit to travel. Hopefully they would be in time to join General McLeod in his assault on the capital, though Adel would storm the duke's palace single-handedly if that was what it took to end this war. Idanox would die, no matter the cost. Whether that death came at the end of a noose or the end of his sword made no difference to Adel. At last, they knew exactly where to find the elusive leader of the Hoyt, and Adel would not rest until he put an end to the evil man. But since no plans could be made yet, he turned the conversation in another direction.

"Ola, do you think it is irresponsible of me to be with Alsea?" he asked, putting to words the question that had been running through his mind since the moment they had kissed in the army encampment. His bliss had over-ruled his doubts in the moment, but with each passing hour, his old thoughts threatened more and more to creep back into his mind. Was he making a mistake? Alsea had refused to allow him to speak yet, so he felt the need to turn to Ola for affirmance that what he was doing was right.

"I seem to remember us having this conversation shortly before we were captured. Is that just my head wound making me remember things that did not actually happen?" Ola asked with a chuckle so infectious that Adel could not help but join in. Before long, it turned into a burst of full-fledged laughter, something he had not experienced for a long time. Finally, fighting down the laugh, he tried to explain himself.

"No, but it may have given you more of a sense of humor, so you will hear no complaint from me. I know we did, but after everything we have gone through since then, I was wondering if your thoughts had changed at all."

This was nonsense, of course, but Adel felt the urge to justify his need for reassurance. He knew he would eventually have to overcome his insecurities to be an effective Master of the Rawl. But since they had yet to bestow the title upon him formally, he felt comfortable asking his questions. He knew Ola would never judge him, no matter how exasperated he might be with Adel's lack of confidence.

"Well, I think I made my feelings known the last time we discussed this. But I have nothing better to do at the moment, so I will repeat myself. I feel it would be irresponsible for the two of you to carry on the way you have been, holding your feelings inside. Look at what happened. How did you feel about the way you left things while you were in that cage and knew you might never see her again?"

"I felt horrible. The thought that I could die and not be able to tell her how I felt was torture worse than anything the army or the Hoyt could ever do to me. But now that we know how we feel, is it irresponsible for me to act on it? If I am to be the Master of the Rawl, as you and Elim have told me I will be, would I be able to make informed decisions without my emotions interfering?" Adel asked.

"Alsea is not a helpless child, Adel. If she were, the fact that she was the one to rescue us last night would say something about our own competency, don't you think? I suspect if she ever thought you were listening to your heart and not your head, she would be the first to let you hear about it. Master of the Rawl or no, she is a grown woman with a mind of her own. She will not allow you to treat her any differently; of that much I am confident. Once again, you are focused too much on your role in your relationship with Alsea. It needs to be a partnership, a bond the two of you build together. It will take time to get used to it. I do not know where it will lead, but I believe you both owe it to yourselves to find out."

He's right, Adel thought. Perhaps he was too worried about his own role in a potential relationship. Maybe it was disrespectful of him to feel that Alsea would not feel comfortable expressing herself to him if he became Master of the Rawl. Their feelings were out in the open now, and he owed it to Alsea and to himself to be transparent about them. After thanking Ola for his advice, he slipped back into the room he shared with Alsea, not wanting to wake her from her slumber.

He turned as he entered to find that she was no longer sleeping in the bed. He spun in every direction, looking for her, only to feel a playful shove on his back. He turned to face her, feeling weakness in his knees at the sight of her smile, which had nothing to do with his injuries.

"Did I tell you that you were allowed to get out of bed yet?" she asked him with a laugh.

"I was just checking on Ola," he began to explain before she waved him off.

"I know where you were. I always know where you are. I'm actually quite clever, you know. It's rather obvious that tabs need to be kept on you."

Adel grinned sheepishly. "I can't argue with that. If not for you, Ola and I would still be in those cages."

"You would have gotten yourselves out of them eventually. I just thought you might appreciate a little help," Alsea said with a grin, then surprised him by leaning in for another kiss, holding it for a long moment.

"Your help is always appreciated." Adel laughed as she pulled away. "I will try not to end up in any more cages. I can't make any guarantees, though."

"Better not. You have a knack for getting yourself into trouble. Well, if you do, I'll start another fire and make sure you get out of it all right. You know, my life just wouldn't be as exciting without you," she said with a reassuring wink.

Adel had so many things he wanted to say and no words with which to say them. He settled for opening his arms and taking her into an embrace, one that he held for a long time, not wanting to ever let her go. He had been a fool for allowing his feelings to go unspoken for so long.

When they finally did break, Alsea immediately forced him to get back into bed, promising to return shortly with food.

She was back a few minutes later with two bowls of roasted garlic soup and bread she had fetched from the dining room. The aromatic smell made Adel realize for the first time exactly how hungry he was. He had done nothing but sleep since their last meal, yet as soon as the food was in sight, his stomach growled ravenously. The soup was delicious and savory. His bowl was empty and his bread devoured within moments. Alsea laughed at how he had wolfed down his food, using a cloth to wipe a few drops of the soup from his chin.

"Do try to have some dignity, Adel. I can't always be cleaning up after you," she joked.

"But you're so good at it," he said before turning serious once more. "I'm sorry, Alsea. I should have told you how I felt a long time ago."

"But you didn't, and that's in the past. It's not like I am blameless. I've felt the same way, but I said nothing either. When I found out you had been captured, I was devastated. I felt like I had lost my chance to tell you how I felt. But I've never been one to take an injustice lying down, so I decided to come and rescue you. You aren't getting away from me that easily," Alsea said with yet another of her knee-weakening smiles that made Adel grateful to be sitting down.

"Out of curiosity, when did you first begin to feel this way?" Adel asked.

Alsea paused for a moment, thinking. "I think the first feelings came after the Battle of Kolig. Seeing the way you so selflessly risked your life to save people you did not know. Then you did so again, putting out the fire in the army camp. I suppose it just told me all I needed to know about the type of man you are. You have done nothing but prove me right time and time again, ever since that day. Looking back on it now, though, you probably should have let General Bern die a horrible death in that fire first."

Adel burst out with laughter that hurt his aching body, but he could not help it. This woman brought him so much joy that he could never have imagined himself to experience, and he did not want it ever to end.

"Listen to me, Adel," Alsea said. "We still have a dangerous challenge ahead of us. We both know what we are going to do once you and Ola are well enough to travel. There will be a time after this is over to figure out how we are going to go forward together. But I want you to know that I want us to be together, always. I will never leave your side unless you send me away."

"I will never send you away, Alsea. I can't imagine a day spent without you. Besides, it would be a pretty dumb thing to do considering how often you tend to save my skin when you are around. I have to believe I will live a longer, happier life with you nearby," Adel replied with a smile.

"That's true. You know, it really is a miracle you managed to survive until I came along." Alsea laughed and gave him another good-natured shove.

They lay in bed talking until Adel's eyes started to droop. Alsea noticed at once and immediately ordered him back to sleep. Too weak to put up more than a token protest, Adel complied, knowing the rest was much needed. The rest of the day and night, he dreamed nothing but pleasant dreams for the first time in a long time. He knew there was pain, blood, and war both behind and in front of him, but those things could be set aside for one night.

The next morning, both Adel and Ola were feeling improved enough that Alsea permitted them to have a brief meeting around the table in Ola's room. She had retrieved lunch for the three of them from the inn's dining room, still not wanting to take any chances of anyone spotting Ola. The Thornatans had likely moved on from the area several days ago, but there was no harm in caution. Besides, people in a village like this had most likely never seen an ogre before. Even perfectly innocent gossip could draw unwanted attention to their presence.

"I assume we are all in general agreement on what is going to happen after we leave this inn?" Adel asked.

"The Hoyt need to be stopped, now more than ever. The longer they are allowed to stay in power, the more soldiers will feel compelled to join them in order to protect their people. The backing of the army will allow them to commit atrocities on a scale I would rather not imagine. The odds against us will grow worse by the day," Ola replied. "We need to put an end to them as soon as possible."

"That is true," Alsea said, raising a hand to ward off the protests she must have known would come from her next statement. "But the two of you are still a week away from being fit to travel, let alone fight. Don't bother arguing with me; you both know I am right."

"We may not have the luxury of waiting a week if Ola is right," Adel protested, earning a stern glare that stopped him from finishing his statement.

"What the pair of you do not know is that as we speak, General McLeod is mustering as many men as he can rally to try to take back Oreanna. He will need time to assemble as many as possible. He will be gathering them on the Ice Fields to prepare for the attack. He will not attack before we arrive; I am certain he will need more time than that. We stand a much better chance of success if we have more numbers behind us. Take the week to rest and recover. You will both need to be at full strength for what awaits us in Oreanna. I promise it will be more horrific than anything we have ever faced before," she explained.

It was true that General McLeod would need time to gather troops. If they did have the week to spare, they should take advantage of it. Ola, in particular, had been severely injured during their capture and imprisonment and needed all the time he could get. If they rushed to battle too soon, they could be signing their own death warrants. Alsea was right, as always; the best thing they could do was wait and head north once they were at full strength.

"Very well, Alsea. I agree with you. We will wait at this inn for one week. Ola and I will be cooperative and rest to heal our injuries. Then we will hurry north to the Ice Fields, meet up with General McLeod, and join the attack on Oreanna. Then we will finally put an end to Idanox, the Hoyt, and this war, which has gone on for far too long."

Chapter Eleven

The Ice Fields of northern Thornata were among the bleakest landscapes that could be found in the entire Empire. A vast desert that had frozen over centuries before, they stretched as far as the eye could see in every direction. Wherever one looked, all they could see was an endless sheet of the purest white ice imaginable, unthawed for hundreds of years. The Ice Fields lay on a towering plateau that stood perhaps a thousand feet higher than the surrounding plains. The bitterly cold air and brutal winds of the high elevation kept these lands frozen during even the hottest of summer months. Few people traversed this barren plain, for there were few reasons for anyone to come here. Only those hunting the pelts of the rare animal species that called this desolate plateau home dared to traverse it. The Ice Fields were utterly cut off from the major cities of the province, and even the nearest small village was over twenty miles away. The remoteness made this an ideal staging location for the forces gathering to launch an attack on Oreanna.

This desolate plain of ice was the place where General Randall McLeod had won his most famous victory, leading a small Thornatan Army patrol to victory over bandits and raiders who'd tripled their numbers. He had fought that day, fully expecting to die on this frozen plain. He had never thought of returning to this desolate place, but all these years later, he had found a purpose for it to serve once more. Such a landscape would act as a natural line of defense. Idanox would not dare send his fighters out to meet them here. It was this place that he had selected to engineer what he hoped would be a far more significant and more meaningful victory. Thus far, however, he saw few signs of hope that this would come to pass.

His journey to Kalstag and Kalskag had not been as productive as McLeod had hoped. While most of the soldiers garrisoned there bore no love for Idanox or the Hoyt, they were hesitant to join him in an all-out assault on the capital. Only two hundred men from the two cities had agreed to make the march north with him, all of them going against their barrack commanders' orders to do so. For the rest, fear of retribution against themselves or their loved ones outweighed their hatred of Idanox and the Hoyt.

In addition to the men he had brought from Kolig and various patrols they had encountered and persuaded to their cause on the journey north, they numbered just under four hundred fighting men in total.

Oreanna was the capital of Thornata, and its physical defenses were among the best of any city in the Empire. A tall outer wall made of solid stone, stores of provisions that could last for years, and gates which had never been penetrated by an attacking force while under siege awaited any attacker. The bulk of the Hoyt forces would be there to defend Idanox, along with an unknown number of Thornatan Army defectors. The city had once been home to the army's largest garrison, with nearly three thousand men stationed there. If even a third of those men now served the Hoyt, they would wipe out this paltry force McLeod had assembled in short order.

The general looked out at the tents of the few men he had managed to gather and sighed. The improbable victory he hoped to lead them to looked more unlikely by the day. In all likelihood, the Hoyt could destroy them in a battle, even in a wide-open field. The formidable defenses of Oreanna only made their defeat more assured.

There had still been no word from Alsea, no indication that she had succeeded in her mission to find Adel and Ola. McLeod feared the girl, capable though she was, had likely gotten herself killed in the attempt. Missing

Adel's powers would be another challenge to overcome, one which may prove to be insurmountable. The young man could have played a devastating role in the battle to come, turned the odds in their favor. But he had learned long ago not to fret over what was not, but rather to face matters as they were. The odds stacked against them were high, and there was no denying it. But hope was not gone until there was no longer a single man alive who was willing to fight back against the tyranny of the Hoyt. So, he would fight until they won or until the bastards cut the last breath from his body.

General McLeod had hoped to oversee the construction of a dozen siege towers, but his men were reporting that sturdy lumber was in short supply. It was to be expected in a place such as the Ice Fields. Soldiers had carried the bulk of the lumber up onto the plateau from the plains below, a tedious process. They had already constructed two towers, and if they were lucky, they might be able to scavenge enough wood to finish a third. The towers were likely to be their best chance of making it over the walls of Oreanna. Attempting to batter open the gates would be far more deadly, exposing men to endless archer fire from above, and they did not have enough men.

The towers were not much more likely to succeed, and McLeod understood this. They did not have enough men to move them quickly into position, and three points of attack would not be enough to overwhelm the Hoyt defenders on the walls. But they were the best option he had, so he put his men to work and tried to maintain an aura of optimism every time he swept through the encampment. It was the duty of a leader to project an image of confidence, no matter how he might feel inside. McLeod understood that his men fed off his own emotions. If he paced the camp nervously with a defeated look upon his face, his men would put off similar energy. He needed them to fight as though they thought they could win. If they did, maybe they could.

Randall McLeod was not a young man, but this day he felt older than he had in any of his many years. This would be his last great battle, win or lose. Even if he did somehow survive the war ahead, he was getting too old for this line of work. War was a pursuit for younger men, most of whom were doomed never to grow old. Those lucky enough to survive those wars may find themselves in his shoes one day, and he did not envy them. He had found over the years that the only reward for victory was another battle to fight. There would always be another enemy; it was the nature of humanity. He had never lost a battle over which he had command, and he wanted to win this one more than he had any other. Yet as he looked out over his far-too-small encampment, he knew it was unlikely he would emerge victorious one final time.

McLeod let out another sigh. It was the curse of a successful soldier. There was always going to be another battle. Men were too warlike for it to be any other way; they had proven it time and time again. Survive enough battles, and you would find yourself leading other men into the next one. Lead enough campaigns, and you were bound to lose one eventually and be doomed to watch the men who had placed their trust in you perish. McLeod wondered if he would have chosen a different path in life if he had known as a younger man where he was destined to end up.

The thought of his own demise was not particularly troubling to General Randall McLeod. He had lived his entire adult life knowing any day could be his last, and he had made his peace with that long ago. However, the prospect of leading these four hundred young men into near-certain death was not one he relished. The Thornatan Army was a strictly voluntary force. Every one of them was here of their own accord, but it did not stop him from thinking their blood would be on his hands. Still, what option did he have? Not attack Oreanna? Leave the province under the rule of Idanox without a fight? As many men as would die in the battle to come, many more would perish under the Hoyt leader's brutal rule. They had to try for the sake of the Thornatan people. Randall McLeod could not go to his grave knowing he had not done everything in his power to liberate Thornata from the rule of a tyrant.

If the commanders in Kalstag and Kalskag had listened to reason, he could've had close to fifteen hundred men right now. With a force that size, they would have stood a more reasonable chance of victory. But here he was with only four hundred men to go up against the bulk of the Hoyt forces, some of their own brothers in arms, and the greatest physical defenses Thornata had to offer. If he died on the field of battle, he could accept that. Nevertheless, he was not ready to face the harsh reality of what that defeat would mean for the future of his people. Would the Empire intervene on their behalf? Would they see Idanox as a threat who needed to be removed from power? McLeod hoped so, but years of experience told him they would likely look the other way. The emperor did not trouble himself with the issues of his provinces unless his own rule was under direct threat. Even Idanox was not stupid or arrogant enough to try to pose a threat to the Empire.

He was shaken from these thoughts by a blasting horn at the southern end of the encampment. Were they under attack? Had Idanox decided to bring the battle to them? He could only hope the Hoyt could be so foolish. The Ice Fields were the type of terrain that would not be kind to an attacking force, as he had proven so many years before. He would be all too happy to decimate any force that Idanox had sent against them. Men were rushing to the south as fast as their feet could carry them, weapons in hand. Randall McLeod hurried to join them, his hand resting on the pommel of his sword. If the Hoyt wanted a fight here, any survivors would regret it.

He reached the southern edge of the camp and looked out over the side of the plateau. There was a force marching toward them, one that was at least close to their own size. The Thornatan Army uniforms were recognizable even from this distance. His heart sunk. Idanox had sent some of his former brothers to weaken them before they attacked the capital. But wait, what were those other uniforms? They were not all Thornatan. Some of the men were adorned in black, though from a distance it appeared to be real armor, not the leathers and rags the Hoyt favored. Had the Hoyt forged their own armor? With Oreanna under their control, they certainly had the resources to do so. *As if the odds were not already stacked against us badly enough*, McLeod thought.

As the approaching force drew close enough for him to get a good look at them, McLeod saw that these were not Hoyt men at all. The star sigil on the breastplates of the men in black revealed their identity; these were Imperial soldiers. The Empire was known for staying out of the affairs of the individual provinces unless intervention was absolutely necessary. What were Imperial men doing here? Was it possible the emperor had sent these men to their aid? McLeod dared not believe it could be true.

The bulk of the force arrived within minutes, line after line of Thornatans and Imperials marching side by side, a sight McLeod had never thought to see in his life. When at last they had all arrived and taken their place in the formation, a lone Imperial soldier stepped forward. He walked with a slight limp. He was not as old as McLeod, but the general could see this was a man who had seen his fair share of war. His limp was not so dissimilar from one McLeod himself was often forced to conceal from his men in cold weather. *It's a gift of old soldiers—the ability to spot another who has seen more than he would care to remember.*

"Greetings. I must assume you are Supreme General Randall McLeod?" the man asked once he was no more than a few feet away.

"Your assumptions are correct, soldier. I must admit I am surprised to find Imperial soldiers this deep into the province. May I ask why you have come all this way?" McLeod responded.

"My name is Captain Thaddeus Dunstan, and until recently I was the commanding officer of Fort Oliver. It is a small fortress operating close to the border with Verizia, meant for keeping the peace between the two provinces. It's dull work, but work that the Empire feels is necessary," the soldier replied.

"Yes, I am familiar with the area. I visited your fortress many years ago. Still, I am not quite clear on why you are here, Captain Dunstan."

"A fortnight ago, a hundred of your men arrived at Fort Oliver along with twenty Hoyt fighters. They intended to force us from the fortress and the province. They were acting on the orders of Idanox, who has declared himself duke of this province, though I assume you know this much already. However, your soldiers turned on their Hoyt companions and killed them. They asked me for my help, a request that I was not able to refuse," Dunstan explained.

"They asked you to come here with them?" McLeod asked, confused.

"No, they asked us to help them ambush another group of their comrades bound for another fortress with the same intent. We succeeded and were able to kill all the Hoyt fighters with that group as well. However, they still managed to assault three other Imperial fortresses and slaughter the men manning them. I have come here with your men, as well as all the Imperial forces from the two surviving fortresses. I am here to offer our assistance for your assault on Oreanna, for that is why you are here, is it not? I seek justice for the Imperial soldiers killed at our fortresses, and the ones responsible are in Oreanna. Our goals seem to be aligned. I believe we can help each other, Supreme General."

General McLeod could hardly dare to believe it could be true. How had Idanox been foolish enough to send forces against the Imperials? Even if all had been successful, the Imperial High Command would be furious and immediately send a retaliatory force. The Empire would turn a blind eye to almost anything, but attacks against their troops would never be tolerated. The Hoyt leader had delivered a gift right into his lap. *Thank you, Idanox. I will make good use of it.*

"Thank you for explaining everything, Captain Dunstan, and thank you for the assistance you have provided my men. I am forever in your debt for the aid you have already given them. May I ask how many of you total have come to join us?" General McLeod fought to maintain his dignity, struggling to hide his considerable glee at the shocking turn of events.

"We have two hundred Imperial soldiers and two hundred Thornatans who turned on their Hoyt captors. We are far from a full invading force, but I daresay we can be of use," Dunstan replied.

"I daresay a truer statement has never been said, Captain Dunstan. Every last man will be put to good use, rest assured of it."

This infusion would bring their total to nearly eight hundred men. McLeod was thinking to himself, the wheels in his head spinning already. It still may not be enough, but it would be enough to give the Hoyt a proper fight at least. Furthermore, it may be enough to help sway scared Thornatan soldiers back to the side of their brothers. It was a boon McLeod had not dared to think may come. Only a few minutes ago, his thoughts had been bleak, their impending failure weighing heavily on him. They still had a difficult task ahead of them; there was no doubt about it. But at least now they had a chance. An opportunity, no matter how remote, was all he had ever needed in the past.

"I am curious, Captain Dunstan. My understanding is that it is standard Imperial procedure to stay out of the affairs of the provinces unless intervention is absolutely necessary. May I ask what you said to convince your commanders of the need to become involved in our conflict?" McLeod asked. He noted that Dunstan shifted somewhat uncomfortably at the question, and he suspected the answer that was coming.

"I will be blunt with you, Supreme General McLeod. I am acting here without authorization from Imperial High Command. It is an offense I will undoubtedly have to answer for once this is all said and done, assuming I'm still breathing. With that being said, I have no regrets. These Hoyt savages butchered several hundred good Imperial soldiers, and I mean to see them answer for it. If Imperial High Command has an issue with that, I am willing to face the consequences of my actions. I may not be doing the appropriate thing, but I do not doubt for a second that I am doing the right thing."

General McLeod had already possessed a great admiration for Dunstan's courage, but now that respect grew tenfold. Acting in the interests of doing what was right, even knowing he would likely face severe discipline for it, was truly admirable. He would love to have a man of morals like Dunstan under his command, though he was sure the bloated politicians at Imperial High Command would see things differently. He decided not to press the matter any further. Dunstan and his men had come to their aid; that was all that needed to be discussed.

"I want room made for our men as well as Captain Dunstan and his men. Have food brought to them as well. They must be hungry from their long journey. Let's get them fed and ready to fight. Captain, we plan to march from this camp in three days. Will your men be ready?"

"Aye, Supreme General, we will be ready to march and ready to fight. Those Hoyt bastards will regret the day they thought they could violate an Imperial outpost without facing the consequences. I'll promise you that," Dunstan replied.

"I expected no less from a man like you, Captain Dunstan. I plan to conduct a final war council the day before we depart. I would like to have you there if you are willing. Your input may prove valuable in the battle ahead of us," McLeod requested.

"As you wish, Supreme General."

"Thank you, Captain. If you or your men need anything at all, please bring your request to me directly."

McLeod headed back toward his tent, plans already forming in his head. Their force had just doubled in size in an instant, and it was up to him to utilize them in a way that gave them the best chance at victory. Their chances were still not great, but at least now there was hope. The men already assembled would be reinvigorated with the arrival of additional forces. They would fight like men who believed they could win; he was sure of it. He sat down at the makeshift table he had set, along with a crude drawing of Oreanna and its defenses.

More fighting men was an advantage—there was no doubt about it—but it would all be for naught unless he could find a way to get them inside the walls. If they took too long to get inside the city, the Hoyt would feather them with arrows from the walls until they were too decimated to launch an assault that could be considered a threat. Two siege towers, even three, was just not enough.

Even if successful, each could only transfer a small number of men onto the walls at once. After the initial rush, his men would have to climb to the top one by one. This would allow the Hoyt to regroup and counterattack. They could not afford to waste time or lives on the city walls. They had to get into the city proper as quickly as possible.

Breaching the gates would be the more effective way to get men into the city, but it was simply not plausible. Oreanna's gates were too strong. By the time a battering ram could get through, all the men wielding it would fall to the archers above. Even if, by some miracle, they did breach the gates, the Hoyt would have time to muster a force within the wall to drive them back. He could quickly lose half of his army in such a battle. The gates could not be breached effectively by any means they possessed; he would have to find another way.

The city could potentially be attacked by the Kival River. He had heard reports that the Hoyt had used this tactic when they'd initially sacked it. But they lacked water-craft and the materials they could use to construct them. With eight hundred men to transport, it did not seem likely they would be able to find lumber to build enough ferries on their way to Oreanna, even if they dismantled the siege towers. In addition, the city had river gates as well. They usually stood open, but with an attack approaching, Idanox would order them closed. While not as formidable as the main gates on land, they would complicate any attempt at entering Oreanna on the water. A best-case scenario would be to breach the city by water, having lost only one or two hundred men. It was not enough. He needed as many of these men as possible inside the city if he was going to win this battle.

Again, General McLeod regretted the loss of Adel. The Rawl wielder could have used his power to open the river gates and freeze the river solid, allowing the men to enter on foot. He could have used his power to devastating effect against the enemy combatants just as he had countless times before. He could have shielded them from enemy arrows. Beyond his use in battle, McLeod had liked the young man a lot, and it pained him to know the fate that Adel had almost certainly met. He almost wished he had never asked the young man to join him after the Battle of Kolig. Perhaps he should have been grateful for the help Adel had given them at Kolig and let him go on his way back to his temple.

Regrets are useless, he scolded himself. *Regrets will not win this battle*. If Adel was dead, he had willingly made that sacrifice in the name of defeating the Hoyt. McLeod would not allow the young man's sacrifice to mean nothing. A good general made decisions based on things that were, not things that could have been. He would have to be more than a good general if he was going to win this one. A good general would not be able to map a victory with the tools he had been given.

Setting aside his regrets, his wishes, and even his hopes, Supreme General Randall McLeod began to devise his battle plan.

Chapter Twelve

Idanox had experienced these situations enough times since taking control of Thornata that he felt he had a good idea of what was happening. Whenever his men informed him they had news on the way with no specific information, he never came away from the meeting feeling pleased. Except, of course, for the night he had learned of the Rawl wielder's capture. That had been a pleasant evening indeed, perhaps his best as the duke of Thornata. The Rawl wielder should be arriving in the city any day now, and there were still many preparations that required his attention. He had little time or patience to deal with the constant mistakes of the bumbling men under his command. Enough Thornatan soldiers had come over to his side that he may just decide to make a point by executing whichever fool had blundered this time. It felt as though his Hoyt had begun to feel secure. Continually getting away with acts of pure incompetence no doubt contributed to this sense of impunity.

So, Idanox sat in the duke's palace, in the great hall where the duke would traditionally accept important guests, and waited for the hammer to fall. His two monstrous bodyguards stood to either side, slightly in front of him, always ready to defend him at any time. Any man who disappointed him this night was running the risk of being on the receiving end of their terrifying wrath. He had not needed to use their skills in weeks, and frankly, he missed seeing them in glorious, bloody action. Perhaps a little bloodshed would be a good exercise for his pets. Idanox had grown accustomed to their constant presence and the unapparelled feeling of security it brought him. He had put aside his apprehension of the mindless creatures, and he could no longer imagine his life without them by his side.

One of his lieutenants arrived at last, accompanying a man in a Thornatan Army uniform. The shoulders of the man's uniform were adorned with a series of stars and stripes that Idanox understood identified him as a general. Was this General Bern, the man who was bringing him the Rawl wielder? Why had he not been informed the boy had arrived in the city? He had given his men a clear protocol to follow for the boy's arrival. He had planned to receive the Rawl wielder in the duke's bunker with Srenpe by his side. *I will have somebody's head for this*, he thought foully to himself. If these fools brought the boy to him here, they were putting his life in danger, an offense he would not tolerate under any circumstance.

"Sir, this is General Bern, commander of the Thornatan Army garrison in Kolig. He has requested an audience to share urgent news with you regarding the Rawl wielder," the lieutenant said, glancing anxiously from the general to Idanox.

Urgent news of the Rawl wielder? Idanox did not like the sound of that at all. A boy being transported in a cage and surrounded by soldiers shouldn't have been capable of producing anything newsworthy. The only news he cared to hear was that the boy had arrived in Oreanna and was ready to join the Hoyt or die. What could have possibly gone wrong this time?

"Thank you, Lieutenant. Welcome to Oreanna, General Bern. It is a pleasure to finally meet you in person. What news is it that you have brought for me? My understanding was that you were traveling to the capital with the Rawl wielder in your custody. Have you brought him here with you?" Idanox asked, anxious to get down to business.

"Greetings and salutations, Duke Idanox," General Bern began, sinking into a ridiculously low bow, which he held for a full thirty seconds. Even Idanox, who never tired of seeing men simpering and bowing before him, found the gesture to be a bit too much. "I am afraid I do not have the Rawl wielder with me, but rest assured, I have my best men searching for him."

It sounded as though Bern had more to say, but Idanox cut the man off before he could go any further. "You have men searching for him? Forgive me if I have received incorrect information, General Bern. But I was under the impression that the boy was already in your custody. Can you please explain the discrepancy? Have I been given inaccurate information?"

Idanox almost felt a sense of admiration for the incredible effort that General Bern was putting into maintaining his sycophantic smile. A less observant man may not have noticed the growing redness in his face or the beads of sweat beginning to drip down the man's beefy forehead. Bern clearly understood that Idanox knew full well he had not received inaccurate information. Idanox could almost see the man's mind at work behind his eyes, searching for an acceptable explanation for his incompetence. He gave a brief moment's consideration to just telling the beasts to kill the fool now but decided on hearing him out first. He had not climbed to the level of duke by making rash decisions; there was no reason to start now.

"No, sir, you were not given inaccurate information. We did indeed capture the boy and his ogre as well. I regret to report that there were complications with their transport."

"Complications with their transport," Idanox repeated, cutting the man off once again. For being a general, Bern was none too skilled at concealing his nervousness. Such weakness would not inspire confidence from men under his command in the midst of a battle. It was disappointing to see. Idanox had harbored such high hopes for the potential of a good relationship with this man, but it seemed as though it was not meant to come to fruition.

"This must have been quite unforeseen, General Bern. After all, what indication could you possibly have had that they may be a challenge to transport? After all, what had this boy ever done, besides display ludicrous, unnatural power on multiple occasions? Choose your next words very carefully, General Bern. Tell me what happened, and tell it truthfully. If I suspect you are lying to make yourself appear to be less of a fool than you are, it will be the last blunder you make in a life that I am certain has been full of them. Speak!"

"The pair escaped from their cages and fled when our caravan was just south of the Bonner Mountains, my lord. Our men were distracted by a fire that had erupted near our supply wagons. We searched for them for several days but found no traces. We were unable to take our horses up into that rocky terrain and were forced to search for them on foot. We lost their trail, which was heading northwest until it vanished. I fear they may have fled to the Temple of the Rawl, which I believe to be hidden somewhere within those peaks." By the time he had finished, General Bern looked to be on the verge of tears.

You incompetent fool. I will give you something to cry about before this night is over.

"How exactly did they manage to escape their cages? I thought the purpose of a cage was to be secure," Idanox said. He did not particularly care; such information was irrelevant. But he was imagining the most entertaining possible ways to have the oaf killed and wanted to take his time to savor the moment.

"As I said, my lord, there was a fire in our caravan while we were camped for the night. My men were fighting to put out the fire, and by the time the blaze was under control, they were gone. It appeared as though the ogre was able to break his chains and force open the doors of the cages. They killed over thirty of my men on their way out; they even killed all our sentries. We had twelve of them surrounding the encampment on all sides. We still don't know how they did it."

"They killed all the sentries, did they? During this fire, which just happened to occur in the middle of the night? So, you believe, after they escaped their cages, they took the time to make a circle of your perimeter just for the purpose of killing your sentries? An interesting detour for two men trying to make a quick escape. Did it ever occur to you that they may have had assistance with this escape? Perhaps from the Supreme General of your army, a man I have heard you had an opportunity to capture but failed? When I heard a Thornatan general was bringing me two valued captives, I was quite excited, I must admit. I was excited about the partnership that could be forged between us, General Bern, and the potential such a partnership would have. I hoped we could do so much for the people of this province, the two of us together. It appears I was mistaken," Idanox said, growing tired of the man's voice and face. He was within seconds of ordering one of his beasts to eliminate General Bern when the great fool began to blubber.

"Please, sir, we can still have the partnership you wanted, I swear it! Please let me prove my value to you. I will do anything you ask of me," General Bern cried out, falling to his knees.

Tears were beginning to flow from his eyes, running uncontrolled down to the floor. It was a pitiful sight to see from any grown man, let alone one who had been entrusted with the command of military forces. Who had made this blubbering excuse for a man into a general? Idanox wondered if this fool had ever seen battle before or if he was the son of some decorated general who'd worked his way through the ranks on his father's reputation. Under his predecessor, there were many examples of such nepotism. It had infected both the army and the ranks of the government. Idanox could only assume General Bern was yet another example of it.

He was on the verge of ordering one of his beasts to disembowel the fool when he had another thought.

General Bern was a blundering fool, and there was no doubt of it. But he was still the highest-ranking Thornatan officer to pledge himself to the Hoyt thus far. Perhaps he could still be of some use after all. Maybe having him killed right now was not the right move to make, despite his incompetence. How much respect could this man command among the army? Idanox did not have high hopes, but perhaps it was worth taking the time to find out.

"I should have you killed for your incompetence, General Bern. I hope you understand that," Idanox began, framing his words like a practiced politician. "But I don't believe in punishing loyalty. I believe that is what you are showing to me by having the courage to come here and deliver this unwelcome news face-to-face. You could have hidden, could have sent one of your men to deliver this news on your behalf. You didn't. While I am frustrated by your mistakes, I admire your courage, and I thank you for it. I would like to offer you another opportunity to prove yourself if you will accept it."

"Yes, Duke Idanox, I am loyal to you and only to you. Please forgive my negligence. I should have performed better. Please, if there is anything I can do to make this right, just say the word, and it will be done. Your mercy only confirms what I already knew to be true. You are the ruler Thornata needs to lead us into the future. I beg you for another chance to prove my value to you. I promise I will never fail you again."

It was done. Idanox had the man wrapped around his finger now. By showing the incompetent fool his merciful side, he had ensured he would have a new devoted follower. He may have had his doubts about the man's intelligence and ability, but perhaps Idanox had enough of those to mask Bern's weaknesses. He had a specific job in mind for General Bern, one that even this fool should be able to manage without too much difficulty. But it was a job Bern was uniquely able to perform for him, and he had nobody else who could do it. If Bern failed, he would die, but if he succeeded, the Hoyt would have a valuable new ally.

"Former Supreme General Randall McLeod is mustering a force to attack this city. You remember him, don't you, General Bern? The same man who managed to escape from under your nose in Kolig? Through no fault of your own, I am sure. As we speak, they are camped on the southern edge of the Ice Fields, according to reports my scouts have brought me. He has already mustered several hundred Thornatan soldiers to his cause. I have no doubt they will move to attack us within days," Idanox began before the oaf felt the urge to interrupt.

"Do you want me to take an attack force and destroy them, Duke Idanox? I would be honored to do so in your name! I can muster a force and depart at once if that is what you w—"

"Do not presume to interrupt me while I am speaking ever again," Idanox snapped, causing the general to go pale with fear once more. "Only a fool would try to launch an attack on the Ice Fields, and this is precisely why McLeod has chosen them as his staging ground. Are you a fool, General Bern? I do not doubt that sending a large attack force against them in the Ice Fields is precisely what McLeod wants us to do. In your professional opinion, is it wise to play straight into our adversary's hand? We will soon come under attack from this force McLeod has assembled. Would it not be your professional military opinion that we would be better off defending ourselves from a position of strength, General Bern?"

"Yes, of course it would, sir. My apologies. I only meant to serve you as best I could. I was too eager, and I overstepped my bounds. You are right, of course you are. I knew what a brilliant man you are in matters of industry. I am pleased to find your military acumen matches if not exceeds your industrial knowledge. How may I serve you, my duke?"

Even Idanox, who never tired of hearing himself glorified, felt the slightest bit sickened by the man's constant praise. *So, this is how he reached this rank. He licked the right boots.*

"Calm down, General Bern. I believe you truly regret the mistakes you have made and are eager to rectify them. I believe I have just the job for you to prove it. Who better to lead the defense of this city than a man familiar with the invaders? Do you think you are equal to this task, General Bern? Are you able to defend this city against your former brothers-in-arms? Do you think you would be able to outwit your former Supreme General on the battlefield?"

"Yes, Duke Idanox. Nothing would give me more honor than to fight to defend this city in your name. Any man in a Thornatan Army uniform who challenges your rule is nothing more than a coward and a traitor to his people. I thank you for this highest of honors, and I intend to prove myself worthy of the trust you have placed in me," General Bern said, sinking into yet another ludicrously low bow.

"I am sure you will prove yourself quite capable, General Bern. I have a feeling this will be the beginning of a fruitful working relationship between us. My men will fill you in on the defenses we have already deployed and the number of men you will have at your disposal. If you succeed, we will require a new Supreme General. I do not doubt that you will prove yourself worthy of the title. We are all counting on you, General Bern. Do not fail us again," Idanox finished, throwing a menacing touch on his final sentence for good measure.

"Thank you again for your hospitality and wisdom, my lord Idanox. I serve at your pleasure," Bern said with one final bow before being led from the room.

This turn of events was not a pleasant one, but he could still manipulate matters to work in his favor. Bern was incompetent and deserved to die for letting the Rawl wielder out of his grasp. Idanox had never made a habit out of forgiving such mistakes, especially from a man as dimwitted as General Bern. But such a senior Thornatan Army officer had value, despite his obvious intellectual limitations. His mere presence could sway any soldiers considering mutiny back to the fold. Seeing one of their highest-ranking officers at peace with the Hoyt could convince them that they should be as well. He doubted the fool had any tactical knowledge that would be of any particular use, but Oreanna's defenses were near impenetrable, and they vastly outnumbered their attackers. Bern was a sycophantic man who would make just the type of Supreme General Idanox desired, one that would never question his orders.

The Rawl wielder's escape was disconcerting; there was no doubt about it. He had looked forward to removing the boy from the fight against him once and for all, one way or another. Could the boy reach the city soon enough to take part in McLeod's attack? It was possible, and he needed to be prepared for that possibility. When the attack came, he would summon Srenpe and retreat to the bunker, just as they had already planned. If the Rawl wielder did come for him, the plan would proceed as anticipated, and the mage would disable the boy. Once the boy was harmless, he would have two options: join the Hoyt or die.

He summoned a few of his lieutenants and began giving orders for the defense of the city. The walls were to be fully manned by archers until they destroyed the attacking force. The Thornatan soldiers inside Oreanna were to be reminded of the punishment for treason against the

Hoyt. General Bern was to be allowed to scheme as he saw fit, but Idanox was to be notified of all his movements. This was a job even an idiot should be qualified to perform, but Idanox had his doubts about the general. With the exception of his two bodyguards, the rest of the beasts would be out patrolling in the city, ready to help the fighters deal with any attackers who made it inside the walls.

The defenses will hold, he told himself after giving the orders and dismissing his men. Soon he would have Randall McLeod's head on a spike atop the city gates, and that would be the end of any attempts to resist his rule. If the Rawl wielder tried to interfere, he would die as well. If he chose to hide in Temple of the Rawl, the Thrawll could go and deal with him later.

This was it. The final threat to his hold on Thornata would likely arrive within the week. One week from this night, it would all be over, and nobody would ever dare to question his power again.

Chapter Thirteen

Adel had never seen the infamous Ice Fields of northern Thornata before, but he had heard many tales of them and had formed an image in his mind. After all, a vast plain made entirely of ice had to be a relatively easy thing to picture. Staring out upon them now, he realized his imagination had not done justice to the beauty and utter desolation of the frozen wasteland. It was an endless sheet of the purest ice he had ever seen, unmarked but for the hundreds of tents that stretched out before them. Even now, in late summer, the wind up on this vast plateau was bitterly cold, the sheet of ice showing no signs of melting. After several days of marching through the brutal summer heat, the chilly air was refreshing, like a cold drink of water for his lungs.

They had made the journey north as swiftly as possible after allowing his and Ola's injuries a week to heal as the trio had agreed. They must've been a sight to behold, especially Adel. His dark green armor was grimy and filthy from his time in captivity and long journey north, the stolen Thornatan Army sword clasped to his waist. He was still upset to have lost the sword Captain Boyd had given to him at their parting. He had resolved that General Bern would pay for that loss if they ever crossed paths again. He had trimmed his beard before leaving the inn, but it had mostly grown back over the past six days as they had made their way north. There had been no opportunity to shave properly, and Adel was beginning to get used to the feel of the extra hair on his face.

Ola did not look much better, a brand-new scar decorating the back of his head, his armor just as scruffy looking as Adel's, if not worse. Ogres did not grow facial hair, so he did not look quite as unkempt as Adel. Of course, Alsea looked as stunning as ever, though Adel thought to himself that he might be slightly biased in that regard. He met her gaze, and as she returned his smile, it was apparent she was just as in awe of their surroundings as he was. As they smiled at each other, Adel found himself wishing they were living in simpler times. If only they could've come to such a remarkable place for the joy of it rather than to throw themselves headfirst into a bitter war.

Their week together in the inn had been perhaps the best of his entire life. Though he'd understood the urgency they needed to move with, he had not wanted it to end. The time he and Alsea had spent alone in that small room was the sweetest memory he could recall, one that motivated him even further to put an end to the Hoyt. They would never be able to live in any semblance of peace while Idanox ruled in Oreanna. As long as the Hoyt were in power, not a single man, woman, or child in Thornata would be able to live in safety.

He was hesitant about his friends joining him once more—Ola because of his injuries, and Alsea because of their new relationship. But he had a duty to carry out, and neither Alsea nor Ola would consider leaving his side. So, they had come to rejoin the army one last time, marching north at a relentless pace, dreading what lay at the end of the journey but eager to see it done. Throughout the march, they'd tried to prepare themselves mentally for a final confrontation with Idanox and the Hoyt. Now that they had arrived at General McLeod's camp, they knew that clash would be upon them soon. Adel called out to a nearby Thornatan soldier as they approached the camp. The last thing they wanted was to be mistaken for enemies upon arrival.

"Greetings, soldier! My name is Adel, and these are my companions, Ola and Alsea. Could you please take us to General McLeod? He will want to speak with us as soon as possible."

"General McLeod is in his final war council. The army marches tomorrow. He asked not to be disturbed," the man replied uncertainly. His words were addressed to Adel, but his eyes did not leave Ola. This was a reaction they expected by now; most Thornatans were quite unaccustomed to the sight of an ogre.

"I understand orders are orders, my friend. But trust me when I say the general will be very displeased with you if he finds out you have delayed us," Adel replied. "We may be able to change the tone of his war council, so I suggest you violate protocol just this once. If the general is angry, I promise you I will take full responsibility for the interruption."

The soldier glanced around, seemingly hoping a higher-ranking officer would come along and take the burden of this decision off his shoulders. No such help was forthcoming, and he finally beckoned uncertainly for the trio to follow him. He led them through the encampment, past Thornatan soldiers and other men wearing black uniforms Adel had never seen before. They arrived at a large tent, and the soldier asked them to wait outside. He stepped into the tent and returned a few short moments later with General McLeod on his heels. McLeod looked as though he had aged five years in the weeks since Adel had last seen him, but his face split into a wide smile at the sight of them nonetheless.

"Adel, Ola, Alsea, I must say that the three of you are a beautiful sight for sore eyes," General McLeod said, clasping each of their hands in turn. "I had held out hope you would join us here, but I must admit I had begun to lose that hope at this late hour. After we became separated in Kolig, I feared the worst."

"We're sorry to have kept you waiting, General McLeod, but it is good to see you again. Ola and I were captured by our dear friend General Bern, but we managed to escape thanks to Alsea," Adel replied with a smile.

"Alsea, I owe you an apology. I owe all three of you an apology. I should have known you were right. I should have known Adel and Ola were alive and helped you set them free. I am so sorry. Words cannot express my regret. I was a narrow-minded fool, and if the three of you had died, it would have been my fault. I hope you can forgive an old man's stubbornness. Those of us who have left our youth far behind tend to always believe we know best."

"All of that is in the past, General McLeod. The important thing is that we are here now, and we hear you are marching for Oreanna tomorrow. Do you have a place for the three of us in your ranks?" Adel waved off the apology, eager to get down to business. General McLeod's past lapses in judgment were irrelevant. In truth, McLeod leaving them for dead had stung, but they had to set that aside. They needed to work together to put an end to the Hoyt before it was too late. McLeod had done what he'd felt to be right, and there was no point in rehashing his decisions.

"You had better believe I do. You have impeccable timing, as usual. I am holding my final war council inside the tent. Please join us. I would love to have your input on the battle plan, all of you. With your arrival, we may need to make some modifications, though you will hear no complaints from me." General McLeod hurried back into the tent, holding the flap open for the three companions to follow him inside.

Adel entered the tent first to find eight men seated around a hand-drawn map of Oreanna. One of the men was adorned in the unfamiliar black armor he had noticed outside; up close, he could see the sigil of a shining star upon the breastplate. Several of the men, including the one dressed in black, had evidently never seen an ogre in person before, their eyes widening and complexions paling at the sight of Ola. General McLeod called for an aide to bring three more chairs for the newcomers, which were set up within moments. He also indicated for them to help themselves to the carafes of water that rested on the table.

"I'll just make a quick introduction," General McLeod said. "These three have fought by my side against the Hoyt repeatedly and have returned to do so once again. I will admit that this is much to my delight. This is Alsea; she is as skilled a scout as you will ever find and equally impressive with a bow or a sword in her hand. Seriously, gentlemen, I would strongly advise against making her angry."

Alsea blushed at the general's compliment.

General McLeod now turned toward Ola. "This is Ola, and I can tell you that he is better than any man I have ever seen with a sword in his hand. He will be a most valuable asset to us in the battle ahead."

Ola bowed his head slightly in thanks. Adel was sure that if ogres could blush, Ola would've been doing so.

"Finally, my friends, we have Adel. Adel is the Rawl wielder that many of you have heard stories about. His powers can do things I would not believe had I not seen them with my own eyes. These three are the heroes of the Battle of Kolig, and they have saved my life on numerous occasions since then. I invited them into our council in the hopes that they may have valuable input to our plans," McLeod finished.

"A Rawl wielder, you say, Supreme General? I must admit, I have heard stories about them but had often wondered about their accuracy. With such tales, it is often difficult to determine the difference between truth and fiction," the man in black exclaimed, looking curiously at Adel.

"This is Captain Thaddeus Dunstan of the Imperial Army. He has come here with two hundred Imperial troops to fight beside us. They have already helped liberate two hundred Thornatan soldiers from the Hoyt. It is largely thanks to him that we have a fighting chance of winning this battle at all. To answer your question, Captain Dunstan, yes, Adel is a Rawl wielder. I have witnessed his powers firsthand on numerous occasions, and as I said, they are truly a sight to behold," General McLeod assured the man.

The Hoyt War

So, the men in black are Imperial soldiers. I wonder what brought them here, Adel thought. He had never seen soldiers loyal to the emperor before, apart from Captain Boyd, who had served in the Imperial Navy many years ago. But Boyd had retired long ago, often waxing on at length about the Empire's new policies of staying out of the affairs of the provinces. He had long complained that the Imperials should march north and help stamp out the Hoyt since the duke had shown little interest in doing it. It was fortunate they had come. The Hoyt had a marked advantage in the numbers, even with their presence.

"I was telling these men before the three of you arrived that we will have three operational siege towers ready for the assault. It will be dangerous, but they may be our best hope of getting inside the walls. The gates of Oreanna are nearly impenetrable, and we do not have enough craft to attack the city by river," General McLeod explained. "I understand that our odds with the towers are not much better than trying to batter down the gates with a ram, but I do not think we have a better option. Perhaps with the added numbers that Captain Dunstan has given us we will have a better chance of success."

"I can breach the gates," Adel blurted out, not pausing to think the matter through.

Every face in the tent swiveled to look at him, some surprised, some doubtful, Thaddeus Dunstan's intrigued. Even Ola and Alsea seemed astonished that he had spoken up so abruptly. It was out of character for Adel, who was always measured and cautious. He knew he should not have spoken up so soon, but he did not want General McLeod to waste his time on inferior strategies when there were better options available. Siege towers would not work; McLeod understood this just as well as he did. They had merely been the best of several ineffective options the general had been forced to choose from. If the gates were open, they would be able to utilize the eight hundred men they had with far greater effectiveness.

"Adel, are you certain you can get the gates open? I will admit that before you arrived, I was wondering if you would have been capable of such a feat. However, I had resigned myself to the fact you were not coming," General McLeod said.

"As long as you don't expect them to be reusable afterward, yes, I can breach them. They will need to be re-built after the battle, but I think you would all agree it's a small price to pay for a greater chance at victory," Adel replied.

"If Adel can indeed open the gates, we can bring the fight to the Hoyt more effectively. It would circumvent the need for the towers entirely. But we will still be signif-icantly outnumbered," Dunstan pointed out. "An all-out assault on the open gates might work, but it will be a strug-gle every step of the way."

"We need to get to Idanox and kill him as quickly as possible," Ola said. "He is the head of the Hoyt snake. Ultimately, if we eliminate him, most of their fighters will flee or surrender. They fight only in his name; no other will command the loyalty he does. The Thornatan soldiers he has brought over to his side will turn for sure, or most of them at least. They fight not out of loyalty but out of fear of what Idanox will do to their families."

"Ola is right, but he presents another problem," General McLeod said. "The duke's palace is as far from the main gates as one can be. We will have to fight our way through every line of defense to reach him. Fighting our way through the streets will pose a threat to civilians. Not to mention the duke's bunker. If he flees there, which I suspect he will, we will have to batter it open. That will take time that his forces will not allow us. Unfortunately, we have to defeat his army before we can kill Idanox."

"What if we don't?"

Once again, every head turned toward Adel. Once again, he had opened his mouth without fully thinking through the plan that was still forming in his head. But he knew he had little choice; he could not allow them to proceed with their plan, as flawed as it was. They could not win a straight fight against the Hoyt forces. The numbers against them were too much, even with the addition of the Imperial soldiers. Besides, the Hoyt had no regard for the innocent civilians who lived in Oreanna and would have no qualms about using them as human shields. They had to get to Idanox and kill him; there was no other path to victory. Counting on a decisive victory at the gates was a surefire way to lose the battle.

"Our army cannot reach Idanox without a catastrophic loss of life, both within our ranks and among the people of Oreanna. The Hoyt will use the innocents as human shields at every turn; I think we all realize that. Until we kill Idanox, the war is not over. Ola, Alsea, and I could enter the city discreetly along with a small group of your best fighters. Once we are inside, I can open the main gates, which will focus their attention on the bulk of our army. If you can keep the focus of the fighting on the edge of the city, near the walls, it will draw the majority of the Hoyt forces away from protecting Idanox. This will also minimize civilian casualties if most of the Hoyt forces are occupied at the gates," he explained, most of the plan still coming to him as he spoke.

"So, your small group would go after Idanox and kill him? What if he is inside the bunker?" one of the Thornatan captains asked.

"If I can open the gates, I can open his bunker. He will no doubt try to run and hide like the sniveling rat he is, but we will get to him, one way or another. His days of slipping away are done. I don't know about you, but I am tired of chasing him. He will answer for his crimes, no matter what we have to do to see to it. There is nowhere for him to hide that we cannot get to him."

"How would you get this small group into Oreanna?" General McLeod asked.

"We will enter the city by river. We can come in from the north once the army has staged to the south of the city. Almost all their eyes will be fixed on you, and we will float right in. I can open the river gates if necessary. The Hoyt will most likely close them as the army approaches, but my powers can get us past them easily enough. Once we are inside Oreanna, I will open the main gates, and that will be your signal to begin the attack," Adel explained.

"I'm assuming this signal will be easy for us to notice?" Dunstan asked.

"I would recommend keeping your forces far away from the walls until after it is done. I wouldn't want any of your men to get hurt by accident," Adel replied, drawing a small chuckle from General McLeod.

"I think Adel's proposal is the best plan that we have available to us," General McLeod declared. "Is there anybody here who has any objection?"

Adel glanced at the faces of the men gathered, trying to gain some insight into their thoughts, but they were indecipherable. General McLeod paused for around a minute, waiting to see if anybody would raise a protest. Adel felt a small sense of pride when none came. He had known his plan was the best available to them. Still, it was a lot to ask of career soldiers, expecting them to trust in the wisdom and skills of a seventeen-year-old boy. General McLeod knew him, but most of these men did not. He knew it was their trust in McLeod rather than their faith in him that was keeping them silent, but it would have to be enough. He would not fail them, he reassured himself; he could not fail them.

"We will march at dawn. I need all of you to have your campsites broken and your men ready to move. I mean to reach Oreanna in three days. This will be a hard march, but not so hard that the men who are making it won't have the strength to fight at the end. If nobody has anything to add, that will be all for today," General McLeod declared, and the soldiers filed out one by one, leaving McLeod alone with Adel, Ola, and Alsea.

"You're the most experienced battle commander Thornata has ever seen, General McLeod. How do you see our odds?" Alsea asked.

"A hell of a lot better than they were before the three of you arrived," McLeod replied with a wry smile. "I've spent the last few days wrestling with the fact that I would be leading these men into a possible, even likely suicide mission. Now I truly feel there is hope. Thank you, all of you, for giving me that much."

"This will work," Adel declared, surprising even himself with the conviction in his voice. "We will get to Idanox, and once he is dead, the Hoyt who are left will give up the fight. I am sure of it."

"I think you are right, Adel," General McLeod declared. "I feel more confident in this plan of yours than I have in anything else we have devised since these bastards started terrorizing this province. This will be the last battle we fight with them, and we are going to win at all costs.

Taking Oreanna was a mistake on Idanox's part, and he won't realize it until it's too late for him. Now he is caught like a rat in a trap."

***

The general had his men arrange tents for the three of them. Adel had barely had time to wash his face in the small basin they had provided when Alsea slipped into his tent. She hurried over to him and hugged him tightly, kissing him as they parted.

"I just wanted to make sure you know how proud I am of you," she said, beaming at him.

"Proud of what?" he asked with a blush.

"You were incredible in there. You told a tent full of seasoned soldiers that your plan was better than theirs and convinced every one of them you were right. When we first met, you never would have dreamed of even attempting anything like that. You've grown so much in the time we've known each other, and I wanted you to know how proud I am."

"Maybe you should wait to see if the plan works before you feel too proud," Adel muttered sarcastically, though, to part of his mind, it was no joke at all.

"It will work. I have faith in you, and I have faith in us. When we work together, we can do anything. I truly believe that," Alsea declared.

"If it doesn't work, that failure is on my shoulders. This is my plan, my strategy that I felt the need to blurt out in there," Adel began, but she cut him off before he could go any further.

"That is why it will not fail. Everything you have been through since the day the Hoyt first attacked your boat has shaped you into the man you are today. That man is the right one to devise this plan and the right one to carry it out. We won't fail. I'll say it again. All of us together can do anything. I believe that more than I have ever believed anything in my life."

Adel reflected on this and was not entirely convinced. But he was sure of one thing. While he may not have fully believed in himself, Alsea did. If there was one person in this world he felt he would always be able to believe in, it was her. If she believed in him, perhaps he would just have to trust her judgment.

He kissed her again, wrapping her in a tight embrace. Her faith would have to be enough.

Chapter Fourteen

For most of the two days following General McLeod's war council, the combined forces of the Thornatans and the Imperial Army marched toward Oreanna, along with Adel, Ola, and Alsea. They made their way down from the towering plateau of the Ice Fields and began winding south and west across the windswept plains of northern Thornata. Each day was a long, hard march, though none of those making it were inclined to complain. It was a journey that would typically take twice as long to complete, but not a single person complained about their breakneck pace. Every man and woman assembled knew the importance of their objective, and their determination overpowered their fatigue.

In no person did this determination burn more fiercely than it did in Adel. He was more energized than he had ever been now that the ending of this war was finally within sight. For the first time since the attack on his barge the prior year, he could envision a life beyond the conflict with the Hoyt. As each day had passed and they drew ever closer to Oreanna, his confidence had grown by leaps and bounds. He understood a terrible battle lay before them, and all their lives were in jeopardy. There would be death and destruction waiting for them at the end of this march. Not all of them would survive; they couldn't. It was unavoidable. But as the days passed by, his faith continued to grow. They would not fail; they could not fail. No matter what it took, the Hoyt would fall, and the people of Thornata would be free from the grip of a tyrant.

His own role in the attack was one with which he was especially confident after his talk with Alsea. Adel knew beyond any doubt that he was capable of blasting open the gates of the city. He knew beyond any doubt that he could get their strike force past any Hoyt defenses on the river. Most of all, he knew once they finally located Idanox, they would not fail to put an end to the Hoyt leader once and for all. No matter how deep of a hole Idanox tried to dig for himself, they would drag him out of it. He could run, but by the time the battle was over, there would be nowhere left for him to hide. Every fight, every training session with Ola and Elim, and every hurt he had endured had been leading to this specific time and place, shaping him into the man he would need to be for him to succeed.

"You've been quiet today," Alsea said, coming up beside him. Her voice startled him; he had spent most of the day marching slightly apart from his companions, deep in thought. Once, this would have led him deep into a hole of his insecurities, but now he found solace in the silence. Everyone knew what was coming. What good would it do to discuss it further?

"I suppose I have been. Each day it seems to loom larger, doesn't it? We are finally at the end of this road. I don't know if I'm excited or nervous or both. One way or another, this will all be over soon. I've always tried to be optimistic, but I won't lie to you. There were days when I thought this march would never come," he replied, taking her hand in his. "Now it's here, and I'm surprised at how calm I am. As I said, the emotions are there, but they're under control, perhaps more than they have ever been before."

"It's because you know you have never been more prepared to face whatever is waiting for us. Let me ask you something I've been wondering about. Have you given any thought to what will come after this is over? Assuming we are still alive to enjoy the spoils of our victory, of course," Alsea said.

Truthfully, Adel had not given much thought to anything that would come after the battle. His mind had been so solely focused on winning the fight against the Hoyt that he had been virtually blind to anything else. The past few days, he had envisioned the future as a utopian paradise, free of strife and struggle, where he and Ola and Alsea could live out their days in peace and happiness. But Alsea had a point. If they were to prevail, which Adel believed they would, there should be some sort of plan for what would come next. His dreams of a blissful paradise were unlikely to come to fruition anytime soon. He could not imagine the type of damage the Hoyt had already done during their brief rule. The government of Thornata would likely need to be rebuilt from the ground up. He could not even begin to imagine how many lives must have been ruined during the brief rule of Idanox.

"I haven't thought much about it, but I suppose I probably should, at least a little bit. Once the Hoyt are gone, a new government will need to be put in place. I can't imagine Idanox has left any part of our old one alive. That will mostly fall on General McLeod, I expect, but if we can help in any way, we should."

"Yes, I agree, but what about after that?" Alsea pressed. "Eventually, there will come a time when the Hoyt are no more than a distant memory."

She wanted to know what would happen after everything was done. *The entire time we have known each other, all we have done is focus on destroying the Hoyt. It's all that we have known together.* Once that was over, Adel knew his world would change completely. For the first time, it crossed his mind that his relationship with Alsea could change. What if the struggle against the Hoyt was all that bound them together? *Don't be a fool*, he told himself. *That's the old Adel talking, the one who has no confidence and is filled with self-doubt. There is no room for him anymore, not if you want to survive the next few days.* Knowing he was right, he gave the only answer he had ever truly considered.

"I still feel like I have so much more to learn about the power of the Rawl. At some point, I need to return to the Temple of the Rawl. I need to finish my training under the Children. I need to know everything I can learn about this power. When it first revealed itself, I didn't know what to think. I have come to see it as a gift, one I should be using for the betterment of the world. If I'm going to do that, I need to know how to use it to its fullest potential."

"Once you have done so, your future will truly be up to you. You will be the Master of the Rawl, our wise, benevolent, and hopefully merciful leader," Alsea said, shooting one of her mischievous grins that had a habit of making Adel feel weak at the knees.

"I still wish I knew more about what that means. Elim told me some things, but I still feel ignorant. He said the most important purpose of the Children is to be ready in case of an attack by the Thrawll. How does one prepare for an enemy that you know nothing about? An enemy who may never come for us at all? The Hoyt are human, an enemy of flesh and blood that I can understand. I can make sense of their motives, even if I find them repulsive. The Thrawll are nothing but a shadow to me," Adel mused. He had not thought much about the mysterious people called the Thrawll, but each time he did, it sent a chill running down his spine. Perhaps his first order of business should be to learn everything he could about the shadowy race of Rawl wielders.

"It's a fair question, Adel. I wish I had an answer to give you, but I don't. But I do have faith that you will find your way. Just know that no matter what, I will always be by your side as you do," Alsea promised, leaning over and kissing him. Once again, he was grateful to have her by his side. He knew he could overcome anything as long as she was beside him.

Adel spent the remainder of the day's march thinking about their conversation. While the future was uncertain, it was still more comforting to think about than the violent confrontation awaiting them at the end of their march. His newfound confidence notwithstanding, he took no pleasure thinking about the bloodshed in front of him. He had known for a long time now that the Children planned to groom him into a leadership role, but it was a position he still found himself uncomfortable thinking about. He hoped more time training in the Temple of the Rawl could help to ease his apprehension.

Seeking more reassurance later that night, he set out through the camp in search of Ola. As usual, Adel had seen little of his friend during their march toward Oreanna, the ogre always out scouting for potential threats. At last, he found Ola sitting near a campfire at the southern edge of their encampment. Adel had suspected that Ola would be found here. His friend was always eager to be as close as possible to the place where any trouble was likely to arise. This would be the direction that any Hoyt attack would be most likely to come from.

General McLeod did not think any attack was coming. His theory was that Idanox would prefer to preserve his forces and utilize every man available to him from a position of strength. It was a thought Adel agreed with, but there was no denying that you couldn't be too careful where Idanox was concerned. Ola turned as Adel approached; his sharp ogre ears had no doubt alerted him to his approach well in advance of his arrival.

"You should be sleeping, Adel. We will most likely reach Oreanna at sundown tomorrow. You are not likely to have another chance at rest until after the battle is over," Ola said as Adel took a seat beside him.

"I could say the same for you," Adel retorted.

Ola smiled, and Adel reflected for a moment on how rare that sight had been in the early days of their relationship. He had once resigned himself to the fact that the ogre would never be more than a stoic, silent protector. But Ola had become so much more in the past year. It was a friendship that he had never thought to find. It had come to the point where he saw the ogre more like a brother than a friend. *Although I don't believe we are the type of brothers that people would get mixed up with each other*, Adel thought, fighting back a chuckle.

"We ogres don't need quite as much sleep as you

do. I got plenty in that inn. By the end of the week, I was going mad with restlessness. I've never slept much anyway, even by ogre standards. After my years as a slave in the fighting pits, I just never cared to sleep away any more of my life as a free man than was necessary," Ola explained. "When you spend time as a slave, you grow to appreciate every breath you are able to take in freedom. All these years later, it still feels the same to me. It made me realize how truly precious life is. Even right now, on the verge of a battle, I can sit here, looking up at the stars, and relish this moment. I was given such an incredible gift, and I don't want to waste any of it, not a single minute."

It makes sense, Adel thought to himself. Ola had spent years as a slave, knowing every day could be his last. After such a long time of knowing he would die in captivity, Adel would likely have felt the same way about enjoying his freedom.

"You still live with those memories every day, don't you?" he asked gently. They had not discussed Ola's slavery since the day Adel had first learned about it. He knew it was a topic that brought his friend pain, and he had taken great care to avoid it. While he appreciated the trust Ola had shown in him by sharing the story, he had no desire to make his friend relive his pain.

Ola was silent for a moment, his face becoming the unreadable mask Adel had become accustomed to seeing in those first days together. "I know that there are countless ogres still enslaved in my homeland, down in Gryttar.

It will be the case for as long as there are wealthy men with money to gamble. I was fortunate that I was set free. Still, every day I think of my brothers and sisters who were not as lucky as I was. I think about those who have no doubt been forced into that life since the day I walked free and those who have died in the years since. There are days where I feel disgusted with myself. What right do I have to enjoy my life of freedom while at the same time my brothers and sisters are being forced to fight and kill one another for the entertainment of wealthy men?"

Adel reflected on this. It must've been a terrible burden for Ola to bear. He couldn't imagine the guilt he would feel if he had managed to escape the Thornatan soldiers but his friend had not. Ola had lived with a similar burden for years.

Seeking to distract his friend from the pain he was reliving, he tried to change the subject.

"Alsea was asking me what I think should happen after this is over. I've been so single-mindedly focused on the Hoyt that I admit I had not given it any thought. Not until she brought it up. Have you thought about it at all?" he asked.

"Something will have to come after what lies ahead. Assuming we survive, of course, which I believe we will. There will be work that needs to be done. The damage the Hoyt have inflicted on Thornata will not be undone by removing Idanox's head from his shoulders. If only things could be so simple. That will merely be the beginning of the healing process, one that may take years, if not decades. Who can say how long it will take for the people of Thornata to heal from this? It may not happen until all of those who have lived through this mess are dead and gone," Ola mused.

"No, there will be a lot of hard work needed to rebuild this province; it is true. But what happens after it is done? I know I have more training to complete at the Temple of the Rawl, but once that is done, what then? I am expected to be a leader of some kind. How will I know which direction to go?" Adel struggled to find the words to explain his confusion.

"You will meet the challenges as they come, and you will find a way to overcome them. I do not doubt you have what it takes, Adel. A true leader follows his or her instincts, and yours are as sharp as any I have ever seen. I have faith in you."

Ola's response was not all that different from Alsea's, which Adel found a bit frustrating. He appreciated their confidence, but he yearned for more specific thoughts. He had sought out their opinions hoping they would lift some of the burden of the unknown from his shoulders. Still, he would take what he could get.

"At least I will have the pair of you by my side. We will meet whatever challenges that come our way together. I wouldn't have survived this last year without both of you," Adel declared, understanding that he would be receiving no better answers from his friends on this night.

Ola shifted and was silent for a moment before responding. "Adel, there is something I need to ask you. You are my friend, and I will be by your side as long as you will have me. I will always fight beside you against any enemy. But when you are the Master of the Rawl, I will need your permission to do something I have wanted to do for a long time."

"What is it you want to do?" Adel asked, perplexed. He had never heard the ogre ask anybody for anything, so he knew it must be meaningful to his friend.

"I would ask for your permission to set my duties to the Children of the Rawl aside for a short time. I have business of a personal nature that I need to see done," Ola answered, just as elusive as he had been when Adel had first been trying to get to know him. It was at that moment Adel realized those days felt like a lifetime ago.

"May I ask what this business is?" Adel asked, confused.

"I am grateful beyond words for the gift of my freedom the Children gave to me all those years ago. I am grateful for the friendship I have received from you and Alsea. These are the greatest gifts I have received in my life. But as I said, I also think of all the ogres who were not so fortunate, and I would like to offer them the same gift that was given to me. I wish to return to my homeland in the Ogra Mountains of Gryttar for a time and free as many ogres from slavery as I can. Until I do this, I will never be able to feel as though I truly deserve the freedom that was gifted to me those many years ago. Once I have fulfilled this, I will return to Thornata and the service of the Children of the Rawl. This is not an attempt to forsake you; you have my word. You are a friend the like of which I had never hoped to find in my lifetime."

Adel was silent for a moment, considering what his friend had just said. Ola had never expressed a desire to return to his homeland before this moment, but this must've been a desire he had been harboring for a long time. He could not imagine how long Ola must have secretly carried this wish, never wanting to request anything for himself. He would never want to deny Ola this request, but at the same time, he knew he could not grant it.

"I'm sorry, Ola, but I'm afraid I can't allow that," he replied.

Adel had grown accustomed to deciphering Ola's various facial expressions, but he had never seen the one that crossed the ogre's face now. It was not anger; he had learned to decipher that one well enough through their various encounters with the Hoyt. His best guess was that it conveyed either confusion or dismay. He decided it best to explain himself before Ola could grow too upset.

"Allow me to explain, Ola. I will not give you permission to travel to your homeland and free your fellow ogres on your own. I won't do this because I will be coming with you. This will be a journey we undertake together, you and I."

"Adel, you are a good man. But I cannot ask you

to face such a dangerous task with me. This is a battle that belongs to me and nobody else," Ola began to protest before Adel cut him off.

"You did not ask me to do any such thing. You told me what you wanted to do, and I agree it is a noble cause. It's a cause worth fighting for, one that would make me proud. But you are my friend, and I would never allow a friend of mine to undertake such a mission on their own. We both know if our positions were reversed, you would not let me go alone either. You have proven that much time and time again over the past year. So, if you want to do this, you will have to accept my company. Do we have an understanding, or don't we?"

"I would be delighted to have you by my side, Adel," Ola exclaimed, his face splitting into a broad smile. "I believe together we can make an incredible difference in the lives of those who have lived for far too long without any hope."

"I think you're right, my friend. I'm looking forward to it."

Perhaps this is the type of thing I should do after this war is over, Adel thought to himself on his way back to his tent. There were people suffering and acts of injustice all over this world. Unlike most people, he had the power to do something to correct those injustices. Maybe that could be his calling once the Hoyt were defeated—defending those who could not protect themselves. It would be a purpose he would be happy to live.

The army marched once more at dawn, knowing the last stretch of their journey was ahead of them. Tensions were high throughout the ranks; it was well-known that they would reach Oreanna by nightfall. The day's journey passed quickly for Adel, the apprehension of the battle ahead reaching its peak. He had found over the past year that when an unpleasant prospect loomed ahead, time had a funny way of speeding up.

At last, just as the sun was falling behind the horizon in the west, General McLeod called for the forces to come to a halt. They were drawing close to Oreanna, and it was time for the plan he had laid out to come into motion. Taking one last deep breath and steeling himself for what lay ahead, Adel prepared himself to play his part, hoping he would be up to the challenge.

Chapter Fifteen

Adel felt as though he were floating through the air above his body. It was a sensation he had not felt since the Hoyt attack on Captain Boyd's barge— the day he had discovered his powers. He was scarcely aware of movement around him or of General McLeod moving about, giving orders. Knowing this was a critical moment, he forced himself back to reality, willing himself with all his might to focus on the moment at hand.

"Begin forming the troops into three companies for the assault. Keep our men far away from the walls, but I want them at the ready just in case the Hoyt decide to come charging at us. I don't think it will happen, but we have to be ready for anything. Adel, are you ready to go?"

Adel could barely hear General McLeod over the pounding of his own heart. He nodded wordlessly, glancing around at Ola and Alsea, finding them smiling reassuringly at him.

Was he ready for this? He had spent the entire journey to Oreanna trying to get himself into the right state of mind for this battle. The past three days had been spent reassuring himself of his abilities. For the most part, it had worked. As recently as a few minutes ago, he had been feeling full of confidence. Now the battle was upon them, and he was not so sure. It was not the fighting that frightened him; he had been in plenty of fights over the past year. It was the innocent lives that were depending upon his plan working. If he failed, their deaths would fall on his hands. He had never been a part of a battle of this scale, yet he had seen fit to interject himself into the planning process. Had he bitten off more than he could chew? Perhaps he should have left the strategizing to General McLeod.

"I don't plan on launching an attack against them until dawn," General McLeod was saying. "Adel, this will give you and your team plenty of time to get north of the city and then inside via the river. I will have the men blow the horns when we are ready for you to open the gate, but please don't do it too early. If we aren't prepared to advance, our element of surprise will be wasted. We're only going to get one shot at this. If we time this right, we can be inside the walls before those bastards know what hit them."

Again, the only reply Adel could muster was a curt nod. He did not want to speak, did not want his shaking voice to betray his fear to the hardened soldiers gathered around him. They were looking to him for hope. If he could not display the utmost confidence in himself, why should they? Perhaps the illusion of certainty would serve as well as the real thing. It was taking every bit of concentration he possessed just to control his breathing. His heart was racing so fast that Adel was sure people must be able to see it pounding through his dark green leather armor.

"I'm going to talk to them a bit before I order the assault," General McLeod continued. "Maybe I can persuade some of the soldiers in the city they have another option, that they do not have to fight for Idanox. I don't want to kill anybody who does not need to die. As soon as Adel has the gates open, we will advance into the city. Any Thornatan soldier who lays down his weapons is to be spared—any who do not are to be fought the same as any other enemy. Make sure we are stressing this to our men. I do not want them to hesitate at the sight of their former brothers-in-arms. It's to be expected, but we simply can't afford it. Such hesitation could lose us this battle. If we lose, Thornata loses."

"We should begin to line up at least some of our attack force. We can put them within sight of the walls but out of range of their archers," Captain Dunstan said. "If we can keep their eyes focused on us, Adel and his team will have an easier time slipping into the city unnoticed. As long as we are out of the range of their archers, there is nothing they can do unless they want to come and fight us out here."

"Agreed," General McLeod replied. "As I said earlier, it would behoove us to be ready if they decide to open the gates and attack us. I doubt they would try it, but you never know what Idanox may have up his sleeve. I've learned to expect the unexpected from that snake."

The plans were laid, and the commanders dispersed to begin ordering their men into formation. Before Adel could depart the camp, General McLeod pulled him aside for a final word.

"Good luck, Adel. This time tomorrow, this war will be over. We are going to win; I know we are. I just wanted to tell you how grateful I am for everything you have done to help us in this fight. I fully plan on surviving this battle to tell you that again, but just in case I don't, I wanted to let you know. I don't expect that Idanox will let you bring him in alive. An arrogant man like him will never allow himself to be executed in front of a cheering, jeering crowd of the people he has tormented. If that's the case, make sure the bastard gets the end he deserves."

"We will, General McLeod. That quivering rat will not live to torment the people of this province for another day. I promise you that," Adel replied, trying to sound as assured as possible, his mind screaming its doubt at him all the while. *At least I managed to keep my voice from shaking.*

Darkness had set in entirely by the time Adel, Ola, and Alsea departed the army encampment with twenty of McLeod's fiercest fighters following them. Alsea roamed ahead, ever the scout. Ola constantly moved from side to side and to the back of the group. Adel was happy to have his ogre ears with them, always listening for any hint of a threat. Adel led the soldiers, relying on Ola and Alsea to alert him to any danger. He wondered if his friends and these soldiers were concealing an overwhelming rush of fear, just like he was. It was taking all his focus just to keep putting one foot in front of the other.

It took them several hours to make their way around the massive city of Oreanna, traveling over a mile to the east of the city walls to avoid detection. Adel knew from his years on Boyd's barge that the Moyie River passed briefly through the northeastern corner of Oreanna before continuing south toward the Bonners. This short stretch of water that passed through the city would be their entry point. Even if the water gates were closed, Adel believed he could use the Rawl to get them into the city quickly enough. It was then just a matter of finding and killing Idanox and hopefully not dying in the process. After he had opened the gates for the army, he reminded himself. That was a crucial job that he had to do right. What had he been thinking, promising such a ridiculous thing?

The company reached the riverbank north of Oreanna a few hours before dawn. Ola had insisted that they travel at least two miles north of the city before moving toward the river, fearing that Hoyt scouts may be out on patrol. They had encountered no such patrols, and Adel's heart was now racing faster than ever. They found the riverbank utterly deserted, the only sign of life the faint torchlight that shimmered from Oreanna to the south. Ready or not, it was time for his plan to spring into motion. They had to get into the city before dawn. If he was not there to hear the horns blowing, he would not be able to open the gates for McLeod's forces, and the battle would be lost before it could begin.

Adel motioned for the first five soldiers to move closer to the edge of the water as he began his work. The Rawl responded to him at once, reacting exactly as he had commanded. The water started to solidify immediately, freezing faster than should've been possible. Within seconds he had fashioned a thick ice raft perfectly sized for the five men to clamber aboard. As he watched them scramble onto the makeshift raft, he remembered how creating his first such tool only months earlier had seemed an impressive feat. He knew this was no time to reminisce, but the thought of the strides he had taken gave him a much-needed boost of confidence. As soon as all five men were on the raft, he shifted the river current just gently enough to move them out into the center of the river, giving himself room to make the next.

He created four more ice rafts in short order. He, Ola, and Alsea climbed aboard his final creation, and Adel immediately turned his attention to the water beneath them. Reaching out with the power of the Rawl, he began to speed the river's current. He did not shift it as drastically as he had when they had fled from the monster on their way to the Temple of the Rawl, rather just enough to propel them gently on their way. The water flowing too rapidly through Oreanna could draw unwanted attention to their stealth mission. It was essential that the Hoyt not suspect they were coming until it was too late.

Adel glanced skyward to find the moon dropping rapidly from the sky. Dawn would be upon them before they knew it, and the final battle of the war would come with it. Anxious to ensure they arrived in the city in time for the assault, he increased the speed of the current ever so slightly. The first slivers of sunlight were just beginning to creep over the eastern horizon when they reached the walls of Oreanna and found the river gate sealed shut. They had expected as much, but Adel still could not help but feel disappointed. *What, did you think Idanox was going to leave the door wide-open for you to walk in and kill him?*

Adel scanned the walls above the river gate anxiously, searching for any sign of sentries. Beside him, Alsea had set an arrow to the string of her bow, ready to drop anybody who might be waiting to betray their position. To their surprise, there was no sign of any Hoyt or Thornatan soldier on this section of the wall. Adel could only surmise that General McLeod's forces had drawn every available fighter to defend the main gate on the southern end of the city. Relaxing ever so slightly, he set to work on opening the river gate.

The gate was a portcullis of dozens of solid iron bars that dropped from the walls above. They ran nearly to the bottom of the river below them. The only way to raise the bars—for ordinary men at least—was with a winch system that could only be accessed by men on the walls above. Fortunately for the attackers, Adel was no average man.

He had given a brief thought to simply obliterating the portcullis but had ultimately decided against it. Too much noise would reveal them to any forces that may be nearby. General McLeod's troops were the hammer of this operation, designed to draw the defending troops' attention. Their mission was dependent on the element of surprise. Any forces who came to meet them would only make it more difficult for them to reach Idanox. Adel would have to find a more subtle way of raising the gate. The solution came to him, one brought to mind by the manner of transport they had utilized to come this far.

Focusing his power on the deepest depths of the river directly below the portcullis, Adel steadily began to freeze a small patch of the river. Unlike an ordinary freeze, he needed to start from the bottom of the river and work his way upward. He had never done this before but did not allow any doubt to enter his mind. He would succeed because he had no other choice. Collecting as much water as he could focus into the small area between the bars and the sand at the bottom of the river, he built his block of ice one small bit at a time. The ice block was maybe a foot tall when the gate made its first visible movement, just a slight jolt upward.

With the gate moving slightly, it was time for Ola to assist. Moving to the front of their ice raft, he took two of the bars in his hands and lifted upward with all his might. It produced only a small movement, but it was enough to create a small bit of space between the bars and the ice block. Quickening his pace, Adel began to expand the ice upward with greater urgency, filling the gaps as Ola continued to strain the gate upward. Every time the iron bars made a slight movement upward, Adel looked to the top of the walls, expecting to find archers about to rain arrows down upon them. It took just over a minute for his block of ice to reach the surface of the water. The bars were now raised high enough that they could swim underneath if needed, but Adel preferred to keep them dry. Being waterlogged would slow them down if a fight happened upon them unexpectedly.

At last, the portcullis had raised perhaps a foot above the surface of the water. Adel paused and sat back to examine his handiwork. It had been no easy task, but the ice block had done its job. The gate was raised, and the defenders of the city were none the wiser.

It was not much room, but it would be enough for them to squeeze under the bars. Adel did not want to expend any more of his energy on this task than necessary. Motioning for the soldiers to lie flat on their ice rafts as he did the same, he once again compelled the current of the Moyie River to continue south. It responded at once, and they were through the gates and inside Oreanna in moments. As soon as all the rafts had cleared the gate, Adel focused his power once more, melting the ice block behind them instantly. The gate descended into the water, leaving no trace of their passage. It would not do for some stray soldier or Hoyt fighter to spot it sitting in the upward position. Adel took a deep breath. They were trapped inside Oreanna, precisely as they had wanted. Now the real challenge was about to begin.

***

Just as Adel and his companions were slipping past the river gate and into Oreanna, General McLeod was preparing to launch his part of the plan. Every man he had under his command had been assembled, eight hundred strong, grouped into three companies before the main gates of Oreanna. They had split as a precaution against an attack, but soon all three companies would converge as one at the gates of the city. They stood several hundred yards back, still too far away for Hoyt archers to open fire on them. The plains surrounding them were eerily quiet, the calm before the storm that was about to erupt and consume them all. This war would end today, for better or for worse. General McLeod had lost any enjoyment he'd found in battle many years ago, but he knew there was no other way. Conceding Thornata to the Hoyt would doom the people he had spent his life serving to lives of hopelessness and brutality.

He understood he might soon be forced to kill men who had once served under his command. Even Randall McLeod, a veteran of more battles than he could easily count, had never faced such a grim reality. This thought was a particularly unappealing prospect to face, but one he could not allow to sway him from doing whatever was necessary to liberate Oreanna. They would have their chance to lay down their weapons, and he could only pray that most of them would accept it. If not, he would have no choice but to fight them the same as he would any other foe. The sun had finally fully risen off to the east. Adel should be inside the city by now, and every second that McLeod delayed put the boy at risk of being discovered before he could carry out his part of the plan. There was no point in waiting any longer.

"Make sure the trumpeters know the signal. When I give it, they need to blast those horns as loud as they possibly can. If Adel can't hear them, this will be a brief offensive," he instructed Captain Thaddeus Dunstan.

Dunstan nodded and began to make his way down the line of troops, making sure the trumpeters knew the signal. The grizzled Imperial captain had become a valued advisor in the days since he had joined McLeod's forces. Dunstan was the type of man who would have undoubtedly risen to the level of general within the Thornatan Army. McLeod allowed the captain a few moments to make his way down the line, steeling himself for what lay ahead. He began to walk toward the gates, his stride relaxed and meaningful. He stopped about halfway between the city wall and his forces. He would be just out of the range of any longbows on the walls but close enough to make his voice heard by the men holding them.

"My name is Randall McLeod, and I am the Supreme General of the Thornatan army!" he cried out, his voice carrying across the silent plains to the men on the walls.

"You were the Supreme General of the Thornatan army, Randall. Now you are nothing but a traitor to your province and your people. You are unworthy of the uniform you wear. Surrender your forces, lay down your weapons, and step forward to face the justice that is due to you!" The response was immediate, the voice familiar. It took General McLeod a few seconds to place it, but when he did, his disgust only deepened.

"Bern, it is quite bold of you to name anyone else a traitor. You are here, serving your new master, licking his boots, hoping for a scrap of riches to fall to you. I'm surprised even a weasel like Idanox found a purpose for a blundering buffoon like you. I always knew you were a coward, but even I never suspected you could sink to such depths. The day one of the generals of the Thornatan Army turned turncoat will forever be a black mark on our name. I regret more than anything that I allowed a man like you to serve in my army. You will face justice for your crimes soon enough," McLeod called back, his rage at finding one of his former generals commanding Hoyt forces palpable. Whatever else the battle ahead held in store, he hoped that he would have a chance to see Bern face-to-face before it was over.

"How many of your own people are you willing to see bleed and die for the sake of your stubborn pride, Randall? You have assembled quite a force, and I admit I am impressed. But you and I both know you do not have enough men here to breach the gates. Even with the Imperial invaders you have brought with you, you still do not have enough. The true black mark on the reputation of this army is the fact that you went begging outsiders to help you fight against your former brothers-in-arms. Your legacy will be of a man who asked Imperial invaders to come into our province and murder our people. There is no need for further bloodshed. Lay down your weapons and swear yourselves to the service of our new duke. He is a just and merciful leader; such a gesture would go a long way toward absolving you of your crimes."

Bern had always been a sniveling coward, but still, finding him so thoroughly set against his own people was a disgusting sight. McLeod wondered if Bern would try to surrender once he realized the battle was lost. It would not save him if he did. The traitor would face justice, either on the battlefield or on the executioner's block. Deciding he might as well make that fact official, McLeod cried out once more.

"We are going to come in there and deal with you and your just, merciful leader. I hereby strip you of your rank and discharge you from the service of the Thornatan Army. As Supreme General of the Thornatan Army, I condemn you, Bern, for the crime of treason and sentence you to death. I hope for the sake of whatever shred of honor you have left that you meet it with your sword in your hand and not quivering like the cowardly rat you are."

"So be it, Randall. When you meet your fate, just remember that I tried to help you," Bern cried back, the arrogant twat. As if he would ever be able to offer help to a man like Randall McLeod.

"I am now addressing any Thornatan soldier inside Oreanna who is part of the defending force. I understand that many of you are acting against your best judgment. You act in the face of threats that have been levied against you or your families. It is the only reason that you serve Idanox and the Hoyt; I understand this. Just know, any Thornatan soldier who lays down his weapons in surrender will be granted mercy. I urge you not to fight against us, my brothers. Please do not throw away your lives in the name of a tyrant," McLeod called out.

He fell silent for a moment, half expecting Bern to have another smug response, but to his surprise, none was forthcoming. *Keeping his silence was actually the smartest thing Bern could have done in that scenario*, McLeod thought. The more the oaf talked, the more the men following him would question their allegiance. There was no point in delaying any further; the morning sun was now fully risen. He hoped some of the men inside would heed his call. Win or lose, this battle was the one he would be remembered for the most. Whispering one final prayer to himself that Adel was in place, he raised his left hand into the air, two fingers extending toward the clouds.

The horns blasted out behind him within seconds, a dozen of them sounding in unison. There was no music or rhythm to their wailing, the trumpeters' sole purpose to sound their blasts as loudly as possible. The volume was so intense that it pained McLeod's ears; there was no way Adel would not hear them if he was inside the city. The trumpeters blew as long as they could, falling silent after a few moments. General McLeod stared at the gate, waiting anxiously. For those brief moments, time itself seemed to stand still. *Please, Adel. We need you to come through for us, now more than ever.*

There was no warning that it was coming, no hint of the destruction that was about to unfold. The lightning bolt appeared from the bright blue sky as if by magic, striking the main gate of Oreanna with earth-shattering force. The noise reminded General McLeod of the night in the warehouse in Kalstag, a thunder blast right on top of him, though this strike was far more powerful. As though it were made of twigs, the gate was blasted into thousands of pieces, a sizeable portion of the thick stone wall crumbling along with it.

Thick black smoke filled the air almost immediately. As the ringing in his ears began to subside, McLeod could hear defenders on the wall retching from the overpowering stench. The smell of burning flesh followed soon after. McLeod did not know how many men had been killed in the blast, but it must have been quite a few to produce such an overwhelming stench of death. Adel had heard the horns and was no doubt making his way toward Idanox now. It was time for the army that McLeod had assembled to do their part. They had to keep the bulk of the city's defenders occupied to give Adel and his team time.

"Forward!"

Chapter Sixteen

Alsea's voice was distant, as though she were calling out to him from the other side of a river. But she was standing right beside him, her hand resting reassuringly on his shoulder. Still, he could barely make out her words over the high-pitched ringing in his ears, her face swimming back and forth before his eyes.

"Adel? Adel, can you hear me?"

"Did it work? Did I blast the gates open?" he asked, the sound of his own voice a distant echo.

"I think so," she replied, her voice becoming clearer as the ringing in his ears slowly subsided. "I saw the lightning come down and heard the blast. I don't think it would have been so loud if it had not found its mark. I can smell smoke too, and where there's smoke, there's fire. We have to get moving, Adel; we have a job to do here."

Yes, a job. We have to get to Idanox, Adel reminded himself, coming out of his daze. He realized for the first time that he had sunk down to one knee. The effort of producing and directing the lightning bolt had been immense. The energy required to destroy the gate had been significant, even greater than he had anticipated. But he knew he could not allow his weariness to catch up to him now. He had no choice but to keep moving and hope his body would not fail him before the battle was won. He rose to his feet, taking in his surroundings. The Oreanna docks were massive, boats and warehouses stretching out in every direction. They would usually be bustling with sailors and workers at this time of the morning, but they had arrived to find them deserted. The workers must have taken shelter to wait out the coming battle, he supposed. After all, nobody in their right mind would be out and about in Oreanna right now.

Far off to the south, the sound of metal striking metal rose into the morning sky, finally becoming audible over the still-subsiding ringing in his ears. It was distant but unmistakable. The battle had begun, confirming that he must have indeed succeeded in destroying the main gate. General McLeod's forces would do their best to win the fight to the south; they had a job of their own to do. They had to get to Idanox and finish him while the attack at the main gate occupied the bulk of his forces. Two separate forces were working toward the same goal, and it was his job to make sure this one succeeded. Already, he was considering a change to their original plan.

"Alsea, give me your opinion. Should we bother with going to the duke's palace first? Or do you think that Idanox has already fled to the bunker?" Adel asked, not wanting to waste any time. Alsea had the best instincts of anyone he had ever met. She would know what to do.

The palace was far from the bunker, and he did not want to make the long trek through the city for nothing. Adel knew the more time they spent running around the streets of Oreanna, the higher the chances of discovery. Furthermore, their numbers were limited. Even a single death in an unnecessary skirmish at the palace was more than they could afford. While most of the Hoyt forces would be engaged with General McLeod, he would be shocked if there were not at least some patrols in the city streets.

"Idanox is a coward. He's shown that at every turn. I would wager every coin I've ever had that he is hiding in the bunker already. That's where he will feel safest. He isn't interested in leading; he will only be worried about preserving his own skin," she replied, glancing at Ola, who nodded his agreement.

"Then let's get to the bunker. Everybody, look sharp. There could still be Hoyt fighters in the streets, and we don't need to get ambushed. Let's avoid drawing attention to ourselves. No talking unless you see danger," Adel said, glancing around at the soldiers to make sure they had heard him over the growing sounds of the distant battle.

They made their way away from the docks and into the streets of Oreanna. General McLeod had advised them that the duke's bunker was located near the western wall of the city. It was in an area anybody not privy to the location would not think to look, surrounded by the homes of relatively poor civilians. The logic of building a bunker in such a place made sense. The houses of the poor would be the last priority for an invading force looking to pillage and plunder. The group of twenty-three made their way westward as fast as their feet could carry them, weaving through streets of shops and homes. There were no civilians in sight; Adel was relieved to find they must've been sheltering in their homes. Hopefully most of them would stay sheltered in place until the battle was over.

They had only traveled a short distance from the docks when they met their first resistance. Six armed Hoyt fighters came flying from an alleyway ahead of them, freezing in their tracks at the unexpected sight of the invaders. Seemingly realizing they would stand no chance in a fight against the superior numbers, the men instead elected to start screaming for help. Alsea loosed her bow twice, silencing two of them within seconds, and General McLeod's soldiers dispatched the rest in short order.

The party froze once their foes were dead, their eyes scanning desperately in every direction. Had the Hoyt screams drawn attention to them? Casting about desperately, Adel could see no sign of enemies approaching and allowed himself to breathe more comfortably for a few moments. Then he saw the look on Ola's face, and his heart sunk. From Ola's expression, he knew the ogre could hear something the rest of them could not. They had not been quick enough to silence the Hoyt patrol, and they were about to pay the price for it.

"We have more incoming, a lot more than we just faced," Ola declared, drawing his sword. The army had given him the most enormous blade they could find, and while not as massive as the one he had lost the night they were captured, it seemed to fit well enough in Ola's hand.

A few seconds later, Ola's prediction came true, a stream of Hoyt fighters and Thornatan soldiers pouring into the street from all sides. Of course, they would have anticipated the possibility of an attempt to assassinate Idanox. It was a tactic the Hoyt leader himself would likely have come up with under similar circumstances. Reports had indicated he had used a similar diversionary assault to distract from his own move against the prior duke.

Adel drew his sword, readying himself for battle, and saw a sight that made his heart sink even deeper. Lumbering into the street along with the enemy fighters were two massive unmistakable figures. These were no ordinary men; they were far too large to be ordinary men.

They had known they might encounter such creatures, though the advanced knowledge brought Adel little comfort. It had taken days of careful planning and perfect execution to rid themselves of the first one. To be faced with two of them at once was enough to fill him with a deep sense of despair. They had heard rumors of such monsters in Oreanna, but he had desperately hoped such stories were false. If they could not defeat these creatures immediately, they could destroy the entire attack force, and the battle happening at the main gates would be for nothing. There was no helping it now. The creatures were here, and they had to overcome them. The power of the Rawl was likely to be their only hope of doing so.

Several Hoyt fighters were the first to attack, crashing into their left side. The soldiers held their ground, repelling the attack effectively, but now the first beast was on the move, bearing down on them. *They will not be able to withstand an assault from this monster. I have to do something now!* Adel focused the power of the Rawl on the ground at the beast's feet, calling all of its moisture to the surface and turning the solid dirt immediately into thick mud. It was a delaying tactic and nothing more, but it spared several soldiers from certain death. The creature sunk in quickly but continued its advance, albeit more slowly than before. Adel had bought himself a few seconds, and he needed to find a way to make them count.

More Hoyt and Thornatan soldiers were crashing in on them now. Adel sent a vicious wind blast outward, ripping most of them from their feet and scattering them like leaves in an autumn breeze. Ola, Alsea, and the soldiers immediately sprang into the offensive, cutting them down while they were off-balance. The brief delay was a costly one; the beast was almost free of the mud. *I need this beast destroyed without hurting anyone else!* Adel thought to himself, frustrated at his inability to find a solution.

It was the power of the Rawl that found the solution. It reacted just as it had all those months ago when he had struggled to move the water from the jug to the goblet. His arm seemed to extend of its own accord; he was not consciously moving it, yet it was moving nonetheless. His index finger pointed directly at the struggling monster, and Adel felt the air at his fingertip begin to change, as if a massive amount of energy was pooling at the end of his reach. The hair on his arms stood straight, as though a midsummer thunderstorm were about to erupt around him.

When the lightning bolt struck, it surprised him as much as it did anybody else. It was much smaller than the massive ribbons of energy that he had previously summoned from the sky, a concentrated bolt that flew directly to its target with deadly precision. Despite its small size, it struck the beast with blistering power, sending it reeling backward. This smaller lightning bolt was not powerful enough to destroy such a monster in a single hit, but it did produce a series of small flames along the creature's rock-hard flesh, and this was all the opening Adel needed.

Focusing the power of the Rawl on the flames, he fanned them all over the creature's body. Once the beast was fully engulfed in fire, he focused all his concentration on intensifying the flames, burning them as hot as possible, just as he had with the first beast they had encountered. Even engulfed in flames, the creature continued to try to press its attack, but it was too late. Within seconds, the raging beast had been burned away to ash. Turning his focus away from the remains of the creature, Adel began to look around for the second.

He didn't find it; it found him. It came crashing through the soldiers and slammed into him in an impact unlike anything he had ever felt before. It was as though he had been struck by a wagon loaded down with heavy metal and moving at full speed. He tumbled to the dirt, his arms and legs spinning in every direction, his sword ripped from his hand by the sheer force of the blow. The durable armor that had been gifted to him by the Children of the Rawl saved him from any broken bones, but it still took him a second to find his bearings. As soon as he had, the beast was upon him once again. This time it was raising a massive axe above its head for a killing strike.

With his sword torn from his grasp, Adel had no weapon with which to defend himself. Even if he had, he likely would not have been able to deflect an attack from such an impossibly powerful foe. It was Ola who saved him, just as he had so many times before. Just as the beast was about to drop the axe down on top of Adel's head, the ogre was there. Ola seized the creature's arms and began fighting with all of his might to hold the blow at bay.

Ola's intervention gave Adel the split second he needed to find his feet. He hurried to put a little distance between himself and the monster. He knew that he needed to be fast; even Ola could only hold it at bay for so long. The fighting was chaotic, and Adel could not make any sense of which Thornatan soldiers were fighting with them and which were trying to kill them. There were too many bodies too close to the beast, and he could not risk killing their own men. Lashing out once more with another mighty wind gust, he blasted everybody clear of the monster, friend and foe alike, except for Ola, who was still trying to wrestle with it.

"Ola, let go of it and get clear!" Adel shouted, raising his hand with finger fully extended once more.

The ogre released the monster and sprang away with an agility that defied his enormous stature. The beast began to advance on Adel at once, but he had already started his assault. The lightning came easier this time now that Adel knew he was capable of such a feat. It flew straight to its mark, blasting the beast backward, flames crackling up across its body. Once again, Adel turned the full focus of his power on the fire. Within seconds the creature was wholly engulfed in a raging inferno, and after a few more seconds, nothing remained but a smoldering pile of ash.

The beasts slain, Adel was able to turn his attention toward helping the soldiers deal with the Hoyt and Thornatan Army attackers. Snatching a sword from the ground to replace the one the beast had torn from his hand, he waded into the fight. He slipped a strike from a sword racing toward his head, his sword opening a gash in the Hoyt fighter's leg as he tried to sidestep. The Hoyt cried out in pain and tried to stagger away only for Alsea to catch him from behind as she moved to Adel's side.

"We have to finish this and get moving again! This is taking too long. If Idanox finds out we're coming, he may try to flee the city," she cried out to him, spinning to face another attacker as she spoke.

She was right. The longer this fight continued, the more opposition would flock to them. Eventually, they would not have enough men left to mount an assault on the duke's bunker, even if Idanox had not fled the city by that time. Their objective was to get to Idanox, and every second spent fighting these men was a distraction they could not afford. If Idanox managed to slip away, this battle and the men who gave their lives fighting it would prove meaningless. Adel would not allow that to happen; they had fought too hard and sacrificed too much to fail now.

Adel looked around, searching for another way to use his power to end the fight quickly. The Thornatan soldiers accompanying them wore green ribbons tied around their arms to help identify one another, but they were difficult to spot in the flurry of battle. One of the beast's bodies was still smoldering nearby. Adel could use the embers to turn the tide of the fight, but he could not risk killing their own men.

His lack of focus on the battle around him nearly cost him his life, one of the enemy soldiers lunging toward him with a spear thrust. He barely managed to sidestep the blow, launching a counterattack as the men stumbled past him, his sword coming up underneath his enemy's arm and sinking deep into his chest.

Still formulating a plan as he did so, Adel began to step away from the still-smoldering body of the beast. There was only one thing to try, and he could only hope that his men would be quick to catch on to what he was doing. Desperately trying to find an open area in the chaos of the battle, he fought his way clear of the crush of combatants and called out to his men. A Hoyt fighter blocked his path, slashing at him with an axe. Adel avoided the first blow, and then the second. He struck back at the Hoyt with a hard kick aimed at the man's knee. The attack worked, buckling the Hoyt fighter and allowing Adel an opening to plunge his blade into the man's gut. After wrenching it free, he stepped around the dying Hoyt, working his way out into the open.

"Green bands! Green bands, form up with me!" he shouted, hoping the soldiers would understand what he meant. They had not rehearsed such commands, an oversight he was now kicking himself over.

To his relief, they seemed to understand the command. One by one, the elite Thornatan soldiers fighting alongside him began to make their way through the battle toward him. Several Hoyt and enemy soldiers tried to charge at Adel as well, but Ola rushed forward to meet them, his greatsword slashing out at them. Adel didn't know how many battles these men had seen in their lives, but it was clear they had never faced an opponent like the ferocious gigantic ogre. Ola's sword met the men as they came, and not one of them was able to breach the ogre's exceptional defenses. Those who were fortunate enough to survive Ola's initial onslaught staggered back to join ranks with their comrades.

As soon as all the green bands left standing had joined him, Adel reached out toward the still-burning beast corpse with the power of the Rawl. Reigniting the flames, he began to spread them toward their attackers. The Hoyt and their allies realized what was happening, but it was too late for some of them. Their clothing went up in flames as soon as the fire reached them, sending them fleeing in every direction, screaming in pain. Their comrades who were lucky enough to avoid the fire scrambled to avoid them as they scattered. Soon the street in front of them was completely clear of adversaries. Knowing it wouldn't be long before reinforcements arrived, Adel turned to the others.

"They will go for help. We have to move fast. Let's go!"

The Hoyt War

He looked around as they moved out, trying to make a fast count. They had lost three men in the struggle. It could have been much worse, but it was still a grievous loss to such a small group. There was bound to be more resistance now, and they could not afford to lose even a single man. Desperate that their mission not prove to be in vain, the company continued westward through the streets of Oreanna. They did not know how the battle at the gates was going, but they knew they were running out of time.

Chapter Seventeen

Supreme General Randall McLeod had seen more battles than he could easily recall in his rapidly advancing age. He had been in the midst of chaos and bloodshed more times than perhaps any man in the history of the Thornatan Army. McLeod had never been a general who led from the rear. He had always preferred to be in the middle of the fighting, never content to sit back and watch his men do the fighting and the dying. This was different. He had to treat this battle with caution, knowing his men would need his guidance if they were to prevail. He had entered the day of the Battle of Oreanna thinking there was nothing that could surprise him. But he had never witnessed carnage that could compare with what was unfolding before his eyes at the main gates of Thornata's capital city.

They had begun their advance as soon as Adel had destroyed the gate, and things had initially appeared promising. For a few moments, McLeod was confident their initial charge would break through the defenders and be inside the city walls within minutes. His attack force surged forward into the breach, the defenders caught off guard by Adel's attack on the gates. But to his surprise, the Hoyt had rallied their troops and were holding the breach more competently than McLeod would have ever suspected them capable. If Bern was still in command of the enemy forces, McLeod was forced to concede that the traitor had prepared more thoroughly than he would have ever expected of the oaf.

To the general's dismay, he did not see any Thornatan soldiers inside the walls laying down their weapons. It saddened him, even if it was not much of a surprise. Fear was a powerful tool, one Idanox had deployed effectively against them. McLeod knew most of them did not want to be in this fight, that they would much rather have been fighting against the Hoyt. They felt as if they had no other choice if they wanted to preserve the lives of their families. He pitied these men, but there was no other option for him. He needed to take control of Oreanna back from the Hoyt no matter who stood in his way. If this meant killing unwilling combatants, he would do what needed to be done without hesitation. There would be no joy in it for him, but there were too many lives at stake to allow his personal qualms to stand in the way of doing what was necessary.

The attacking soldiers were held up at the breach where the city gates had once stood, unable to press farther into the city. For every Hoyt or Thornatan soldier who fell to their assault, two more seemed to appear from within the city to replace him. General McLeod had thought if they could find a way through the gates, they could neutralize their enemy's superior numbers in the narrow city streets. He was beginning to think he had been mistaken in this assumption. The Hoyt were fighting as though their very survival was at stake, which was admittedly an accurate assessment. The outlaw band seemed to sense this battle would determine whether they would live to see another day and were fighting accordingly.

Deciding there was little to be done from the back of the battle, General McLeod drew his sword and began working his way through the ranks of his men. There was no point in hanging back to direct a force that would be too decimated to put up a fight once they got inside the city. It was time to throw caution to the winds. If this battle was to be lost, he would rather die where the fighting was thickest, fighting to give his men a chance at victory. No observations he could make from a distance would help them now. There were no commands he could give that would simplify what they needed to do. This was no longer a contest of strategy and planning, but rather one of willpower and sheer brute force. Perhaps his presence on the front lines could offer inspiration to the men under his command. As he neared the chaos beneath the city walls, Randall McLeod could see up close the toll this battle had already taken.

The remnants of the walls where the gates had once stood were charred black from Adel's lightning strike. The stench of smoke and charred flesh grew even more intense the closer he drew to the heart of the conflict. McLeod blinked away the tears that were surging to his eyes in response to the smells and pressed forward. The smell of death was one which McLeod would never become accustomed to, even if he lived another hundred years and fought another thousand battles.

There were too many dead to count, and countless more were wounded, struggling to stay alive under the crush of fighters from both sides. It was nigh impossible to distinguish between the men who fought beside or against them. The green bands he had ordered his men to wrap on their arms were difficult to spot in the chaos of battle, and he immediately cursed himself for not developing a better strategy. The stench of blood flooded his nostrils, joining the burnt smell of the lightning strike and its aftermath, forming a sickening scent cocktail that made even the seasoned general want to retch. McLeod was no stranger to death on the battlefield, but it was clear this battle would be the costliest he had ever seen.

"On me, lads. We're breaking through their ranks if it's the last thing we ever do! Make these Hoyt bastards pay for everything they have done to Thornata ten times over! If they draw a drop of blood from you, draw fifty from them. If they take an inch from us, we'll take a foot from them. Forward!" he cried out, charging the Hoyt front line with reckless abandon.

Randall McLeod had made his living as the Supreme General of the Thornatan Army by recognizing the techniques necessary to win any conflict he encountered. He understood immediately that a patient, strategic approach would not work here. Their only path to victory was through sheer force of will and reckless violence, a tactic he had seldom employed in his decades of leadership. In most instances, he believed it to be bullheaded, but this was different. They needed to engage the Hoyt and their Thornatan Army allies in close quarters, and they needed to be willing to fight dirty. In short, they had to fight like the Hoyt if they wanted to beat the Hoyt. If he fell in the attempt to reach the gates, hopefully his sacrifice would inspire his men to fight their way through the enemy lines and into the city.

A black-clad Hoyt fighter charged toward him, his sword swinging wildly for McLeod's head. General McLeod brought up his own sword in defense, parrying the sloppy blow and then the lower attack that followed it. He counterattacked, aiming for his opponent's neck. The Hoyt barely managed to parry the strike but was knocked off-balance by the force of McLeod's blow. *Not so old after all, am I?* The next attack found its mark, a thrust sliding deep between the man's ribs. General McLeod wrenched his sword free and turned to face his next attacker.

The next man to attack him was no Hoyt, but rather a Thornatan soldier. The sting of seeing one of his men trying to kill him wounded General McLeod deeper than he would have thought possible. There was no time to wallow in self-pity; the attacker was right on top of him before he could dwell too long on what he was doing. The fury of battle did not make it any easier to cut the man's life away. The man's expression as the general's sword found its mark was one McLeod knew would haunt him until his final day. But there was no time to dwell on it. If he did, that day would come much sooner than he wanted.

General McLeod continued to press forward, desperate to breach the logjam of Hoyt and Thornatan soldiers who fought to hold the ruins of the city gate. He was surrounded by utter pandemonium, men on all sides hacking away at one another with reckless abandon. He could smell and taste blood as he fought his way through the combatants. An arrow would occasionally fall from above, archers on what remained of the walls firing down indiscriminately into the crush of bodies. Thankfully, he suspected there was no way for the men above to recognize him in the frenzied crush of bodies. If they had, there would no doubt be more arrows coming his way. He would scream the occasional order into the uproar, though he was not sure if anybody obeyed or even heard them. Everything around him blended together into a dizzying whirlwind of blood, death, and mayhem.

General McLeod did not know how long it took him to fight his way through the Hoyt forces to the remnants of the main gates. Once he reached the remnants of the gates, the fighting got worse, the Hoyt and opposing soldiers fighting with a renewed fury, desperately trying to keep the general from cutting his way into Oreanna. McLeod did not know how many men he'd killed so he could finally breach their line. He did not know how many wounds he'd suffered during his charge, but they were numerous; he could feel that much. He was covered in blood, and he could sense that a significant amount of it was his own. All he knew was the deafening sound of war and the smell of fire, sweat, and blood mingling as one.

When he did break through the line, it came as a surprise. It had felt as though there would be no end to the Hoyt forces, that the battle would rage on until all the attackers were dead, McLeod included. It happened quite suddenly; one moment he was pressing forward through a horde of combatants, and the next he was looking out at the relatively empty streets of Oreanna. The city before him looked like it might on any morning just before dawn. If someone were walking even a few hundred yards away, they might never suspect the chaos that was unfolding at the gates were it not for the horrific sounds and smells rising into the morning air.

McLeod spun, fearing the Hoyt forces might attack him from behind. His fears were well-founded; a black-clad Hoyt warrior was charging at his back with a battle-axe in hand. McLeod crouched into a defensive posture, but the man never reached him. The attacker was within a few feet when he came to a sudden halt, an expression of shock etched across his face. He tumbled lifelessly to the ground, Captain Thad Dunstan pulling his spear from the man's back as he fell.

General McLeod nodded a wordless thanks as the Imperial captain made his way toward him. More of their forces were breaking through the defenses now, reinvigorated by the courage of their leader. Many of the Hoyt were beginning to flee deeper into the city, realizing there was no way to regroup and retake the gates. To his relief, McLeod saw many Thornatan soldiers dropping their weapons, their hands raised in surrender. He was already thinking the surrendering soldiers could bolster his own diminished forces for the next phase of the battle. He did not know how many men he had lost. There would be no time to count until the fighting was over, but he knew he needed more.

"I wasn't sure we were going to make it through for a while," Thad Dunstan remarked, his voice barely reaching McLeod's ears over the deafening roar of the battle. The Imperial captain was covered in blood, a sight that McLeod realized mirrored his own appearance. "The Hoyt may lack skill, but they make up for it in ferocity. I'll give them that much. Your men fought well, Supreme General."

"We knew it was going to be a battle. The Hoyt are fleeing into the city, but they'll regroup and come at us again. They won't give up that easily knowing their very existence is at stake," replied General McLeod. "Idanox will have fled to the bunker by now, and we need to regroup and start moving that way. Hopefully Adel has reached it by now. He may need backup, especially if the Hoyt head there to support their leader."

"What about the men who have surrendered?"

McLeod addressed his answer to everyone who could hear him. There was no time to fret about the fact that these men had been trying to kill him only minutes earlier. He had no time to worry about putting them on trial or asking them to justify themselves. The pain he had felt at their betrayal had to be set aside. At that moment, all that existed was the battle and the need to win it. Sometimes the need to make peace was greater than the need to seek justice.

"Brothers, thank you for seeing reason and laying down your weapons. Take them back up now and join us once more. It is time to put an end to the Hoyt disease that has plagued this province for far too long. Their reign of terror is at an end. With me!"

***

Contrary to General McLeod's belief, Adel had not yet reached the duke's bunker. Every step his party took had become fiercely contested by the Hoyt forces within the city. Adel no longer had any doubt as to the Hoyt leader's location; the determination with which the Hoyt fought to keep them at bay left no room for it. Little did he know, the force resisting them was being bolstered by their comrades who were fleeing from General McLeod's attack on the gates. Onward they pressed, Adel deploying the Rawl in every manner he could conceive to help clear their path. The closer they drew to the bunker, the stouter the resistance became. Their ideas of a relatively smooth path through the city were long forgotten. Every foot of ground they wished to gain was going to have to be earned the hard way.

So, with no other option available to them, they fought. They fought their way through Hoyt warriors and Thornatan soldiers alike; it did not matter. Anybody in their path was an enemy who needed to be defeated. It was by far the most prolonged conflict Adel had ever been a part of. His limbs ached from the strain of combat, yet he knew he must keep fighting. If he allowed himself to stop long enough to assess his pain, his body would fail him. After a time, everything seemed to disappear into a blur around him. He was aware only of the space immediately in front of him and of the men who stood in the way of his goal. Everything else was irrelevant, a distraction that could prove fatal if he allowed it.

Ola led the company forward, his massive sword cutting a path through any who sought to stand in their way. He had been wounded in return for his efforts, perhaps a dozen cuts all over his body that Adel could see, but the ogre paid them no mind. Adel knew his friend had felt unimaginable pain many times before and had learned to compartmentalize it and fight through it. He would not allow his wounds to slow him. His friends depended on him to clear them a path to the bunker. He would not fail them, no matter how many injuries he sustained in return. Idanox had to be dealt with; if the Hoyt leader escaped again, they would not have enough men left to go after him. The future of Thornata depended on the outcome of this mission, and Ola would not allow them to fail.

Alsea wound her way through the battle like a shadow, her sword cutting the life from her foes before they even knew she was there. Many times, her sword found an enemy seconds before they could deliver a fatal strike to one of her companions, and then she'd dart away before they even realized she had saved them. Every time Adel caught a glimpse of her, he could see the exhaustion etched across her face. But still, she never slowed, knowing she must press on, that without her skills they would not reach the bunker. If Ola was the hammer of their party, she was the utility knife, mostly unnoticed yet supremely important to the job at hand.

It came as a surprise when they reached the bunker at last. In the seemingly endless fray, the group had lost all sense of how much farther they had to travel. All the streets had begun to run together in their minds in the midst of all the chaos. They burst out of a side street, and there it sat. Looking out at their objective, they found their battle was not about to get any easier. No fewer than a hundred men were gathered in front of the only entrance to the stone bunker, and it only got worse from there. Standing alongside the Hoyt and Thornatan soldiers were four more of the monstrous unnatural beasts. Idanox had reserved the most powerful of his defense forces for his own safety, much to Adel's displeasure, if not his surprise. He motioned his party to fall back, taking cover behind a nearby house in case the defenders were to open fire.

"Adel, your battle is hopeless. You must realize it by now!" came a cry from within the ranks of the bunker defenders. General Bern emerged from the crowd, his sneering arrogant face unmistakable. "No more of you need to die here. Surrender to me. Lay down your weapons and beg Duke Idanox for mercy. He is a just and gracious ruler, and he will hear you out if you are willing to see the error of your ways. I will admit I was once a skeptic, just as you are now. But Duke Idanox did not punish me for my past sins. He has shown me he is truly the leader Thornata needs to lead us into the future."

None of them had any intention of surrendering, yet they also understood their chances of fighting their way through such a force were not promising. They had lost more men on their way through Oreanna; only a dozen of McLeod's men still fought beside them. It did not matter. Adel was unwavering in his will to fight until his last breath.

Ola, however, had a different idea. He turned to Adel, ducking behind a few of the soldiers so nobody could see him speaking.

"Adel, you have to find another way into the bunker. We will attack and fight for as long as we can, but we cannot get through them. There are too many of them. If we all attack in the hope of reaching the door, we will all die, and the battle will be lost. If you can get inside and kill Idanox while we create a diversion, we may still have a chance," Ola muttered.

"I'm not leaving you all out here!" Adel protested.

"Ola is right; you have to go. You are the only one here who might be able to get inside the bunker another way. They have the door completely covered, and Ola is right. We will never be able to get through all of them, especially with those monsters fighting with them. We don't have time to argue about this, Adel. Get out of here, get around their forces unnoticed, and find a way to use the Rawl to get in there and end this!" snapped Alsea, who had silently approached from behind.

"What will it be, Adel?" General Bern shouted. "Are you going to see reason and surrender, or are we going to kill every last one of you? It's your choice, boy, but don't keep me waiting too long! Duke Idanox is kind, but he is not patient."

Adel hesitated for a moment, but Ola did not. Raising his sword above his head, he cried out for the soldiers to charge the bunker. They did so without hesitation, and

The Hoyt War

Adel was left behind as his comrades slammed into the Hoyt forces in a reckless all-out assault. He did not like this. He wanted to stay and fight with his friends, but Ola was right. Getting to Idanox was the key to winning this battle, and he had to try. Every second wasted was another second that his friends were fighting against impossible odds. They were as skilled as any fighters in all of Thornata, but even they could only hold out for so long against so many foes.

***

Turning away from the battle in front of the bunker, Adel backtracked and then began making his way down alleyways at a swift jog. He needed to approach the shelter from behind but could not risk being seen by the defenders. He was confident that Idanox had left the bulk of his personal defenses outside of the bunker. If he could slip in unnoticed, he should be able to overcome whatever the Hoyt leader had in store for him inside. He moved as fast as he could, knowing that every second wasted could cost his friends their lives. When he felt he had traveled a safe distance, he darted out of the alleyways, crossing the street and ducking behind the buildings adjacent to the bunker. He could hear the commotions of the fighting to his side but dared not turn his head to look. He knew himself well enough to understand he would be unable to resist the urge to go to the aid of his friends. They would keep Bern's forces occupied well enough for him to get into the bunker unseen; he was sure of it.

Adel broke into a full run, desperate to get into the bunker as quickly as possible. He came up behind the building and found, just as he had feared, there was no entryway on the back of the building. There was not even a window, just solid stone walls on each side. He could blast it open with a lightning blast as he had with the gates, but his comrades were too close; it was too dangerous to risk. Besides, as soon as he did, the defense force would swarm to his location before he could get inside and kill Idanox.

Was the floor of the bunker also made of stone? He had not thought to ask General McLeod this question, but now he realized he should have. Somehow, it had never occurred to him that he might have to enter the bunker through means other than through the door. *There are a great many things that never occurred to you, you fool!* It was possible he could tunnel into the shelter from below, but only if the stone did not extend to the floor of the structure. With few other options, he knew he had to try.

He focused the power of the Rawl on the ground beside the bunker wall, and the earth began to soften. It turned immediately to mud as he drew up moisture from deep underground. As soon as the earth softened, he shifted it to the side and immediately hardened it once more, forming a makeshift tunnel. He found that the walls of the bunker extended perhaps three feet into the earth. As soon he had gone deep enough to squeeze under the wall, he began working sideways, creating a small passage under the building.

Adel dropped into the small hole he had created, using his power to widen it ever so slightly, giving himself just enough room to move. Once he had extended the hole just far enough underneath the bunker that he would be able to crawl under, he dropped to his hands and knees and began to burrow his way through. Adel cleared the wall within seconds and began to tunnel his way upward like a wild animal desperate for air. After a few seconds, he knew that he must be right below the floor of the bunker. Now it was time to find out if he could breach the floor of the shelter or not. Taking one last deep breath, he pushed upward with all of his might, breaking through the earth and emerging into the bunker.

Chapter Eighteen

The battle outside of the duke's bunker was not going well for Ola, Alsea, and General McLeod's men. The attackers were vastly outnumbered by the Hoyt and the opposing Thornatan soldiers, and the presence of the massive mindless beasts didn't make matters any easier. In the chaos, Ola did not have a good perspective of how poorly the battle was going for them, though he understood the reality of their situation. This wasn't a fight they were going to win; it was a fight to buy time. His sole focus was on the opponent in front of him and then the one who came after that. He had rushed directly toward General Bern as the assault began, hoping to cut the traitorous worm down where he stood. Of course, the cowardly man had slinked his way to the back of the battle, preferring to let other men do the fighting and dying. Ola doubted Bern had ever willingly been in a fight in his entire life. It did not matter. One way or another, the traitor would answer for his crimes before the day was over.

Had Adel found his way into the bunker yet? Ola had no way of knowing for sure, but he felt the young man would have rejoined the battle by now if he had failed to find an alternative way of entering Idanox's shelter. If he had gained entry, Idanox would be dead soon, and hopefully his forces would fall apart without their leader. Idanox was the heart, brain, and soul of the Hoyt, and they could not possibly operate for long without him. Ola had the utmost confidence in his young friend's ability to do what needed to be done once he got inside. He had spent more than a year training for this exact moment, and he would not fail now. Of course, Adel could have been killed or captured trying to get inside the bunker, but Ola refused to entertain such a possibility. They had come so far; they would not falter now.

Ola was not sure how long the fighting went on. Amid the violence and bloodshed, it was impossible to tell. Seconds, minutes, hours—it made no difference. He had to fight until there was nobody left to fight; it was simple enough. He did not keep track of how many enemies he'd cut down, knowing if he paused for even a moment it would likely be the end of him. When one of the massive mindless beasts came for him, he hacked away at it with wild abandon, chopping away its arms and legs in a frenzied counterassault. They would regrow, of course, but that was not Ola's concern at the moment because as soon as it fell to the ground, another was there to engage him.

***

Alsea had been in her fair share of fights, but she had never experienced utter pandemonium quite like this. Did the blood covering her clothing belong to her, a friend, or a foe? Was the pain on the left side of her head a wound, or was it merely her ear throbbing from the continued deafening din of the battle, of the endless clash of metal striking metal? There was a faint metallic taste in her mouth. Had she bitten her tongue, or was it the result of a far more grievous injury inside her body? How many of these soldiers were friends, and which were enemies who would not hesitate to cut the life from her? In the chaos, she couldn't take the time to look for the identifying green armbands. Her mind was flooded with questions, but she knew that if she paused for even a second to seek the answers, she would die.

It seemed as though Adel should have emerged from the bunker by now. How long had he been gone? Five minutes? Ten? There was no way of knowing, but she was anxious. What if he had been hurt or killed? What if they were fighting in vain, their failure inevitable? She should've been with him, just as she had planned to be for this final confrontation with Idanox, but they hadn't had any other choice. She could not allow herself to dwell on these thoughts. There was nothing she could do to help him now. Adel was capable, and he was a survivor. He would put an end to Idanox, and that would be the end of this war. If she wanted to be there to see it, she needed to keep fighting.

A Hoyt fighter came rushing for her, swinging a massive axe. Surmising that he was likely much stronger than she was, Alsea elected to sidestep his attack rather than try to parry the blow. She barely avoided it, colliding with a Thornatan soldier in the process. She was used to fighting in more open areas. These close confines did not suit her fighting style well at all, and they restricted her ability to use her catlike quickness to its fullest potential. The Hoyt was bringing up his axe again, but it was a heavy weapon, and the man wielding it was not fast enough to stop her. She lunged forward, cutting deep into his arm with her sword. The axe tumbled from the man's grip as he howled in pain. Her next attack ran him through completely, and he fell to the ground with his lifeblood rapidly pooling beneath him. She wrenched her sword free, moving on to her next foe while the previous one was still dying on the ground.

Alsea guessed that of the soldiers General McLeod had sent with them, less than half were still standing. Those who remained fought bravely, but they were severely outnumbered and could not hope to hold out much longer. Every minute that passed there were fewer of them, and soon they would be entirely overwhelmed by the Hoyt forces.

***

Ola was aware of nothing except for the opponent in front of him, and then the one who came after that man was struck down. The violence in front of him was all that existed in the world at that moment. He retreated to a dark place within himself, a place he had not visited since his days as a slave in the Ogre Pits. In those days, he had discovered the only way to survive the horrific cruelty and violence he was subjected to daily was to block out everything familiar about the world around him. However, as he cut his way through yet another group of foes, he found that he was looking at a familiar face, and the realization shook him from the dark pit into which he had banished his mind.

To his surprise, Ola had cut his way through the bulk of the enemy forces and reached the walls of the duke's bunker. There was General Bern, the cowardly traitor, hiding as far from the thick of the fighting as possible. He had clearly not counted on Ola fighting his way through, and even Ola was somewhat surprised, yet he had done so nonetheless. He shot the general a ferocious smile as he advanced. Ola was a man who took no pleasure in killing, but this time might be a rare exception.

One of Bern's massive bodyguards shoved the general behind him, shielding the coward with his own body. The other stepped forward to meet Ola's attack head-on.

The Hoyt War

Ola recognized this man; he was the same man who had struck Adel while they had been Bern's prisoners in those cages. He wondered if the man would be as brave now as he had been when hitting a defenseless boy in a cage. Remembering the promise he had made to this man all those days ago, Ola stepped forward without hesitation, sword at the ready.

Surprisingly, the bodyguard attacked first, striking with a misguided bravery Ola had doubted him capable of possessing. The attack was powerful but slow and sloppy, just as Ola had suspected it would be. He parried without difficulty and counterattacked, kicking straight forward and connecting with tremendous force to the bodyguard's stomach. The large man staggered backward from the blistering force of the blow but regained his composure with surprising quickness and came forward once more.

The second attack was just as clumsy as the first, though it had more power behind it. Once again, Ola deflected the blow with minimal effort. It was evident that the bodyguard was used to overpowering opponents with brute force, and against most opponents, this strategy would be sufficient. With each passing second, however, it was obviously dawning on the man that he would not be able to do so with Ola. The bodyguard was incredibly strong, but compared to Ola, he may as well have been a child swinging a stick. Ola struck back, this time with his sword. The bodyguard parried the blow but was rocked backward yet again by Ola's superior strength. For the first time, a flicker of doubt flashed across the bodyguard's face.

This time, Ola did not relent, pressing forward as the bodyguard struggled to regain his footing. He attacked once more, and again the bodyguard managed to block the strike, but the force tore the sword from his hands, sending it clattering to the ground. Ola struck one last time, his sword catching the bodyguard in the torso. It landed with such force that it ripped right through his chain mail before finally coming to a halt deep in his chest. The bodyguard stared up at Ola, his face a sheet of pain and confusion, the color rapidly fading from his skin.

"I told you I would do this," Ola hissed as he wrenched the blade free, allowing the bodyguard to collapse to the ground before stepping around his dying body. "Consider my promise fulfilled."

The second bodyguard took a few steps forward now, though he was in no apparent rush to attack Ola after seeing him dispatch his comrade with such ease. General Bern's eyes were darting in every direction, searching for a path of escape. Determined not to allow the sniveling weasel to slip away, Ola went on the attack once more. The second bodyguard was also immensely strong, and he possessed a fraction more technical skill than his fallen comrade, but not enough to save him. Three precise swings of Ola's sword was all it took to break past the second guard, leaving his body in a bloody mess on the ground.

General Bern met Ola's eyes for the briefest of moments before fleeing once more, this time right into the

heat of the battle, the color fading from his face. Faced
with the choice of facing Ola or racing into a chaotic skirmish, Bern decided the latter was the more appealing prospect. Ola chased after him but was met almost immediately by one of the monstrous beasts. The creature struck
at him with a large axe, and this time even the mighty Ola
struggled to deflect the attack. Before he could counter, the
beast was attacking again, forcing him into a steady backward retreat. Instantly, General Bern was out of sight and
out of mind. All Ola could think about now was surviving
the onslaught of the monster that sought to butcher him
where he stood.

***

Alsea had just finished off yet another foe when the face
of General Bern flashed across her vision for the briefest
of moments. The rage racing through her body at the sight
of the man was palpable, everything he had done to her
friends flashing through her mind. The coward was attempting to flee the battle, and she would not allow that to
happen. He would face the same justice as his new master.
Bounding after him, weaving her way through the crush of
combatants, she sought to cut him off.

She avoided foe after foe, her feet too swift for any
of them to force her into a direct confrontation. Within
seconds, she had planted herself firmly in General Bern's
path, right on the edge of the battle. Their fellow combatants were too preoccupied with the mortal struggle they
found themselves in to pay Alsea and the traitor any

mind. *It's just the two of us, General Bern.* He froze at the sight of her before drawing his sword, a sneer twisting its way across his face. Alsea smirked in satisfaction herself. Apparently, Bern thought a woman would be unable to best him in a fight, and she was all too happy to prove him wrong.

"Leaving so soon, General Bern?" she asked, bringing her own sword up into a defensive position.

"Get out of my way, you stupid little girl. If you have any brains in your head, you will get out of this city and this province before it's too late. Your battle is lost; just look around. You're merely delaying the inevitable by continuing to fight. Why are you so determined to die in vain? Run and hide in the deepest hole you can find, because after I've finished your friends, I will come for you," he spat back defiantly.

"Why are you leaving then? Why not just finish me off right now? Don't you want to enjoy the sweet taste of your heroic victory? I'm sure Idanox will be happy to let you kiss his rings after such a remarkable performance. You have displayed such tactical brilliance here today, General Bern. I'm sure he won't mind what happened to the gates. I'm surprised you aren't there, trying to hold them."

"McLeod and his band of rats are dead, you foolish girl. Your boy's magic trick was impressive, but we slaughtered them like cattle nonetheless. Nobody is coming to save you."

For a moment, Alsea was filled with despair. If McLeod and his forces had all been killed, there was little hope the rest of them would survive this battle. They had been depending on enough men surviving to help them restore order to the city after the death of Idanox. *He's lying*, she told herself. *He's trying to get under your skin and take your mind off the fight. Focus your mind and put an end to this traitor once and for all.*

"Last chance, you insolent little rat. Get out of my way, or a quick death is the best you can hope for," Bern was saying.

Alsea did not bother with a response this time, instead relaxing her stance and bracing herself for the wild charge she knew would come. Come it did, a few seconds later, General Bern screaming in rage as he bore down on her. His sword was racing in with crushing force, but it never found its mark. She had found that men with the temperament of General Bern were always predictable in their attacks. She easily sidestepped his wild bull rush, kicking out with one leg as he passed. Her shin caught him under the ribs, and while his chain mail absorbed most of the impact, it still knocked the clumsy man off-balance, denying him an opportunity to flee. By the time he had regained his balance, she was already advancing on him.

Bern swung again, more wildly this time, a desperate attempt to halt Alsea's advance. The blow was so wild that she did not even have to evade it. She simply continued walking straight toward him as it whistled harmlessly past her right ear. A quick slash of her sword opened a deep cut on Bern's sword arm, causing the blade to fall to the ground as its wielder howled in pain. For a man of his military rank, Bern was far from a gifted warrior. *No wonder he needed bodyguards*, Alsea thought, wondering what had happened to them. Her moment of distraction cost her. More desperate than ever, Bern charged at her once more. This time, she did not react quickly enough, making the grave mistake of underestimating her disarmed foe. He slammed into her with his shoulder and drove her to the ground. His large frame crashed down on top of her. The impact pushed the air from her body as the entirety of his weight landed on her chest.

Alsea leaned back in revulsion, the general's vile face hovering only inches from her own. Her sword arm was trapped beneath his body, and she could not bring it to bear. Instead, she struck with the palm of her other hand, smashing into Bern's face and shattering his nose. He howled in pain once more, blood spurting from his nose. But this time, he did not give up any ground, pressing his weight down on her even more forcefully. One of his hands found her throat and began to squeeze.

Alsea struck with her free hand again and again, slamming Bern repeatedly in his wounded face. Blood gushed out more rapidly than ever, drenching them both, but he would not release the viselike grip that he had secured on her throat. It was becoming more difficult to breathe with each passing second. Alsea knew she had to end this fight immediately if she wanted to escape with her life. Bern was in a crazed rage, and her attacks were no longer affecting him. Her free hand reached out in desperation, trying to shift some of his weight off her, grasping for anything she could find to use as a weapon.

Just as she was losing hope, her vision beginning to blur, her hand grazed against something hard, something metal. Grasping it, she realized it was a dagger in Bern's belt. He had not thought to draw it and finish her quickly, or perhaps he had wanted the pleasure of watching her die slowly. She wrenched it free as his twisted, enraged face drew closer to her own, blood falling from his broken nose all over her. He was too close to her now for her to bring the dagger against him, his chubby neck pressed too tight against her for her to find it with the blade. She didn't have enough leverage to drive it through his chain mail. Desperate, knowing she had only seconds before her world went dark, she used the last weapon she had available to her: spitting directly into Bern's face, right into his eyes. He recoiled in disgust for the briefest moment, never loosening his grip on her throat, but the moment of distraction was all she needed. As soon as his head jerked backward, she struck, plunging his own dagger straight into his eye socket.

Bern's grip still did not loosen immediately, but as he began to collapse, Alsea was able to release her throat with her free hand, gasping for breath as she did so. Straining, she was able to shift General Bern's still-twitching bulky body off her and climb to her feet. There was no time to regain her breath; no sooner had she found her feet than a Hoyt fighter was bearing down on her.

Fighting through the pain and numbness in her sword arm, she parried the Hoyt's attack. Her fingers still tingling from the weight of Bern's body on her arm, the impact nearly tore the blade from her hand. Not hesitating, not wanting to give the man another opportunity to attack, she slipped under his guard, her sword opening a deep gash in the man's torso. No sooner was he falling to the ground than another was there to take his place. Once again, Alsea was thrust into the heart of the battle. Within seconds, General Bern's defeated body was a distant memory in the dust only a few feet behind her.

***

The beast was stronger than Ola, though it did not possess his skill. It seemed to matter little, though. No matter how many wounds he managed to open on its body, it continued to press forward. When he took off its right arm, it picked up the axe in its left hand and continued to attack. When he drove his sword deep into its chest, the beast bellowed and pressed on. When he slashed a grievous wound open across its face, it showed not the slightest hint of pain. No matter the severity of the injury he managed to inflict, the creature never slowed for even a moment.

Fueled by desperation, Ola charged the beast in a final attempt to stop its maddened killing spree. He hacked and hammered with his sword at any part of its body that he could reach. The aggression of his attack cost him, his sword lodging so deep inside the monster's shoulder that he could not wrench it free before the beast counterattacked, swinging with the axe. It caught him with the side of the blade, fortunately not cutting him open but still knocking Ola weaponless to the ground.

He found his feet quickly, a veteran of more fights than he could count. He had seen enough fights in his life to know how fast things could go wrong for you once you found yourself disarmed. His sword was still lodged in the monster's shoulder, and it was already advancing on him once more. With no weapon to use, Ola charged the beast with nothing but his own body. He wrapped his arms around its waist and dragged it to the ground with all the strength he could muster.

As they clattered to the earth, Ola's eyes darted in every direction, searching for any weapon they could find, as the beast thrashed to free itself of him. He found one at last, a heavy cobblestone that had been dislodged from the street lying just within reach. Snatching it up, he raised it high and then brought it down onto the beast's head with as much force as he could muster. Once, twice, three times, he struck as hard as he possibly could. The creature continued to strain, so Ola continued to swing the stone, crashing down on its head with bone-crushing force each time, losing counts of how many blows he delivered. He didn't stop swinging until the beast finally struggled no more.

Ola staggered back to his feet, his wounds aching

in protest. His ribs felt broken from the impact of the axe, but he was not likely to find a healer anytime soon. He had no choice but to keep fighting. The battle continued to rage on all around him, but time seemed to move more slowly for Ola as he reached for the pommel of his sword and wrenched it free of the beast's shoulder, its leatherlike skin resisting him all the while. He stood straight, his eyes casting about for a new opponent. He had just begun to advance on a nearby group of Hoyt fighters when a spear plunged into his back.

***

Alsea was aware of nothing but the sound of crashing metal and the stench of blood in the air. She knew that she was wounded, but how many wounds and how severe they might be was a mystery to her. She did not know how many Thornatan soldiers still fought beside them. For all she knew, everyone else was dead and she was the last holdout, fighting desperately against impossible odds. Her focus was entirely stolen by one foe and then the next. She did not know if this lasted for a minute or several hours. All concept of time was lost to her.

The noise around Alsea seemed to be growing louder, which confused her. With as many men as had died in the battle, there should've been less noise, not more. *Wait, was that an Imperial Army uniform?* It dawned on her suddenly: General McLeod and his forces had breached the outer walls and come to their aid! In her struggle for survival, General Bern's lie had completely slipped her mind. McLeod and his forces had not been destroyed at the gates, as the traitorous snake would have had her believe. A moment later, her theory was confirmed as General McLeod's voice rang out above the deafening din of combat.

"Lay down your weapons! The battle is lost. You are outnumbered and outmatched. Any man who lays down his arms will be given a fair trial. Any man who wants to keep fighting will die right here and now. It's your choice, but I, for one, have had enough of this bloodshed."

Alsea readied herself for more fighting, doubting any would accept this offer. To her shock, several black-clad Hoyt fighters dropped their weapons, expressions of shocked defeat upon their faces. Several Thornatan soldiers followed suit, and soon weapons were falling to the cobblestone street left and right. Alsea dared not believe her eyes. Could the battle really be over?

A flood of relief overcoming her, she spun to search for Ola in the crowd. To her surprise, she did not see him immediately. His towering figure was usually easy to spot, even in the thickest of crowds. At last, she found him, and her joy turned to horror as she realized he was kneeling on one knee. She rushed toward him, her panic only growing when she saw the spear protruding from his back.

"Ola, stay still. I will find a healer!" she said as she arrived at his side, reaching out to help him lower himself more gently into a sitting position. He could hardly hold himself up, and most of his weight shifted onto her shoulders. She eased him to the ground as gently as she could, barely able to support his incredible weight.

"It's no use," Ola rasped. Alsea had never heard his voice so hoarse.

Now that she was right beside him, she could see he was right. The wound from the spear would have already killed almost any other man by now. There was no way to remove the weapon without doing more harm than good. Examining him further, she found that was only the beginning. The more she studied his body, the more wounds she found. It was shocking to her that he was still alive at this point. She looked around in amazement at the ogre's fallen opponents, strewn across the ground around him. There must've been at least two dozen of them, if not more. One of Idanox's mindless beasts lay closest to him, its head an unrecognizable mess.

"We won, Ola," she reassured him, taking his hand in hers. "We've won, and we could not have done it without you."

"It was all worth it. When you go back to the Temple of the Rawl, thank Elim and the others for me. They gave me a chance to have an actual life. If not for them, I would have died years ago in a slave pit so that a wealthy man could turn a profit. I was able to be free for many years, and words cannot express how fortunate I feel for that. Thank Adel for me too. The two of you were the finest friends a great dumb brute like me could have ever asked for. Look after him, Alsea. He will blame himself for this; you know how he is. He will need you. His life won't be an easy one. I'm sure you know it as well as I do. I wish I could be there to watch over him, but I know you will do so in my place." Ola's voice was more pained by the second, and tears flooded Alsea's eyes. He would be gone any second now, and there was so much she needed to say to him.

"I will, Ola. Thank you, my friend. Thank you for everything. I would have died alone in the wild as a little girl if not for you. I owe you my life, and I will never forget that. Everything I have ever accomplished or ever will is because of you and the lessons you have taught me," she said, fighting to keep the grief from her voice, trying to be strong for him as he had been for her so many times. She took his head in her arms, holding him close.

It was over a moment later, and Ola was gone. Alsea gently closed his eyes and rose to her feet, fighting back against the tears that were streaming down her face. She realized that General McLeod had quietly approached from behind. If there was an inch of McLeod's body that was not covered in blood and gore, she couldn't see it. He looked down at Ola's body, and Alsea was surprised to see that the hardened general appeared to be fighting back tears of his own.

"I'm so sorry, Alsea. We fought our way here as fast as we could, but they resisted us every step of the way. If we had arrived sooner . . ."

"It's not your fault, General McLeod," she cut him off. She would not allow him to take the blame for Ola's death. "This was the doing of Idanox and the Hoyt, nobody else."

"Speaking of Idanox, what do you think is going on in there? I don't see Adel. I can only assume he went in there after Idanox?" General McLeod asked, gesturing toward the bunker.

Alsea had momentarily forgotten about the bunker in the depths of her despair. How long had it been since Adel had left to find a way into the building? It could have been minutes or hours for all she knew. What had happened inside? Shouldn't he have come out by now? Idanox was the one responsible for Ola's death and the deaths of so many others, and he needed to answer for that. If Adel hadn't already made him do so, she would. Picking up her sword, she started toward the bunker door. She would batter it open herself if that was what it took to get justice for Ola, for everyone who had died this day.

"Let's go find out."

Chapter Nineteen

Adel pushed his way through the floor of the bunker, scrambling to find his footing on the uncertain ground. He was covered in dirt and mud from crawling through his makeshift passageway, but he paid it no mind. As he rose to his feet, he looked around, taking in the scene, his hand immediately reaching for the pommel of his sword. He had no idea what awaited him, but he knew he needed to be ready for anything. It was unlikely Idanox would be sitting alone in this bunker without a final line of defense.

The bunker was made up of a solitary room and was relatively unadorned. A few torches lining the walls provided a small amount of light, and a lone chair sat at the far end of the room. Sitting in that chair was a lean man dressed all in Hoyt black with a few pieces of gaudy jewelry and a makeshift crown resting atop his head. A self-satisfied smirk was stretched across the man's face, not dissimilar from the one Adel had often imagined would be there. There was little doubt as to this man's identity, but he spoke up to verify Adel's suspicions anyway.

"Hello there, young man. Welcome to my bunker. My name is Idanox, and I am the leader of the Hoyt and the duke of Thornata. I have wanted to meet with you for quite some time. I am happy to finally be able to greet you in the flesh. It's a shame we have not crossed paths sooner. So much death and destruction could have been avoided. There is much we have to discuss, you and I."

"My name is Adel. I've wanted to meet you as well, but I don't think you will like how this meeting ends," Adel replied, drawing his sword and walking toward Idanox without hesitation.

Idanox seemed relatively unconcerned, smiling and tapping his fingers on his chair as Adel approached as though he had not a care in the world. His calmness was somewhat unnerving, but Adel refused to halt in the face of his misgivings. It was time to finally put an end to this. Leaving all his men outside had been a miscalculation on the part of Idanox. The Hoyt leader was about to realize that. Adel took note of the torches mounted on the wall, reassuring himself that he could use the power of the Rawl to utilize them as weapons if the need arose.

"Please, Adel, there is no need for hostilities between us. It's good to finally be able to call you by your name. Actually, it's a funny story; all my sources inside the Thornatan Army kept giving me different names for you, but I don't think any of them ever got it right. Sheathe your sword, and we can discuss our differences like gentlemen. I can understand you may have certain frustrations with me, but there is no reason that we cannot resolve them in a civilized manner," Idanox said as Adel drew close.

"Don't worry, Idanox. This won't take long," Adel spat in response, eager to sink his blade into the arrogant man and end this conflict once and for all. Idanox wore a sword at his belt but had made no move to draw it. Was he just going to sit there and allow himself to be killed without a struggle? He must've realized by now that he could not talk his way out of this. Was he such a coward that he would not even fight to try to save his own life?

"Very well." Idanox sighed. "Let's teach this little boy some manners, shall we?"

The air behind the Hoyt leader seemed to shimmer, stopping Adel in his tracks. What was happening? The thin air was rippling like the gently rolling waters of a mountain lake. To his horror, the shimmer began to take shape, two monstrous forms materializing behind Idanox. Two beasts nearly identical to those stationed outside appeared as if from nowhere, massive broadswords in each hand.

Adel immediately reached out with the power of

the Rawl, searching for the flames in the torches. The Hoyt leader was overconfident in the ability of his mindless monsters. He could burn these creatures to ash in moments and then deal with Idanox. But even as he was thinking it, he was finding something was wrong. His power could not find the torches. He looked to the wall, and sure enough, there were the flames. But his power was unable to reach them. He had never experienced anything like this before. How could this be happening? It was as though somebody had erected an invisible wall between him and his powers, and they were not responding to him.

"What's the matter, boy? Are things not working out the way you expect them to? I'm sure you never expected such a thing could happen. It's a rather unpleasant feeling, isn't it?" said a voice from the far corner of the room.

The air seemed to shimmer once more, and this time a man appeared, clad in dark red robes and holding a long wooden staff. *A mage*, Adel thought, the truth dawning on him. It was all beginning to make sense now. This must've been the man responsible for creating these monsters. It was a feat Idanox was not capable of performing on his own. Adel took a cautious step back, his sword coming up defensively, shifting his eyes continuously from Idanox to the beasts and then to the mage. The mage was somehow preventing him from using the power of the Rawl, something he would never have thought possible.

"Are you sure it's working, Srenpe?" Idanox asked

the man, never taking his eyes off Adel.

"It's working all right. Your power isn't working for you, is it, Adel? You're trying; I can tell you are. I'm terribly sorry about that. There's no need to worry yourself about it. It's just a precaution. We wouldn't want you to go and do anything rash, would we? You still possess your power, of course. I've merely dulled your senses a bit, so you may find you have a hard time summoning the power of the Rawl. Fear not, though; I have not interfered with your ability to feel pain, should you find yourself in need of that," the red-robed mage explained, pacing around the room before coming to a halt directly behind Adel.

Adel tried again and again to summon his power, but it failed to respond. He still had the sword, but he knew that if he made a move toward Idanox, the beasts would step forward to defend him. His skills with the blade had advanced considerably, but he did not harbor any delusions about how such a direct assault would end for him. He lowered his sword ever so slightly, signaling a willingness to hear the Hoyt leader out, though he had no interest in anything Idanox had to say. In truth, his mind was racing, searching for a new path forward. *Let Idanox talk*, he thought to himself, *while you try to find a way to turn the tables on him. You've come too far to lose now. It won't end like this.*

"There you go, Adel. There's no need for any violence between us. In fact, I was hoping we could eventually become friends, you and I. I'm sure you are skeptical; it's understandable. To be perfectly honest, I would consider you a fool if you were not. But just give me a little bit of time, and I know I can help you see reason. Do you like my guards? Srenpe here created them for me. Magnificent beasts, aren't they?" Idanox asked, talking as though they were old friends sitting down for a drink. "They will obey any order I give them without question. Isn't that amazing? It has made my life immeasurably easier."

"They are impressive specimens, but not quite invincible, as the first one you sent after me discovered," Adel shot back.

"My apologies for that nastiness, my young man. You must think so terribly of me, and I will admit that I have brought much of that upon myself. I am human, and I can err just as easily as any other man. You must understand, I had come to believe I would never have an opportunity to speak with you face-to-face. But I could not allow you to continue your campaign with McLeod, butchering my men at every opportunity. You proved to be quite a formidable adversary, albeit a misguided one. You required a more forceful response than my men could provide. Make no mistake, I am pleased you survived so we can have this little chat."

Adel did not trust a word Idanox said; in fact, he was hardly paying attention at all. Every ounce of inner focus he could muster was focused on attempting to summon his power, but his efforts were continuing to prove fruitless. The man called Srenpe had placed some type of block on him, and he could not extend his powers in any way. He locked eyes with the mage, finding a malicious grin staring back at him. Srenpe could tell precisely what he was trying to do, but it did not seem to worry the mage in the slightest. It was as though he could see the flames in the torches but his power could not. No matter how he begged or pleaded for it to come to his defense, it would not respond.

"I suppose I am rambling," Idanox said, interrupting Adel's train of thought. "I respect you, Adel. You have fought valiantly for a cause you believe in. I admire such devotion, even if I believe your cause to be a false one. You have been deceived about a great many things, but this is not your fault. You are still a young man, Adel. There is still so much you can learn. You have shown courage and dedication unlike any I have ever seen. You have my admiration and utmost respect for that. I think we could work quite well together if you are willing to hear me out."

"You say I have been deceived, that your cause is the righteous one. Can I ask you a question?" Adel knew he needed to keep Idanox talking. The second Idanox believed the discussion to be over, it would be the end for him.

"Certainly," Idanox replied, taken aback by his request.

"The first time I encountered a Hoyt fighter, I was a deckhand on a shipping barge. Hoyt archers opened fire on us from a cliff in the Bonner Mountains, killing several friends of mine. They never spoke a word to us. They opened fire without warning. Their friends downriver talked to us, though, and they explained that they wanted to rob us. When we refused to give up our cargo, they opened fire as well, killing more of my friends. Can you please explain the righteousness of the actions your men took on that day? Can you explain how they were working toward bettering the lives of the common people of Thornata? After all, that is your goal, is it not, Idanox?" Adel's voice was cold and hard as steel, his eyes staring at Idanox with icy intent. He would find a way to kill this man, he promised himself, even if it cost him his own life.

"I am deeply sorry for the loss of your comrades, Adel. You may not believe that, but it is the truth. You must understand," Idanox began before Adel cut him off.

"You seem to enjoy telling me what I must understand. You've used those words quite a few times now. I will decide what I must understand, Idanox. Quit wasting my time and answer my question. What was the justification for your men murdering my friends?"

"Sacrifices must sometimes be made in the name of the greater good. The Hoyt are the architects of the greater good, Adel; you must understand this. Your friends were the sacrifices that were required. It's as simple as that. It's not an easy thing for you to hear, I'm sure, but it's the hard truth. Tell me, would it be more merciful to allow the men, women, and children of Thornata to continue suffering in poverty and hunger under the rule of the former duke?"

"As opposed to suffering under your rule? Because that is so much more humane, isn't it, Idanox? You are such a benevolent and just ruler, aren't you? I've seen your rule firsthand, and I've seen what you and your men do to people. You are trying to sway me to your cause because you want to use my powers to solidify your own position. You can try to dress it up all you want. I can see through your lies. How stupid do you think I am? You won't succeed, so you may as well quit wasting your breath."

A plan was finally coming together in his mind. He would only have one chance. He would have to be perfect, though the idea was far from it. Several possible complications were totally beyond his control. But there was no point in stalling any further. People were dying outside, and he had to act. He had no choice but to make his peace with the fact that his plan could fail spectacularly, resulting in his inevitable death.

"I'm sorry to hear that, Adel. Just know that your death will serve no purpose. We could have achieved great things together, you and I. Instead, I will go on as duke of Thornata, ushering this province into a new age of prosperity. Everything you have fought to preserve will be burned to ashes. Your name will be forgotten, your friends and allies buried at the bottom of the ocean beside you. You will die with your life having no meaning," Idanox gloated, raising one hand to signal the beasts behind him.

Adel was already moving, his sword coming back up. The Rawl was not available to him; he would need to use his own body and mind to overcome this. He broke into a sprint, running as fast as his feet could carry him. He reached his target, his sword coming down lightning fast with as much force as he could muster, not at Idanox, but rather at Srenpe. The mage was the one blocking his powers, and the towering beasts did not stand guard over him. Perhaps striking down the mage would remove the block Srenpe had placed on his ability to use the Rawl. Once his powers were restored, he could eliminate the beasts in short order and then finally deal with Idanox. To Adel's horror, however, his blade seemed to strike an invisible wall as it drew close to Srenpe, glancing away harmlessly as the mage began to laugh in delight.

"Do you think I was born yesterday, boy? Did you honestly think it would be that easy to strike me down? You have guts; I'll give you that. But I have found that brave men usually end up as dead brave men," Srenpe mocked, laughing harder as Adel repeatedly tried and failed to cut through the magical barrier that surrounded him. His sword was met by an invisible block each time, just like the power of the Rawl. "Don't kill him. Disable him and make it hurt. Remove his arms and legs if you must. Don't worry, Adel, I can keep you alive long enough for you to tell us what we need to know."

Adel turned toward the beasts; both were coming toward him now. He could not beat them, he knew that, but he would fight them to his last breath nonetheless. Maybe if he was quick enough, he could dart past them and take one swing at Idanox. He thought for a moment of the first beast he had encountered and the relentless abandon with which it had pursued him, slaughtering everything that dared stand in its path. That was what he faced now, a mindless killer that would let nothing stand in its way, only now there were two of them and his friends were not here to help. At least Srenpe only wanted him disabled for the time being. They would not fight to kill. But why? Realizing he had just stumbled upon a possible solution, Adel snapped out of his memories and into action.

Srenpe had warded himself against Adel's sword, but how thorough were those wards? There was only one way to find out. Throwing caution to the winds, Adel spun on the spot, swinging his left fist with all his might. To his delight, no ward sprang up to block it, and it caught Srenpe square in the face. Srenpe had thought only to defend himself against weapons. Blood spurted from the mage's nose, and he howled in pain. Srenpe stumbled backward, trying to bring his staff to bear, but Adel was already attacking again, swinging his fist as hard as he possibly could once more. His next punch connected hard with Srenpe's mouth, and Adel felt a wave of relief wash through him as he heard the satisfying crunch of breaking bones.

He lunged forward, seizing Srenpe by the front of his robes. Spinning around, he shoved the mage with all his might, straight at the creatures coming forward with single-minded determination to kill him. They were mindless animals who would eliminate anything in their path without a second thought. At the moment, their own master stood in their way. Adel could only hope he had injured Srenpe's jaw sufficiently enough that the mage would be unable to rescind his own order.

The first beast lashed out at Srenpe with its broadsword, trying to swat him aside, but the weapon glanced harmlessly off the mage's ward. The creature swung again, roaring in rage, and then again, the sword crashing down on the invisible shield with crushing force. It's fellow soon joined in, both swords hacking desperately at the man who had created them, the man who was now planted in between them and their prey, believing him to be standing in their way. Srenpe tried to cry out but was only able to produce an incoherent gasp. The creatures paid this no mind, continuing to relentlessly hammer away at his wards.

"Stop! Stop attacking him!" Idanox cried out, realizing Srenpe could not speak in his own defense.

If the monsters had heard Idanox, they did not show it, continuing their relentless attack on Srenpe. Just as Adel had suspected, Srenpe had ensured his creations would follow his own orders above all others. How else could he be sure Idanox would not be able to use them against him? Idanox had been arrogant enough to believe he was the true master of these creatures, just as he thought he deserved to be the duke of Thornata. In the end, the Hoyt leader's arrogance would prove to be his undoing. Srenpe was trying to yell something, but his words were indecipherable, coming from his badly broken jaw.

Again and again, the beasts struck at their master. Srenpe fell to his knees, his staff raised above his head, trying with all his might to maintain the wards that shielded him. But he could not hold out forever. Adel knew he would exhaust himself sooner or later. It was something Adel himself had experienced countless times when wielding the Rawl. The use of such power took its toll on the user, and it was no different for Srenpe. Any mage could only hold out for so long, no matter how powerful. The end came sooner than Adel had expected, a blow from each creature breaking through the magical barrier simultaneously, cutting the life from Srenpe in an instant.

Both beasts now turned their attention toward Adel, their intended victim, as their master fell to the ground in a bloody heap. He was already preparing his attack, reaching out for the torches on the wall, hoping his power would come to his aid. To his shock, the power still did not respond. He spun to look at the torches to find them fading from sight. Within seconds, the only light in the room emanated from two narrow windows high above their heads. *They were fakes! Srenpe wasn't blocking my powers. There never were any torches in the first place!* Seconds later, both beasts crumpled to the ground beside the mage, the magic that had sustained them dying along with their creator.

There were a few moments of deathly silence in the bunker. Idanox and Adel were staring at each other, one with deadly intent, the other searching for a way out of his predicament. Idanox climbed slowly to his feet with his hands held out wide. He smiled at Adel, not the same condescending smirk as before, but rather as though he were pleading with an old friend to see reason.

"You are a remarkable young man indeed, Adel," he began, taking a small step toward the door and utterly failing to keep it inconspicuous. "Srenpe was a powerful mage, but his powers were inconsequential compared to yours. I profess myself amazed at your abilities. I knew you were an impressive young man, but I never imagined you could possess such cunning. I am now more certain than ever that you would be a fine addition to our ranks."

Noting Idanox's continued moves toward the door, Adel stepped forward, moving purposefully to block the other's path. There were no beasts to protect him, no mage to save him, and this reality seemed to be registering in the mind of the Hoyt leader. It was just the two of them now. It was a moment Adel had hoped for ever since the day he had witnessed Donil's lifeless body tumbling from the barge while he could only look on helplessly. Now Idanox knew how he had felt that day, knew how so many of the people of Thornata had felt under his rule. He now understood what it meant to feel helpless.

"Don't be stupid, Adel. How will killing me benefit you in any way?" Idanox tried to reason. "Just take a moment and think this through please. I am rich and powerful. You are already very powerful, and I can make you very rich as well. Think about the life you could live, Adel. A life of luxury for you and your friends. I will pardon them of their crimes; of course I will. You can all go free with a wagon full of gold within the hour if you wish. Go where you wish, do as you please; none will interfere. None of my men will ever pursue you again. Name your price, Adel. Fifty thousand? One hundred thousand? Just say it, and I will make it so."

"You must understand, Idanox," Adel began, mocking the Hoyt leader's oft-used quote. "I did not come looking for you in search of riches or glory. I did not seek you out to benefit myself. I came here for the good of the people you are oppressing. I came here to serve justice in the name of those who have died and suffered in your name. I suppose you could say I came here to serve the greater good. We have something in common after all, don't we? So, draw that sword if you want to try to escape with your life, because one of us is not leaving this bunker alive. If you don't have the guts to fight for yourself, then just shut up and die already."

Adel walked toward Idanox deliberately; he was done talking. Idanox smiled for a moment longer, then, apparently not thinking of a better plea, drew his sword. He moved into a defensive posture similar to one Adel might have used in the early days of his training with Ola. Adel smirked. As he had suspected, Idanox was no fighter. One glance at Idanox's feet told him the Hoyt leader had done a poor job of balancing his weight. This was a beginner's mistake, one that would allow him to be easily knocked off-balance. It was a mistake Adel had made numerous times himself until Ola had beaten it out of him. Adel doubted whether Idanox had ever allowed anyone to teach him a thing. His real power had been his ability to manipulate others to fight for him. But there was nobody left for him to deceive. There were only the two of them, and Adel was done listening to the bile pouring from his mouth.

To his surprise, the Hoyt leader attacked first, lunging forward as Adel drew close. He swung twice, his attacks wild and desperate. Adel slipped the first attack and parried the second with relative ease. Idanox's technique was just as sloppy as his footwork. Idanox scrambled a few steps backward, trying to buy himself time to attack again, but Adel was on top of him immediately, swinging his sword repeatedly, putting the Hoyt leader on his heels. He pressed forward, not willing to give the snake even a second to gather himself.

Idanox managed to sloppily parry or avoid several attacks, scrambling backward the entire time, but Adel's sword inevitably found its mark, finally opening a deep cut on the Hoyt leader's inner thigh. Idanox let out a rather satisfying yelp of pain before stumbling back, looking down at his leg in shock. The sight of the hated man's blood sent a rush of euphoria through Adel. This was it; he was finally about to put an end to this war.

"Have you never seen your own blood before, Idanox? It's not a nice feeling, is it? Don't worry, it will all be over shortly," Adel jabbed, moving forward once more.

Adel continued pressing Idanox backward, the

Hoyt leader now staggering backward on his wounded leg. There was no path for Idanox to reach the bunker's door that did not go through Adel. He could only retreat deeper into the room. Adel braced himself, preparing for one final desperate assault. He was certain Idanox, realizing he was beaten, would come at him in a final reckless charge. It did not come; instead, Idanox hurled his sword wildly in Adel's direction and made a break for the remainder of the tunnel Adel had used to enter the bunker.

Adel avoided the clumsily thrown blade easily, reaching out with the Rawl to ensure the tunnel shifted sufficiently the prevent Idanox's escape. The power responded to him at once, there for him, just as it always had been. The Hoyt leader clawed frantically at the dirt with his fingers, searching for an escape, but found his efforts more futile with each passing second. Adel had already directed the power of the Rawl, hardening the earth and ensuring there would be no path to freedom. Disgusted, Adel walked up behind Idanox, seized him by the back of his neck, and dragged him to his feet.

By the time Adel saw the dagger, it was almost too late. His head moved back instinctively at the flash of metal in the dimly lit room, but the blade still grazed his face, opening a small cut below his left eye. He flung Idanox to the floor, but the other man sprang right back to his feet like a predator that could smell the blood of its prey, desperate to go in for the kill, lunging at the first sign of weakness. Idanox made one last charge with the bloody dagger clutched in his right hand, but Adel was ready. His first attack removed that hand and the dagger clutched in it. A split second later, his second took Idanox's head clean off.

Adel stood in silence for a moment, staring down at the bloody husk that was all that remained of Idanox. He had yearned for this moment for so long, but now that it was here, it felt hollow and empty. Idanox was dead, and justice had been served for the innocent lives he had stolen. But it would not bring them back, would not ease the pain of their loss. The Hoyt may have been defeated, but the wounds they had inflicted upon Thornata would take years, if not decades, to heal.

The pain from the cut that Idanox had opened under his eye set in a moment later, the rush of battle wearing off. He raised his hand to his face and brought it away to survey the extent of the damage. Bloody, but not as severe as he had feared. There would likely be a scar, but he had escaped this war with only minor injuries, something so many others could not claim.

Sheathing his sword, Adel made his way to the door of the bunker. He was not sure if the battle outside still raged on. If it did, he could only hope that word of Idanox's death would bring it to an end. If not, he would call on his power once more and fight until it was over. Anybody who wanted to continue to fight on in the name of their fallen leader would meet his fate. This war would end before the day was over. Too many had given their lives for him to accept any other result.

Sliding open the series of latches that secured the bunker door, he threw it open and stepped out into the blinding sunlight.

Chapter Twenty

The brightness of the sun momentarily blinded Adel, his eyes blinking furiously against the midday light as he stepped out of the bunker. He realized at that moment that the battle must have raged for hours. To him, it had felt like both an eternity and no time at all. It felt as though they had just passed under the water gate a few minutes ago as the sun was beginning to creep into view on the eastern horizon. Yet, at the same time, it felt like his desperate search for a path into the bunker had happened a lifetime ago, though his mind told him the confrontation within had lasted only a few minutes.

The Hoyt War

As he tried to blink his eyes open against the sun, he realized how quiet it was. The battle outside of the bunker must've been over. The screams of anger and pain and the clash of metal on metal had all stopped. Had his friends been defeated? He moved into a defensive crouch, bracing for a possible attack by Hoyt forces. He did not know how much strength he had left, but if needed, he would give every last ounce of it to finish the Hoyt. A few seconds passed, and nobody seemed to be coming forward to attack him.

When his eyes finally adjusted to the light, Alsea was the first person he saw. She was covered in blood from head to toe, her skin and clothing barely visible. Her beautiful face was a mask of blood and horror, and her eyes betrayed the fact that she had seen things she would likely never be able to forget. She was only a few feet from the door, her sword still in hand, but it fell to the ground as soon as she saw him. She rushed forward, wrapping her arms around him. Adel returned her embrace, feeling soft sobs emanating from her chest as he did. She clung to him as a frightened child might cling to a parent, and he knew that the battle outside of the bunker must have been far more traumatic than the one inside. He ran his fingers through her hair, realizing as he did so that they were caked in blood that he could only presume had belonged to Idanox or Srenpe. *In the old stories about the glorious wars of the past, they never mention all the blood*, he thought to himself.

"It's over, Alsea. Idanox is dead. It's finally over. It's all going to be okay," he whispered gently, trying to soothe her.

"Adel, I'm so sorry." She sobbed into his chest, never looking him directly in the eye.

"It's all going to be all right, Alsea. The war will be over. We won't have to fight anymore," Adel tried to reassure her, but he could feel her head shaking.

"It's not that. Adel, it's Ola."

Adel looked up, searching for the ogre. Oddly enough, he did not spot him. Ola was always such an imposing figure that he stood out in any crowd. After a few seconds of scanning, he did spot General McLeod, leading him to assume the attack on the gate must have been successful. McLeod must have come to their aid, allowing them to defeat the force Idanox had staged outside of the bunker. He scanned more, but still no sign of Ola. Had the ogre gone off scouting the streets for hiding Hoyt fighters? It was the type of thing he would do, but it did not feel right to Adel. Would Ola walk away without knowing what was happening inside the bunker? *No*, he thought, *Ola would have been kicking down the door, assuming I was in trouble, that I needed his help*. Why was Alsea so distraught? His heart already knew the answer, but his brain was refusing to catch up, not wanting to confront the horrible truth.

"Alsea, what happened? Where is Ola? You can tell me. It's okay," he said, the truth beginning to dawn on him, though he still refused to accept it until he heard it from her lips. It wasn't possible; it could not have happened.

"Adel, you know how he is. He always puts himself where the fighting is at its worst. If it weren't for him, we would all be dead right now. He killed one of those monsters with a cobblestone. He cut down more of the Hoyt and enemy soldiers than we can count; the bodies were all around him. But he didn't make it out of the fight, Adel. He was just too badly wounded. I'm so sorry, but he's gone."

Adel's legs gave out on him, though he was scarcely aware of it. One moment he was standing, the next he was sitting on the crumbled remnants of the cobblestone street. Alsea fell to the ground beside him, her sobs no longer subdued, the tears flowing freely down her face now.

War was a dangerous endeavor; Adel had known this from the beginning. But Ola had always been so strong, so steadfast, he had never truly thought it possible that his friend may not survive. He had been sure that nothing could kill Ola, that the mighty ogre was too skilled and too durable for anyone to overcome him. Now Ola was gone forever, just like so many others who had died for the greedy ambitions of one man. At that moment, Adel wished he could kill Idanox all over again. He wished he could spend the rest of his life killing Idanox over and over for all the suffering he had caused.

The weight of it all fell on Adel like a boulder. There were no tears, though it was not due to any sort of refusal to cry, but rather from the shock that would not allow him to register what he had been told entirely. His mind was racing, and he was trying to accept the truth while part of his brain was still in denial. General McLeod had made his way over and was standing in silence, allowing Adel and Alsea to share their grief in peace.

Adel didn't know if minutes or hours passed before he was finally able to climb back to his feet. As soon as he did, he asked to be taken to see Ola. The Imperial captain Thad Dunstan stood vigil over Ola's body along with two of his men. They had covered his friend with a sheet but lifted it upon Adel's request. He was unsurprised to find his dearest friend covered in more wounds than he could count. The expressions on Ola's face had always been a challenge for him to read, but here, in death, it seemed peaceful, perhaps more peaceful than he had ever seen it in life. The ogre's life of battle after battle was over, and he could finally rest. At least that was what Adel tried to tell himself, though the reassurances did not stop him from feeling empty inside. He could not help but think if he had managed to kill Idanox a few minutes sooner, Ola might still be alive.

After some discussion, it was agreed they would build a pyre for Ola, as ogres preferred. Adel insisted on helping to build it himself, refusing to pay any heed to the protests of Alsea or General McLeod that others could handle it. He was injured, but in the wake of Ola's death, he hardly noticed his wounds. He worked all afternoon alongside a handful of Thornatan and Imperial soldiers, painstakingly constructing every piece of the pyre by hand. By nightfall, the pyre was complete, and Ola was sent to his final resting place. Every soldier still able to stand came to send him off to the next life, their spears raised in salute to his sacrifice. It was a powerful moment, so many men who would have assumed Ola to be nothing more than a bloodthirsty beast such a short time ago now honoring him as the hero he truly was.

***

The days that followed were a blur for Adel, a whirlwind of grief, relief, confusion, and guilt. It did not feel right that he had survived when Ola and so many others had not. He kept reliving the final confrontation with Idanox and Srenpe in his head. When the Rawl had not been there to save him, it was the skills Ola had taught him that had allowed him to survive the terrible struggle. Not only the skills with the blade, but the ability to think fast under pressure, the value of being able to improvise in stressful situations. Had it not been for his training with Ola, he would have been dead in the bunker. Some mornings he woke up from his nightmares wishing he had been.

For much of the first few days, Adel was beset by an overwhelming feeling of guilt. He could not shake free of the message that kept running through his head. If he had managed to kill Idanox quicker, perhaps Ola might still be with them. His friend had saved his life so many times, but when Adel had the opportunity to save him in return, he had failed. It was a nagging belief he couldn't shake, and it crept into his thoughts at every turn. He expressed these feelings to Alsea once and was sharply rebuked. She told him in no uncertain terms that Ola's death was not his fault, that the blame lay with Idanox and the Hoyt and nobody else. He was nothing short of a hero for what he had done in that bunker, and nobody thought any less of him. General McLeod, Captain Dunstan, and everybody else who got close enough to talk to him told him the same thing.

Adel smiled and gave thanks when this compliment was bestowed on him, but he knew he would never see himself that way. He had achieved what he had set out to do, but he would always see the final battle with the Hoyt as an utter failure. Now that it was over, he realized in full what a naïve fool he had been. He had set out with the best of intentions, thinking he could make a difference. He knew in his heart that he had—he had helped to win the war—but at what cost? Maybe he should have fled the province with Captain Boyd and his crew.

Alsea was by his side through everything, sharing his grief and giving him a shoulder to lean on when he was weak, which was most of the time. He was grateful beyond measure for her, and she equally so for him. Adel had thought that the end of the war would be a happy time; now he realized what a foolish assumption that had been. If he had not had Alsea, he likely would have slipped into madness from the weight of his grief. But she would not allow him to do so, her very presence giving him the motivation he required to fight through his anguish every day.

Almost a week had passed since the Battle of Oreanna, the final battle of what was now being called the Hoyt War. Adel was sitting in silence in the garden of an inn where he and Alsea had been sleeping. General McLeod had offered them rooms in the duke's palace for as long as they wished, but Adel could not bring himself to stay in the home Idanox had called his. Even the thought of the leader of the Hoyt filled him with a rage he doubted would ever entirely subside. Idanox was dead, but many of those he had subjugated would feel the pain of those days for the rest of their lives.

The past week had been a whirlwind for Adel; there had been so much to do. He had recovered well from his injuries, though he now had a scar below his left eye where Idanox had slashed him in their struggle. The healers said it might never fully fade, and Alsea assured him she found it ruggedly handsome. It did not bother Adel; the physical scar was nothing compared to the one he bore in his heart. Each day, he wondered if that wound would ever stop bleeding.

It was midday, the hot sun beating down on him. He was reminded of his first few days with Ola, of the forced marches through the blazing sun on their way to the Temple of the Rawl. He could not have known then what good friends the two of them would become. Those days had been spent merely trying to avoid being a burden to his silent companion. Nor would have suspected that now, over a year later, almost everything would remind him of the taciturn ogre.

"You're thinking of him again, aren't you?"

Adel jumped slightly at the unexpected sound of Alsea's voice. She was right behind his left shoulder, smiling softly at him. He had been struggling with sudden noises, and she had startled him despite the care she had taken to speak softly. General McLeod had told him such reactions were common after the trauma of a battle like the one they had just endured. He had told Adel that they would become less frequent in time, though they may never leave him altogether. He supposed, just like the lessons Ola had taught him, such things were a part of who he was now. Alsea took a seat next to him, placing a calming hand on his shoulder.

"It's hard not to. It seems like everything I see reminds me of him in one way or another. Today it's the sun. It reminds me of those first few days, marching across southern Thornata in the blazing heat. I thought he was going to kill me with his pace. He never seemed to want to take a break. Now I'm just so grateful for those days. I was a soft, weak little boy back then. I probably wouldn't have survived this war if he hadn't toughened me up on that journey," Adel replied with a sigh.

"I know what you mean. It's been nearly a week, and sometimes it still feels like it can't be real, like Ola can't really be gone."

"I've been thinking about him almost nonstop for the past week. In a way, he isn't gone," Adel began, deciding to try to put his feelings into words. "I was just thinking about everything he taught me. How many times would I have been dead in the past year without all those lessons? I know I haven't talked much about what happened in there, in the bunker. I don't know if I'll ever want to talk about it, but I would have died in that bunker if not for him. I've been thinking a lot these past few days about what I am going to do now. I don't have all the answers, but one thing I want is never to let those lessons die. As long as they live on with me, Ola will live on with me in some way. Maybe one day I can even pass them on to others. Then, if they do the same, Ola will never truly die."

Alsea looked at him thoughtfully for a few seconds. Perhaps his incoherent rambling had convinced her he was a fool. These worries were laid to rest as she smiled at him reassuringly, taking his hand in hers.

"I think you are right, Adel. As long as we keep our memories of him alive and pass on the lessons he taught us, Ola will never truly be gone. I can't think of a better monument to his life than that. So much of who we are has been shaped by him. Not to sound too full of myself, but I think he did a great job."

They burst out with laughter simultaneously. It was the first real feeling of joy that either of them had felt since before the battle. The laughter was long and impossible to contain, Adel's eyes full of tears before it finally faded. It felt good to cry from joy rather than misery for a change. Adel climbed to his feet, wrapping Alsea in a long embrace. The pain of Ola's death would not pass anytime soon, but he knew they would survive it together. As long as they were together, they would survive whatever came their way.

"What comes next, Adel? What do we do now? We've been here for a week, and it seems like there is nothing else for us to accomplish here. General McLeod has everything under control, and he doesn't need our help. To be honest, I think I'm ready to leave this city. I'm glad we saved it, but I would be just as happy if I never had to come here again. It's home to so many bad memories that I doubt will ever fade. So, what do we do now?" Alsea whispered after a few minutes of silence.

"I asked Ola the same question the night before the battle. It was the last real conversation I ever had with him, come to think of it." Adel swallowed heavily, fighting back tears of grief before continuing. "I would never have expected the response he gave me. He asked me for my permission to leave the service of the Children of the Rawl for a time. He wanted to go back to his homeland in Gryttar and free ogres who still live in captivity. He wanted to give them the same gift that had been given to him all those years ago."

"I would never have suspected he had any desire to go back there," Alsea said. "But it is like him to want to help those who cannot help themselves, isn't it? I suppose it should not come as much of a surprise."

"I told him I would go with him. I wanted us to do this together. After everything he had done for me, it felt like the least I could do to repay him. He can't go anymore, but I am going to keep my promise to him. I will go south to the Ogra Mountains, and I'm going to put an end to every last ogre slaver I can get my hands on. I'm going to give as many of his fellow ogres the same chance at life the Children gave Ola. I think this is what Ola would want, and it's another wonderful legacy for him to leave behind. Once I am done with that, I will come back to Thornata, back to the Temple of the Rawl. There is still a lot for me to learn. I keep thinking about how many people must be like I was, how many possess a power they don't know anything about. I want to find those people, and I want to help them. There is so much good to be done in the world if only we can find the people to help us do it. I have also been thinking a lot about Idanox and what his plans were. They don't make sense to me. Why did he attack the Imperials? Doing so helped lead to his own demise. He was far from brilliant, but he did have a mind for self-preservation, I will give him that much. There was more at play than we know about, more that we will have to discover when the time is right."

"So, when do we leave?" Alsea asked.

"Alsea, I should do this by myself. It will be dangerous," Adel began to protest, but he froze in his tracks at the sight of the deathly glare she was giving him. "Which is why I am going to be happy to have you along with me. After all, we both know how much trouble I get myself into in such situations."

"You're getting smarter." She laughed.

"I don't know about that, but I know better than to argue with you."

"As I said, you're getting smarter," she quipped, sending them both into another fit of hysterical laughter.

***

They remained in Oreanna for another week, doing what they could to help repair the damage the Hoyt had done to the city. They both knew it was mainly a reluctance to leave Ola's resting place behind that held them in place for so long. But at last, it was clear that General McLeod, who had been named acting duke until elections could be held, had things entirely under control and had no further need for their assistance. They were not needed here, but they could be of service elsewhere. The remainder of the Imperial forces were taking their leave as well, and Captain Dunstan offered them passage as far as Verizia on the ships he had chartered for his men.

They arrived at the city docks just after dawn, the hustle and bustle of the morning a stark contrast to the eerie quiet they had found on their last visit. They found General McLeod waiting for them next to their ship, saying a final farewell to Captain Dunstan.

"The people of Thornata can't thank you enough for your help, Captain Dunstan. I hope you don't catch too much grief from Imperial High Command over coming to our aid," McLeod was saying.

"It's been an honor, if not exactly a pleasure, Supreme General Mcleod. Or is it Duke McLeod now? I'm sure I have a reprimand waiting for me, but heck if I care. Sometimes doing what is right and doing what is approved are two different things. Besides, this old war dog thinks retirement is looking more appealing by the day," Dunstan replied, clasping McLeod's hand.

"Retirement? I might have thought the same thing not too long ago, but this job has a way of pulling you back in. If you get the chance, take it, my friend. This is a job for younger men than you and I."

Dunstan boarded the ship with a nod to Adel and Alsea that he was ready to depart when they were. General McLeod smiled at them both, clasping each of their hands in farewell before pulling each into an embrace.

"I wish you both good fortunes on your journeys. This mission you are embarking on sounds dangerous for you and far more so for anyone who tries to get in your way," he said with a laugh.

"Farewell, General McLeod. It has been an honor to fight alongside you. We leave knowing that Thornata is safe in your capable hands," Adel replied.

"Capable, eh? I appreciate you saying that, but I'm a soldier, not a governor. I'll be relieved when a new duke is selected and I can go back to the barracks where I belong. Though the food in the palace is much better, I won't lie to you on that count. Will you come back to Thornata once you are done with your business in Gryttar?"

"Eventually," Adel replied. "I don't know when exactly. Once we have dealt with the slavers, I want to look for others like me. I want to find other Rawl wielders and help them the way Ola helped me."

"I can think of no better legacy for him to leave behind than the one the pair of you are setting out to forge. I hope our paths meet again one day, albeit under more pleasant circumstances. I can't thank both of you enough for everything you have done for me. Thornata has a chance at a bright new future. That is in no small part thanks to you. Goodbye, Adel. Goodbye, Alsea."

With that, McLeod was gone, returned to the palace or other parts of the city that demanded his attention. Adel turned to Alsea to find the radiant smile he had fallen in love with beaming back at him.

"Are you sure you're up for this? I don't need you slowing me down," he teased.

"Careful now," she warned with a playful shove.

The two of them boarded the ship, Adel already looking for places he could pitch in. *Once a cabin boy, always a cabin boy*, he supposed. Those days felt like a lifetime ago, yet here he was, back on a ship, setting off into the complete unknown. He could not have been happier to have Alsea by his side and could not have been prouder to be carrying on Ola's legacy. The second he'd set foot on the barge, he'd felt like his life had purpose once again. He thought for a moment of his last day as a cabin boy on Captain Boyd's barge. That young cabin boy had come a long way since that day. He remembered a young man who was apprehensive about confronting the unknown, but now he could not wait to face it.

The next trilogy of the Thrawll Saga is coming soon!

Acknowledgments

A trilogy has been completed. I didn't know if that would ever happen when I first started writing The Path of the Rawl Wielder in early 2015. From that day to now, publishing the third book in the span of fifteen months, there are so many people to thank.

As always, my wife Mercedes must come first. I would never be sitting here typing this today if she had not encouraged me to pursue this dream in the first place. She has been by my side every step of the way, and I could ask for no better supporter! Thank you, my love!

My editor, Natalia Leigh of Enchanted Ink Publishing, has also been with me for this entire trilogy. She had meticulously poured over every word of this story, catching my typos, correcting my errant commas, and pointing out when my sentences have gotten hard to follow. If you have enjoyed this story, she is as much to thank for that as I am!

Do you want a know one of the most remarkable aspects of being an author? Looking at a pile of words that fell out of your head and seeing a work of art. My good friend Joseph Gruber has provided the artwork for every one of these books, and I think they keep getting better. Joe, thank you for sharing your exceptional talent with me. You are a great artist and an even better friend.

Of course, this section couldn't possibly be complete without thanking you, the person reading this. Thank you for picking up this book, whether it is your first experience with my work or if you have read the entire series. I hope you feel it was money and time well spent! Your readership means more to me than you will ever know!

The Thrawll Saga will continue with a new trilogy, the first book likely to be released in the second half of 2023. It will feature a new cast of characters, though you can expect to see at least one or two familiar faces. Don't worry; Adel's story is far from complete, and he will return in future stories. Speaking of future stories, it's time for me to get back to work on them. Again, thank you so much for sharing this experience with me. I hope you will return for more adventures!

~Pete Biehl

If you enjoyed this book, please consider

writing a review! Thank you!

About the Author

Pete Biehl, the author of the Thrawll Saga, has been an aspiring author for as long as he can remember. This is his debut novel. When not writing, he enjoys reading and traveling. He lives in Idaho with his wife, dog, and way too many cats that she keeps bringing home, but that he wouldn't trade for anything!

Please visit:

www.petebiehl.com

www.instagram.com/petebiehlauthor

www.facebook.com/petebiehlauthor
www.goodreads.com/petebiehlauthor

Lightning Source UK Ltd.
Milton Keynes UK
UKHW011838061222
413480UK00004B/138